FLESH AND BLOOD

An Eden House Mystery

Bill Kitson

GW00633982

201598867

Published by Accent Press Ltd 2015

ISBN 9781783757275

Copyright © **Bill Kitson** 2015

The right of **Bill Kitson** to be identified as the author of this work has been asserted by him in accordance with the Copyright, Designs and Patents Act 1988.

The story contained within this book is a work of fiction. Names and characters are the product of the author's imagination and any resemblance to actual persons, living or dead, is entirely coincidental.

All rights reserved. No part of this book may be reproduced, stored in a retrieval system, or transmitted in any form or by any means, electronic, electrostatic, magnetic tape, mechanical, photocopying, recording or otherwise, without the written permission of the publishers: Accent Press Ltd, Ty Cynon House, Navigation Park, Abercynon, CF45 4SN

WEST SUSSEX LIBRARY SERVICE	
201598867	
Askews & Holts	13-Apr-2016

For Val.

Proof-reader, copy-editor, unpaid agent, publicist, events manager, wife, lover, and best friend, with all my love and admiration.

Acknowledgements

My thanks to Hazel Cushion and the team at Accent Press for their hard work and professionalism, especially to Greg Rees, whose meticulous editing went far beyond correcting my punctuation and grammar.

Finally, to my wife Val for the countless hours she spent getting the manuscript into order.

Chapter One

1982

I had been opening a champagne bottle to celebrate the royalty cheque received from my publisher earlier that day, when the phone rang. Eve answered it, and a moment later called out, 'Adam, it's somebody called Jeremy Powell. He says you know him.'

I took the phone from her, whispering, 'He's a lawyer. Used to work for the TV company I reported for.'

After a lengthy conversation with Powell I said, 'Let me have a word with Eve and I'll get back to you.'

Eve eyed me curiously. 'What was all that about?'

'He was asking for a favour, well actually, it's for his younger sister, Alison. Her boyfriend's brother has been murdered, but the police don't know how. Apparently the wound was like no other they've ever come across and he wondered if I'd seen anything similar anywhere on my travels. The wound was perfectly circular, like a gunshot, but when they did the post-mortem they couldn't find a bullet. But a core of skin, flesh, tissue, and bone had been removed, right the way to his heart. He'd been cored.'

I saw Eve grimace. '*Cored?*'

'I told him it doesn't ring any bells with me, I can't say I've encountered anything as unusual as that, and I've seen some strange sights. He wanted to know if I could make a few enquiries. I told him I'd have to check with you first.'

There was no doubt the snippets of information Powell had given me were intriguing, but I was cautious about promising anything. 'I don't understand what could have caused a wound like that,' Eve said. 'Are you sure he's got his facts right? I mean, it sounds a bit unlikely, doesn't it? If the police told his sister-in-law's boyfriend, he repeated it to her, then she relayed it again to her sister, and *she* told her husband. By the time he phoned you it was fifth-hand. The original message could have been totally different to the one you heard.'

'You mean like send three and four pence, we're going to a dance,' I said.

'What?'

'It's a story from World War One. It may be apocryphal, but it's about a message getting distorted in the retelling. The commanding officer in the front line sent a message to HQ which said, "send reinforcements, we're going to advance." It got passed from one unit to another, and by the time it reached headquarters, it had become, "send three and four pence, we're going to a dance."'

'Ah. Yes, that was what I meant. Well, I suppose there's only one way to find out, and that's by talking to the people involved.' She eyed me suspiciously. 'That was what you were hoping I'd say, wasn't it?'

There was a time when I'd have denied it, but I wouldn't get away with that now. Eve knew me far too well. I had to defend myself somehow, though. 'Come off it, Evie, you're as curious as I am!'

'Ring Powell back and tell him we'll talk to his sister and her boyfriend.' It was as close to an admission as I was going to get.

An hour later, we'd arranged to see the couple the next day.

'That's a bit quick,' Eve commented.

'I know, but Jeremy seemed to think Alison is really spooked by this, which I suppose is only natural.'

'Ought we to be getting involved?'

'Let's be honest, Evie, wild horses wouldn't keep either of us away after that tale. Besides which, the police are baffled. Added to all of that, according to what Jeremy told me, the detective in charge of the enquiry is our old friend Detective Inspector Hardy.'

'Perhaps we ought to ring him before we go haring off. He might not want us sticking our noses in.'

Eve's suggestion was a good one, but when I tried to contact Hardy the following morning, I was told by a less-than-helpful telephonist that he was unavailable and that they couldn't tell us when I would be able to speak with him. Having made the effort in vain, we were on the road by mid-morning. As we drove, we discussed what little we knew.

'Where is the place this murder was committed, do you know it?' Eve asked.

'The house is called Barton Manor, on the outskirts of a village called Barton-le-Moors, but we're not going there. We're going to talk to Alison Powell and her boyfriend. They're staying at the King's Head in Barton-le-Dale, the nearest town.'

'You were on the phone with your lawyer friend for quite a while; did he tell you anything about the boyfriend or his family?'

'There isn't anyone else, apparently, and he reckons Robert Pengelly is a really decent bloke who's had a rough time of it. He didn't go into too much detail, but he did say Robert wasn't on speaking terms with his brother Stephen, the victim.'

'That doesn't sound good. I mean, it suggests a strong motive.'

'I agree, but he also said that Robert hasn't seen Stephen in years, and hasn't been anywhere near Barton Manor.'

'Did Jeremy say what Robert Pengelly does for a living?'

'He's some kind of boffin. He works for an electronic

equipment manufacturer in Leeds, on the development side. He met Alison in Leeds. She's a postgraduate history student at the university.'

We arrived at Barton-le-Dale, a sleepy market town located at the very north-western tip of the county, almost where North Yorkshire becomes Cumbria. The region is sparsely populated. The buildings are mostly grey limestone, weathered over the centuries and blackened by the soot from the chimneys of countless open fires. Combined with the dark, brooding moorland that surrounds the town, this lends the area a sombre effect, which was accentuated that day by grey clouds that scudded across the sky driven by a strong, cold north-easterly wind.

We parked in the cobbled marketplace in front of the hotel. As we got out of the car I shivered. 'It's a coat colder up here.'

'Yes, and we've still got winter to come,' Eve said as she turned her collar up and thrust her hands into her pockets.

I held the hotel door open and ushered Eve inside, adding, 'At least it hasn't started snowing yet.'

I've never counted weather forecasting as one of my talents. Perhaps it's as well I don't rely on it.

I think the most accurate description of the King's Head would be that it was comfortable. All the furniture and fittings in the lounge were long in the tooth, well-worn but presentable. There were only four people in the lounge, all seated at one of the coffee tables. The younger couple I assumed to be Alison Powell and her boyfriend. We stepped forward and as we identified ourselves, Alison introduced the others.

'This is Robert Pengelly, my boyfriend, and this is Mr and Mrs Jolly.'

Alison invited us to sit down and ordered more coffee. When it arrived, she poured fresh cups for everyone as

Robert Pengelly explained the reason for the older couple's presence.

'Mary and Frank worked for my brother and it was Mary who found Stephen's body. They have just been at the police station giving their statements to the detectives, so I asked them to join us here.'

'I acted as Mr Stephen's cook and housekeeper,' Mary Jolly told us. 'Frank worked as his chauffeur, gardener, and general handyman. We live at the lodge to Barton Manor.'

'All we know is what Alison's brother told us on the phone. He suggested there was some confusion as to what killed your brother.'

'I think that's putting it mildly,' Robert replied. 'To begin with, the police were convinced I'd killed Stephen. There was certainly no love lost between us, and as I am the only surviving relative, they thought I had a strong motive for killing him as I now inherit the estate.'

Having said that, Robert Pengelly seemed to think there was nothing more to add. I found that a little puzzling, but then, we didn't know much about him or his circumstances at that stage.

'You don't sound too upset by your brother's death,' Eve pointed out, 'nor do you seem particularly excited by the thought of your inheritance.'

'I'm not.'

The answer was nowhere near as curt as it looks on paper, but it was definitely less than forthcoming. I decided it was going to need some probing to get Robert Pengelly to open up, so I began questioning him, mixing my reporter's style with that I imagined a detective such as Hardy would use. 'When did you last see your brother?'

'It was seventeen years ago. That was when he sent me to boarding school. I was ten years old.'

'In all that time you've never seen him, not even briefly? Never visited your home?'

'That's correct. I doubt if I'd have recognised him if I passed him in the street. I'm certain he wouldn't recognise me.'

'What about the fact that you've now inherited the Barton Manor estate?' Eve asked him. I think she'd guessed what I was up to and decided I needed help.

'Inheriting the estate might seem like a motive to you, but I'm not interested. I haven't given the place a thought in years. My memories of Barton Manor aren't particularly happy ones, to be honest. I'm sorry, but if the police want to find the killer they'll have to look at someone a lot closer to my brother. I admit that I detested him, but not to the extent of wanting to kill him.'

'Did Stephen pay for you to go to public school?'

'Yes – and no. What I meant is that Stephen made the payments, but the money came from part of the sum set aside for my education in the terms of my father's will, not from affection, believe me.'

'You said that you hadn't seen Stephen,' I commented. 'Did you have any form of contact with him?'

'Yes, but it was one-way contact. I wrote to him three times a year as I was instructed to by my tutors. The last letter was on my eighteenth birthday, the day he ceased to be my legal guardian. By then I was glad to be rid of the chore, and I'd guess Stephen was bored rigid by the turgid drivel I sent him.'

His account did much to explain his seeming disinterest in his brother's fate, or the manor he was in the process of inheriting. 'This is how things were as I grew up in what I laughingly refer to as my family. Stephen didn't like me, and neither did my father. I'd go further than that and say they both hated me. My mother died giving birth to me and they blamed me for causing her death; and they made that fact perfectly clear from the moment they judged I was able to understand the meaning behind their words. Stephen didn't want anything to do with a much younger brother he referred to as "the brat", and as a consequence I soon learned to feel the same about him. I'm not in the slightest bit bothered that he's dead, or that he was murdered, because I couldn't care one way or another. I shan't miss him, but I won't dance on his grave either. To be honest, hearing about his death was a bit like getting news that someone you met a few times long ago and didn't particularly like had been killed.'

My strategy had worked, in that Robert was now talking freely. 'Weren't you at all bitter at the way you'd been treated?'

'Of course I was bitter, wouldn't you be?' For the first time Robert showed some emotion. 'Not that I blame Stephen entirely. I believe some of his feelings came from my father, whose favourite remark about me was addressed not to me, but to my nanny. He'd say, "Get that little brat out of here; I can't stand the sight of him". Nice, that, don't you think? Quite the doting parent. As soon as I was old enough, he sent me away to prep school. I was nine when he died. The headmaster told me the news, broaching the subject with great tact.' Robert smiled. 'The poor man was shocked when he started talking about travel arrangements for the funeral and I said that I didn't intend to go.' He paused and sipped his coffee, which must have been cold by then. He stared moodily into the liquid, and I guessed his thoughts were as dark as the coffee.

'So Stephen became your legal guardian?'

'Yes, and I was brought home for one last time, to make preparations for moving on to senior school. Stephen told me that he was going to give me a handsome allowance, which in fact was also from the fund set aside in my father's will. He kindly told me that he didn't want me at Barton Manor any longer. After that, I was farmed out to teachers, who were well paid to look after me during the holidays.' He gestured to his surroundings. 'This is the closest I've been to what you could call my home since I was ten.'

As Robert finished speaking I glanced round. I could tell Eve was shocked by Robert's account of his callous treatment, as were Frank and Mary Jolly. Alison too was moved, although I guessed she'd heard some, if not all, of it before.

'Why were they so cruel and unpleasant to you?'

Robert looked at Eve, his dark eyes laden with sadness, amounting almost to pain. 'Not only had my mother died when I was born, but my twin sister was stillborn. As far as I'm aware, the only thing I did wrong was to survive. Father and Stephen hated me for that, and made sure I was aware of their feelings.'

'Is that all there is to it?' Eve persisted and was rewarded with another insight into the Pengelly family.

Robert shrugged. 'Possibly, possibly not. Perhaps they realised I wasn't going to turn out like them, even from an early age.'

'What does that mean?'

'I believe that my father was totally unsuited to married life. I'm going by what I heard and saw as a young child. It surprises me that many adults don't realise that small children can hear everything that goes on within earshot, even if at the time they don't understand it. I didn't have many people to talk to, so I learned to listen to everything that was being said, whether it was intended for my ears or not. Much of it I didn't grasp at the time, but later, when I recalled it, what I'd heard made sense. My father had lots of women visitors when I was growing up, and when they came I was forbidden to leave my own quarters. Of course I had my nanny for company. That was OK until she'd had her third gin, when she usually fell asleep. She snored, so I couldn't follow suit. Anyway, from rumours I heard, it sounded as if my father had been carrying on with other women long before my mother died.'

'And you say Stephen was of the same inclination?'

'Yes, although he wasn't hampered by the inconvenience of having a wife to answer to.'

'How did you find out? About Stephen, I mean?'

'I eavesdropped on a row he had with my father. I didn't understand much of what they said, I was too young, but I was intrigued by the argument as it was such a rare event.'

'I take it the subject was a woman?'

'Yes, it must have been from what was said. My father was shouting and carrying on, and I remember him saying, "If you can't keep it in your pants at least check the bitch's birth certificate. This is going to cost me a small fortune". That was when they really started having a go at one another. Stephen came back with "At least I wasn't shagging my way around every slut in the county distressing my wife". I was really enjoying listening, but then my nanny came along and dragged me away. She wasn't at all impressed when I asked her what the word shagging meant.'

Out of my eye corner I saw Frank and Mary exchange glances, before she spoke. 'I know you shouldn't speak ill of the dead, but Mr Stephen did have lots of women friends stay at the manor. Not the sort of women you'd class as ladies, either. It was difficult keeping up with their names, at least until about a year ago.'

'How long have you worked at the manor?' Eve asked.

'We've been there ten years. What will happen now, I don't know.'

I looked at Robert, who seemed taken aback by Mary's comment. 'I hadn't thought of anything like that,' he admitted.

I decided it was time to concentrate on the reason for our visit. 'You said earlier that Mary found the body, would someone tell us exactly what happened, if it isn't too distressing?'

Again, Mary and Frank exchanged glances before she

spoke, and I noticed that he held her hand throughout. It was obvious that both of them were distressed by what had happened, even if Robert Pengelly wasn't. I wondered if that was out of affection for their late employer, or doubts over their own future.

'It happened last Friday afternoon,' Mary began. 'I hadn't planned on being at the manor, but Mr Stephen had been difficult that day. Out of the blue, he demanded that I prepare three guest bedrooms. I didn't mind the extra work, but it would have been nice if I'd had a bit more notice, or if he'd asked in a more polite manner. It took me a long time, and by four o'clock in the afternoon I hadn't finished, and I still had Mr Stephen's meal to prepare.

'The cleaning had made me hot. I remember that as I crossed the Minstrel's Gallery I shivered, and noticed that the house felt colder than it should. That was when I glanced down the staircase and saw that someone had left the front door wide open. I didn't think any more of it until I reached the head of the stairs.'

Mary stopped speaking, her face twisted with pain as she recalled what happened next. 'At first I thought it was a sack someone had left there. I ran downstairs and saw that it wasn't a sack ... that it was ... Mr Stephen. I could see all the blood ... and I knew ... knew he was ... dead.'

Frank took over the narrative, as much to give Mary chance to recover, I guessed. 'I was in the garden all afternoon, cutting back a load of brush and dead wood. It was an ideal day for it, clear and bright. I'd almost finished when I heard Mary scream. I'd stacked the smaller cuttings for composting and started a bonfire with the woodier stems. Nothing goes to waste. I even dig the ash from the fires into the flower beds to enrich the soil. Anyway, I'd just stacked the wheelbarrow with the final load when I heard Mary, and knew at once there was something terribly wrong. I rushed up to the house and saw her standing over Mr Stephen's body.'

'Did you see the wound?'

Frank shook his head. 'No, he was lying face down. I checked his neck for a pulse, but there was nothing, not even a flicker.'

'Did you hear any other sounds before your wife screamed?' Eve asked.

'Like a gunshot, you mean? No, the police asked me that, several times. I explained that I knew none of the estates round us were shooting that day, and I'd have noticed if I'd heard any gunfire. We do get a bit of trouble with poachers and I'd have gone to investigate if I'd heard a shot.'

'Can either of you think of anyone who might have had a motive for killing him?' I glanced at Robert and smiled apologetically. 'Present company excepted, that is.'

'The police asked us that, too,' Frank responded immediately. 'The answer is no, but that's partly because Mr Stephen was very reserved, especially about his private life. Secretive, you might say.'

'What about his social life?' Eve asked. 'Did he entertain often? Dinner parties, that sort of thing?'

Mary Jolly answered this, choosing her words carefully. 'He didn't have anything like that. He was a bit of a recluse. And when his lady friends came to visit him he used to see to the catering himself.' She paused, before adding, 'I have no proof, but I believe that they might have been … professionals.'

'You mean prostitutes?'

'That would be my guess. But in the last year or so, there has only been one regular visitor. She wasn't like the others. A class above, I'd say. She was at the manor most weekends, and occasionally during the week. When she visited, I wasn't asked to prepare an extra bedroom,' she added diplomatically.

'Can you tell us anything about her?'

'Not much,' Mary replied. 'Her name is Kathy King,

and she lives in Barton-le-Dale. Frank could tell you where, because Mr Stephen occasionally asked Frank to drive her home.'

'Didn't the police ask you about her, or about Pengelly's social life? I'm surprised, because we know Detective Inspector Hardy, and those are the sort of questions he would ask right at the outset.'

'It wasn't him we spoke to. It was a detective sergeant called Holmes, and he seemed more concerned with searching the house and grounds, looking for the weapon. He did ask if Mr Stephen kept any strange knives or similar things.'

'I wonder why Hardy wasn't there. Did he interview you, Robert?'

'No, it was Detective Sergeant Holmes. He told me he had taken temporary charge of the case in Hardy's absence. Holmes was the one who phoned me at work.'

'Perhaps it would be an idea to tell the police about this Kathy King woman,' Eve suggested.

I agreed, and as we were discussing it, Alison interrupted, speaking for the first time. 'Does that mean you'll stay and help us? Help Robert, I mean?'

'I suppose it does, but first, I think we'll have to find somewhere to stay. It will be a bit of a long haul driving to and fro on a regular basis. We could book in here, I guess.'

'Why not stay at the manor?' The suggestion came from Robert. I looked at him, surprised by the comment in view of his hostility to Barton Manor.

Eve was rather more forthright. 'I thought you said you detest the place?'

'I did, but as we were talking I realised that whatever my feelings are, I have responsibilities, and they can't be shirked. However, I don't fancy going there on my own. To be fair even with Alison along the place would seem empty, too much like before. The place holds too many bad memories. Perhaps if new people came to stay it might help erase some of them.'

'If you're going to have guests at the manor, Mr Robert, there will be a fair amount of work to do,' Mary pointed out. 'There will be bedrooms to air. The rooms will need the central heating on as well. And I'll have to do some shopping. Mr Stephen was very frugal, and there isn't much in the freezer or fridge, and virtually no fresh stuff. It's not a problem, but even with Frank's help I'll need a bit of time.'

Robert realised his mistake. 'Sorry, I didn't mean to spring it on you like that. How about you tell us when you can have the house ready, and we'll work round that?'

'I suppose I can sort the rooms out today, and I could do the shopping tomorrow.'

'No, that won't do. How does this sound?' Robert smiled reassuringly at Mary, then looked at Alison for confirmation as he spoke. 'If Frank can run Alison and me to the railway station, we'll go back to Leeds and collect some clothing; we only brought an overnight bag. We'll need to let people know where we'll be, so that will take us a day. Then, if you can manage to prepare things tomorrow, Frank can take you shopping in two days and you can pick us up when the Leeds train gets in.'

'That would be fine, Mr Robert.'

'Would you do me a favour, Mary? Please drop the mister bit? Robert will do.'

'Yes, Mr Robert.'

'Is that OK with you?' Robert asked us. 'Will you come and stay at the manor for the time being?'

'Yes, we'll go home and collect some clothes and come back the day after tomorrow,' Eve told him.

'And on the way we'll call in at the police station and tell DI Hardy we've been asked to help and that we're going to be staying at the manor. We can mention that woman, Kathy King, too. Hardy's sure to want a word with her. Can you give us her address, Frank?'

As I was speaking I looked across and saw Mary whisper something in her husband's ear. I stood up, preparing to help Eve on with her coat, but before I could move, Frank said, somewhat hesitantly, 'Mary would like to know … er … how many rooms to prepare.'

Chapter Two

'That was tactful of Mrs Jolly,' Eve said as we walked to the car.

'Yes, they seem a really nice couple. It must be difficult for them though, given that they will be extremely worried.'

'Worried about the murder, you mean?'

'Actually, I was thinking more of the future. Their employer is dead, and they've just heard Robert Pengelly say in no uncertain terms how much he dislikes Barton Manor and that he has no interest in taking over the estate. I assume the lodge where Frank and Mary live is what's known as a tied cottage, so they face the twin threats of unemployment and homelessness.'

'I hadn't thought of that, but you're right, they must be extremely concerned.'

We travelled the short distance to Barton-le-Dale police station and pulled up outside the building. Anything less like Scotland Yard would be difficult to imagine. A two-storey building that I guessed had started life as a private house before the need for law enforcement demanded a police presence in the town.

As I drove, I told Eve I was puzzled by Hardy's failure to question either Robert Pengelly or Frank and Mary Jolly, or to instruct his sergeant to enquire more thoroughly into Stephen Pengelly's personal life.

'It does seem a bit unlike him not to get involved in person,' Eve agreed. 'Perhaps he had other priorities and will come back to that later.'

The reason for the omission became apparent within

minutes of meeting Detective Sergeant Holmes. That didn't take place until long after we entered the police station. I asked to speak to Hardy, but as with my phone call earlier, was told that he was unavailable.

'In that case, perhaps you would be kind enough to ask Detective Sergeant Holmes to spare us a few minutes.'

'Can I ask what it's about?'

I was getting a bit annoyed by the stalling tactic. 'You can if you want, but it doesn't mean I'm going to tell you,' I snapped.

Having given our names to the desk sergeant, we waited. And waited. And waited. Eventually, having spent almost half an hour staring at a wall that was in urgent need of the attentions of a painter, I remarked in a loud voice, 'I wonder if anyone has spotted those bodies in the river yet.' I glanced at my watch, before asking, 'What time did you set the bomb for? Was it quarter to the hour or quarter past?'

My intended has very sharp elbows. I hadn't realised quite how sharp until that moment. 'Will you behave yourself,' she demanded in an angry hiss any cobra would have been proud of.

Out of my eye corner I saw the desk sergeant reach for his phone.

'Say what you like,' I told Eve, 'but I bet we'll meet this sergeant within a couple of minutes.'

Even I was surprised by the speed with which Holmes appeared. 'What's this about a bomb?' he demanded as he bustled into the reception area.

'What bomb?' I tried to look puzzled.

'The desk sergeant told me you said something about a bomb and some bodies in a river.'

'I think he must have been drinking. Either that or he needs his ears testing. I did ask my fiancée what time our friend Tom was setting off for York. Oh, and I also asked her if she'd spotted anybody on the river when we were driving here. I know a lot of canoeists use it. But the reason we asked for you is that we were given your name by Robert Pengelly. We actually wanted to speak with Detective Inspector Hardy who is a friend of ours, but you appear to have mislaid him, which seems rather careless of you.'

'Is this about the Barton Manor murder?'

I looked at the detective sergeant for a second, long enough for Eve to guess that I was about to deliver a sarcastic reply. 'That's correct, Sergeant,' she interposed.

'What do you know about it, Mr Daley?'

'It's Bailey, not Daley,' I corrected him. 'See, I told you your colleague's hearing was bad. As to what we know about it, the answer is more than you do, I reckon.'

'OK, OK, let's start from scratch. Would you come through to my office and we can talk there?'

We followed him into a cubicle that could, with a certain amount of imagination, be described as an office. We sat down and the tiny room seemed full. 'First off, tell me how you know DI Hardy.'

Between us, we explained about the three cases we had been involved with, and as he listened Holmes relaxed.

'I remember reading about them. I'm sorry to have to tell you, but DI Hardy is in hospital. He was seriously injured in a road accident and it's not certain yet whether they will be able to save his leg, which was badly mangled.'

'That's terrible. How did it happen?'

'Nobody knows yet. Hardy was unconscious when they got to him, and then they took him straight to theatre to operate. He's still under sedation at the moment. The whole thing was a heck of a mess. For some reason Hardy swerved and went off the road. Strange as it seems, that may have saved his life. Shortly afterwards a van skidded on a large patch of black ice fifty yards further along the road. The van overturned and the driver was killed. His passenger survived, but he's in a bad way. If DI Hardy had hit that ice, he would probably have died. So I suppose you could say he was lucky.'

I wondered if Hardy would view it in that light.

Holmes didn't appear to be relishing the responsibility that had been thrust upon him, and I could see we would gain little by proffering information at this stage.

'What is your involvement in the case?' he asked.

I explained about the phone call from Jeremy Powell, and said, 'I believe there is some doubt regarding the weapon used.'

'I'm afraid I can't divulge any of the details of the case to members of the public,' he told us. His manner suddenly became stiff, formal, and straight from the manual, I guessed.

'Well, in that case we won't take up any more of your valuable time.' I said as I got to my feet. I saw Eve wince, but the sarcasm was lost on Holmes.

'You said you had some information, or implied as much.'

'Yes, but I only impart it on an exchange basis.'

Holmes frowned. 'You must know that it's an offence to withhold information from the police.'

'I do; the question is, what are you going to do about it?'

'I could have you arrested.' Holmes was now on his feet.

I was about to reply, but Eve nipped in before me. 'I wouldn't do that, Sergeant. The publicity could be very damaging to your career.'

'What publicity?'

'The coverage in newspapers, television, radio, you name it. As a former TV journalist, Adam is something of a celebrity. All I would have to do is pick the phone up and they'd be clustered ten deep outside your door within hours.'

I listened with admiration. I thought I was good with words, but Eve was far better. Holmes seemed to agree but instead of cooperating, all he said was, 'That's enough, I have work to do. Can you see yourselves out?'

'In a moment. First of all, would you tell us which hospital DI Hardy is in?'

'Thorsby General. Why do you want to know?'

'I told you, he's a friend of ours. We'd like to visit him. That's the sort of thing friends do.'

As we drove back to our home in Laithbrigg, we discussed our abortive meeting with DS Holmes.

'The thing is, he didn't seem at all a bad bloke,' Eve said.

'No, it was only when it came to the details of the case that he changed. I reckon he must be feeling the pressure. He's fairly young and I guess he hasn't had much experience of handling a big case like the murder of a prominent landowner. Speaking of which, what did you think of Robert Pengelly?'

'He seems a nice, well-adjusted young man, which is a little surprising if his story about his childhood is true. He's obviously intelligent, otherwise he wouldn't have such a good job,' she added.

'Yes, I don't see him as a vengeful, embittered man striking back at his brother, or wanting rid of him to inherit the estate.'

'And if his brother detested him that much, what I'm keen to know is: did he leave the estate to him? There doesn't seem to any other family that could inherit.'

'It depends if Stephen Pengelly died intestate. If that was so, and Stephen didn't make a will, I believe the law states that the property would have to be shared amongst all living relatives, and if Robert was the only one, he'd get the lot,' I said. 'Of course, there may be a will and all our supposition could be proved wrong.'

'I don't think it will be easy for him returning after all this time, but I suppose there will be a lot for him to sort out; his brother's affairs for one thing.'

After what we had heard about Stephen Pengelly earlier that day, 'affairs' seemed a most appropriate word.

That evening, as I was preparing dinner, Eve made enquiries about Hardy at Thorsby General, and learned that he would be able to receive visitors next day. The following afternoon we arrived at the hospital for the beginning of visiting time, and were shown to a private room alongside the orthopaedic ward. We knocked and entered. Hardy was lying in bed, his lower limbs shielded from view by a blanket-covered cage. He looked to be in some discomfort. Alongside the bed, a slim, attractive woman with blonde hair was seated, holding his hand. I recognised her, although we'd only met her once, very briefly.

Hardy looked up as we went in, and stared at us in surprise. 'How on earth did you know I was here?'

'Hah! You're not the only detective in these parts.'

Hardy's visitor giggled.

'Syl. This is Adam Bailey and Eve Samuels. My wife, Sylvia.'

'We've met already, I think the accident has affected your memory.' She smiled at us. 'How kind of you to come.'

'You can bet that they'll have some ulterior motive or other.'

'There's gratitude for you,' I told him. 'I've a good mind to eat these chocolates myself.'

'Chocolates? What chocolates?' Hardy's eyes lit up as I produced the huge box we'd bought that morning. 'Thank you, that was very kind. They're my favourites.'

Sylvia laughed. 'Come off it, all chocolates are your favourites. Clever of you two to spot his weakness, though.'

'Anyway, how are you?' I asked, sensing Hardy's embarrassment.

'Not too bad, all things considered. This is just a nuisance.' He pointed to the leg.

'He's fibbing,' Sylvia told us. 'He's in a good deal of pain, and he's only being polite because you're here. He can't remember much about it, but they spent hours setting the leg, because it was so badly broken. Even now there are pins holding it in place. It looks like a child's Meccano set under there.'

'Are you going to let me into the secret of how you found out I was in hospital?' Hardy seemed anxious to change the subject.

'It was Detective Sergeant Holmes who told us you'd been injured,' I explained.

'Holmes? How did you meet him?'

'We went to ask him about Stephen Pengelly's murder, and to offer some information, but he wasn't interested.'

Hardy groaned. 'Don't tell me you've got involved in that. I suppose that means the county will soon be littered with corpses.'

Eve and I smiled politely at what we considered to be the absurdity of Hardy's comment. Eve explained about Jeremy Powell's phone call, and the mystery weapon that had intrigued us. 'We went to talk to Robert Pengelly and as a result we're going to stay at Barton Manor for a few days. That was what we went to tell you, but Holmes was a bit dismissive and got Adam annoyed, so we left without explaining what we'd learned.'

'Holmes is a good lad and will make a decent detective in the long run, but he's a bit wet behind the ears and it's unfair on him to be saddled with the responsibility of a murder case at this stage in his career. I'm going to speak to him later this afternoon, and I'll tell him to get in touch with you at Barton Manor. Is that OK? I'll suggest he listens to you.'

'Barton Manor? Isn't that where your accident happened?' Sylvia asked.

'Yes, there or thereabouts.' Hardy seemed suddenly uncomfortable, and I guessed this was another subject he found embarrassing.

Despite his unwillingness, I pressed him for details. 'Care to tell us what happened, or can't you remember?'

'I can recall bits and pieces, but to be honest most of it is a bit of a blur.'

'He's fibbing again,' Sylvia told us. 'What he really means is that he can remember fairly well, but he doesn't want to talk about it because he's afraid that people won't believe him or that they'll think he was hallucinating, or simply that they'll laugh at him.'

'I don't think that should worry him, not where we're concerned,' Eve told her. 'Let's be honest, we've told him plenty of incredible things ourselves, and he didn't laugh at us. Mind you, he didn't always believe us either, until they were proved correct.'

Hardy looked at Eve, then at me, and after a moment's pause, began to speak. 'I'd to drive from Thorsby, so it was almost dusk by the time I passed through Barton-le-Moors. I'd arranged to meet Holmes at the manor. I'd almost reached it when something on the car radio distracted my attention for a split second. When I looked up, I was horrified to see the shape of a large animal directly in front of me, in the middle of the road.'

Hardy paused, reached over to the unit alongside the bed and took a sip from the glass of water on it before continuing. 'I know it was the wrong thing to do, but my reflexes made me swing the wheel to avoid hitting it. In doing so I must have clipped the grass verge and next thing I knew, the car was on its side, then on its roof, before ending face down in the ditch. That's all I remember. I must have passed out, because when I woke up I was here.'

'I don't see why that should embarrass you. It seems a perfectly natural thing to have done,' Eve told him. 'What was the animal you saw? Was it a deer? Did you hit it?'

Hardy looked even more embarrassed. 'It might have been a deer. It must have been a deer. But, no, I didn't hit it, although I can't understand why not.'

'How do you mean, it must have been a deer? Either it was a deer or it wasn't.'

Hardy looked at me for such a long time that I thought he wasn't going to answer. Eventually, when he spoke, his voice was barely above a whisper. 'I said it must have been a deer because there's nothing else that big in this country, and yet it didn't look like a deer. I only got a fleeting impression of it. One second it was there, the next it had vanished. But in that brief glimpse, I'd say it was taller than a deer, and more erect, not on all fours, so to speak.'

I realised that Hardy did have some idea as to what he thought he'd seen, but wasn't prepared to admit it. 'What happened to it? You say you didn't hit it.'

'That's the other thing I don't understand. The thing was in the middle of the road, right in the path of the car. I was travelling at close on sixty miles an hour, and yet I didn't touch it. It was as if it vanished before I reached it, but no animal I know of can move that fast.'

'Come on; tell us what you think it was. I promise we won't say a word to anyone.'

Reluctantly, he said, 'I thought … at least I imagined … it must have been imagination, but it looked a bit like … a bear. Either that or a barghest.'

Sylvia shook her head in disbelief. 'Don't tell me you subscribe to old legends like that?'

Hardy looked from me to Eve and back again, clearly looking for signs of our amusement. I didn't feel at all like laughing. For some reason, his words sent a chill down my spine, and I could tell that Eve was similarly affected. 'By what DS Holmes told us,' I said, 'it sounds as if you were doubly lucky. Obviously, surviving a crash like that was fortunate, but he told us about what happened to the van that hit black ice further along the road. It sounds like your crash was the lesser of two evils. And perhaps what you thought you saw actually saved your life.'

Sylvia's statement had been right, the tale was difficult to credit, and had it been anyone less down-to-earth than Hardy, we might have scoffed at what he'd told us. Even now, what he said is almost beyond comprehension.

Chapter Three

Barton Manor wasn't quite a stately home or a mansion, yet it bore the unmistakeable signs of affluence.

The grounds were extensive and well-kept, an indication, I thought, that Frank Jolly was good at his job. Beside the drive, banks of rhododendrons provided a natural screen. Behind them, massive poplars acted as sentinels. As we approached the house, I got occasional glimpses of huge evergreen shrubs that had been shaped into beautifully symmetrical circular mounds, I wondered if the outstanding topiary work was down to a visiting expert, or if the credit was due to Frank Jolly. Surrounding the large shrubs was an immense lawn that stretched to the low stone wall where the drive opened out in front of the house. The focal point of the frontage was a three-tier fountain. I parked just past it, next to a shallow flight of steps that led to the lawns beyond. These were immaculately clipped, and although the growing season was past, I could still make out the razor-straight lines made by the mower. Whatever his other faults, Stephen Pengelly had obviously cared about the appearance of his property.

I looked across at the house. The grey stone walls were covered with ivy that threatened to encroach on the leaded windows. Age had weathered the stone, softening the hard lines to give a pleasing, almost welcoming impression on the eye. Having parked up, I took our holdalls from the boot and followed Eve to the sturdy oak door, which, framed by a stone arch, formed the front entrance. I glanced around, taking in the splendid setting once more, the beauty enhanced if anything by the soft light of the early November afternoon, which was beginning to fade towards dusk. Eve pressed the ivory-coloured button, for all the world like a giant eyeball, set in a highly polished brass surround. From somewhere deep within the house I heard the lazy clamour of an ancient bell.

As we waited, Eve pointed, directing my gaze to an irregular, slightly maroon stain on the large stone flags directly in front of the door. I guessed that these marked the place where Stephen Pengelly had bled out, and that Mrs Jolly had been at work trying to eradicate the grim reminder of his violent death. Even the repeated application of bleach and hot water would not totally remove the evidence, it seemed. I dismissed a fleeting thought about Lady Macbeth as inappropriate.

A few seconds later, the door swung open and Robert Pengelly peered out. 'Oh, hello, I thought it might be the police. Come on inside, out of the cold.'

We stepped across the threshold into a truly magnificent entrance hall. To our left, a stone hearth almost the size of a football goal housed a huge log fire, whose cheerful blaze provided the perfect welcome. The draught from the open door caused fragrant woodsmoke to waft into the air. At the rear of the hall, which had sufficient space to cope with even the biggest influx of guests, a broad central staircase rose to the upper floor, flanked on either side by beautifully carved and highly polished wooden balustrades.

'Why did you think it might be the police?' I asked after we had taken in our surroundings.

'There's been a break-in. We think it must have happened overnight, because the police were here until early evening, added to which Frank and Mary were in the house until past eight o'clock, getting things ready for our arrival.'

He gestured to our bags. 'Leave those here. I'll get Frank to take them to your room later. We're all camped out in the kitchen at the moment. Come through and have a cup of tea.'

He walked to the midpoint of the entrance hall and opened a door on the right which led to the dining room. 'We only arrived here half an hour ago. As we pulled up, Alison noticed a small pane in the window of Stephen's ... in the study was broken and the window was wide open. When we looked inside, the room had been trashed. Fortunately, for whatever reason, the thieves concentrated on the one room. Either that or something disturbed them, because there's no sign of damage elsewhere.'

'Whereabouts is the study?' Eve asked.

Pengelly gestured towards the front of the house. 'To the front of this room. But the kitchen's this way.'

He guided us through a doorway into the dining room. It was as impressive as the entrance hall. The centrepiece was a huge dining table, which I guessed would have seated a couple of dozen guests without cramping them. Despite its size, the table didn't dominate the room, and neither did the huge dresser and sideboard that stared at one another from opposing, oak-panelled walls. As we walked down the room, my eye was drawn to a portrait hanging over the slightly smaller but still more than adequate fireplace. It was of a young woman, and I couldn't help but notice the striking similarity to our host.

Eve was also admiring her surroundings. 'How old is the house?' she asked.

'Early Georgian, I believe, but there has been a dwelling here since long before that. The manor of Barton is mentioned in the Domesday Book.'

'Has it been in the Pengelly family all that time?' I asked. I was curious, because Pengelly isn't a Yorkshire name. To me, it seemed more in keeping with Devon or

Cornwall perhaps.

'No, we're relative newcomers.' Robert smiled. 'One of my ancestors, Oliver Pengelly, was a banker and took the house from a defaulting debtor around a hundred and fifty years ago. Before that, the family was based in Cornwall and around the West Country.'

He opened the door leading to the kitchen, which was in as grand a scale as the rooms we had already seen. There was another huge fireplace to the left, but this one, instead of an open fire, housed an Aga range cooker, and a separate boiler, which between them not only cooked the guests' food but also warmed their bedrooms via the central heating. On either side of the inglenook were storage units with worktops where food could be prepared for immediate transfer to the oven or hob. I was struck by the absence of fridges and similar white goods. These, as I learned soon afterwards, were stored in a separate utility room adjacent to the kitchen.

Mary and Frank Jolly were seated at the kitchen table, which would have done justice to most dining rooms, and Alison was standing alongside them pouring tea from a large teapot. 'Two more for tea,' Robert told her.

We were greeted with enthusiasm, which I guessed was in part from relief. No matter how law-abiding people might be, there is something daunting about having dealings with the police. We sipped our tea, listening as Alison and Mary described their actions since arriving at the manor from the train station. 'Once we knew about the burglary,' Alison told us, 'I said we shouldn't touch anything unless we had to, because of fingerprints, and even then to cover our hand with a handkerchief or cloth. Did I do right?'

'I'm no expert, but I'd say you took all the precautions you could.'

'I had to open the freezers and fridge to put some food away,' Mary added, 'otherwise it would have been spoiled.'

'I hardly think that would have been their target, do you, Adam?' Eve asked.

'No, I doubt very much if they would even have come into the kitchen.'

I was pleased to see that our tea was presented in mugs rather than cups. Everything at Barton Manor seemed to be on a grand scale. We had just about finished ours when the police arrived. There was no advance warning; no wailing sirens or flashing lights, merely the tolling of that doorbell. 'That should be them,' Robert said. He left to answer the door, and a few minutes later returned, accompanied by DS Holmes. Robert asked Mary to pour another mug of tea, and as he sipped it, Holmes made notes about the time the burglary was discovered, and everyone's actions since then.

He finished his tea and stood up. 'I'm going to check on the room where they got in and have a word with the fingerprint officers. Would you come with me please, Mr Pengelly?'

We watched them leave, and after the door closed Eve looked at me. Her expression clearly showed her belief that Holmes was determined to ignore us. I shrugged, and had resigned myself to the fact that we were to be excluded from the inquiry, only to find within a few minutes how wrong I was.

Robert returned, and said, 'DS Holmes would like a word with you and Eve. He's waiting in the hall for you.'

The detective was standing with his back to the log fire. He looked thoughtful, as if he had much on his mind. 'First off, I must apologise for yesterday,' he began. 'I was a bit uptight, with what happened to the governor and this being such a big case.'

Eve gave him one of her reassuring smiles.

'DI Hardy rang me and put me straight about a few things; said how helpful you've been to him, uncovering

29

details in other cases.' Holmes paused and took a deep breath. 'To be honest, I'm not sure I'm cut out for this job. I thought I'd be OK, but being left in charge of a murder case wasn't exactly what I'd imagined for this stage of my career. The expression "golden opportunity" doesn't come to mind. On the contrary, I think poisoned chalice would be more fitting. If I had any doubts on that score, I've just been reminded of how difficult this investigation is likely to prove.'

'Have you any specific reason for thinking that way?' I asked.

'Before I came here today, I spent a couple of hours transcribing my notes from the house-to-house enquiries I carried out in the village after the murder. Nobody admitted having seen or heard anything unusual on the day. No one reported having seen any strangers in the vicinity, or anyone acting suspiciously. What they did convey was the almost unanimous impression that Stephen Pengelly would go unmourned, and that both he and his father were loathed and detested by virtually everyone who came into contact with them.'

'Did anyone suggest a motive for the murder?' Eve asked.

Holmes smiled slightly. 'Apart from making the world a better place, you mean? No. Although I reckon they could have told me of lots of folk with strong reasons for wishing Pengelly dead, they certainly weren't forthcoming with them.'

'It sounds to me as if Robert Pengelly is the one who has been handed the poisoned chalice,' I suggested, 'if the family as a whole is so widely detested.'

'Actually, I think that rather depends on him, and how he behaves,' Holmes replied. 'He seems a likeable enough chap, and one or two of the older villagers remember him from when he was a small boy. They were sorry for him, because word had got round of the way his father and brother mistreated him. I said to one bloke that Robert Pengelly seemed all right. The man said, "In that case he must have inherited his mother's character, which is a good thing." I asked what he meant by that, and he said that Robert's mother was a beautiful woman, and a real lady in the proper sense of the word. Anyway, that showed me what I was up against, and I wanted to say sorry, and to ask if you would let me know if anything does turn up. To be honest, I now realise I need all the help I can get.'

It takes guts to offer an apology like that, and I felt it merited a response of equal generosity. 'DI Hardy told us this is your first major investigation, and that because of what happened to him, you've been thrown in at the deep end without having learned to swim. I'd guess that standard practice would be for you to accompany a senior officer for some time, listening and learning as you go.' I smiled sympathetically. 'Let me tell you something. When I started out as a TV reporter, I was so nervous that the first interview I had to do was recorded three times before the producer was satisfied that I'd asked the right questions. I don't think anyone is born with the gift. I think you have to learn on the job and profit from your mistakes.'

'Thanks. I appreciate that, and I would be grateful if you can help. However, I must be off in a few minutes. I'm due to meet the Chief Superintendent at the hospital. Between them, he and Hardy are going to want a briefing from me, and to know what I intend to do from now on.' He grimaced. 'That should be fun.'

I glanced at Eve, who, as always, knew what was in my mind. 'How about we meet up with you tomorrow morning in Barton-le-Dale and we can tell you what we've found out? If anything,' I added.

'That would be a great help. Sorry to have to cut this short, but I really will have to leave.'

'One thing before you go, will it be in order for us to

have a look at the study as soon as your people have finished? And I think it will be sensible to devise some means of making the house secure until the window the thieves smashed can be replaced.'

'I can't see any objection to either of those ideas.'

We watched Holmes leave, and as I closed the front door, Eve said, 'That was big of him, don't you think?'

'I certainly do.'

'Did you invent that story? The one about your first TV interview?'

'No, but I exaggerated. There were only two takes.'

'We returned to the kitchen, where the subject of security was under discussion. 'We can't do anything until we get the all clear,' Robert said.

'Yes, but we can't leave the house wide open for anyone to climb in and out at will,' Alison objected.

'Don't panic,' Eve told them. 'DS Holmes has given permission for a temporary repair to that window, that will be some deterrent.'

'I can see to that when the fingerprint men have finished,' Frank Jolly volunteered.

'That will mean more dusting,' Mary said with a despairing sigh. 'Anyway, if you're going to be busy with that, Frank, you won't be able to help me prepare dinner. I'd better make a start, or it won't be ready until breakfast time.'

'We'll help you,' Eve and Alison said in unison.

'Yes, and Robert and I will help Frank with the defences,' I suggested.

'Good idea, Adam,' Robert agreed.

'Just don't let Adam near a hammer, unless you're prepared for the language when he hits his thumbnail instead of the one he's aiming at,' Eve warned him.

'You'll have to give Eve detailed instructions,' I told Mary, 'she has to open a recipe book to boil water.'

'Are you certain you two aren't married? It certainly

sounds like it,' Robert said.

Robert and I followed Frank out through the utility room, passing a bank of freezers, a laundrette-sized washing machine, and a dryer. He collected a couple of torches, which he handed to Robert and me. 'It'll likely be dark by the time they're finished,' he commented.

Armed with these, we went across the yard at the rear of the building, to where a long terrace of what I guessed had once been stables were now used as garages and workshops. In the first of these, I saw a large, gleaming Mercedes saloon, obviously almost new. Plainly Stephen Pengelly didn't believe in stinting himself when it came to life's luxuries. Passing through the garage, Frank opened the side door and switched the light on in the first workshop, from which we collected two sets of stepladders, a large square of plywood, and some battens, plus hammers and nails. Fully equipped, we set off for the front of the building, where we made our preparations for the boarding over of the window.

One of the fingerprint officers looked out of the window. 'Shouldn't be much longer,' he remarked.

The plan was for Robert and Frank to mount the steps, fixing the plywood into position against the wooden window frame and adding the battens for extra security. My task was to ensure the stepladders were secure and to shine the torches on the workers as they completed the job.

Once we'd started work, it took less time than I'd anticipated; which was good, because the air already had a frosty feel to it. As they stepped off the ladders, I heard a chink as Robert's foot dislodged something. I shone one of the torches on the ground and stared with interest at what it revealed. I moved the beam, and within seconds my wild idea was confirmed.

'Let's store this stuff and get back inside,' Robert told us. 'I'm not used to this outdoor life.'

I agreed, because I wanted to take a look into that study

before Mary began tidying it.

We returned to the kitchen, where a minor argument was settled at once by Robert. 'There are only four portions here,' Alison was saying.

'That's right,' Mary replied.

'No it isn't,' Robert intervened. 'What about you and Frank?'

'We'll eat at the lodge later, Mr Robert.'

'No you won't. I'm not having you go home to prepare and cook another meal. You dine with us.' He smiled sweetly at her. 'And that's an order.'

Eve looked across at me. 'No bruises?' she asked.

'None, partly because I didn't go near a hammer. How are your fingers? Any cuts?'

'None, and I've just about finished, so I think if nobody objects, I'll go for a shower. Or at least I would, if I knew where our room is.'

'Before you go dashing off, Evie, I think we should take a look at the study.'

'I'll take everyone's bags upstairs, Mr Robert,' Frank said.

We followed Robert to the study and waited while he opened the door and groped for the light switch. We followed him inside, but stopped just over the threshold, shocked beyond measure at the sight before us. The room was a scene of utter devastation. Much of the damage was superficial, but some of it was savage, vindictive, sickening.

Alison gasped aloud, 'Oh, Robert, this is awful.'

Alongside me, Eve shuffled, her agitation obvious in her voice, which was little more than a shocked whisper. 'This was not a robbery,' she said thoughtfully, 'whoever broke in here came looking for something. If they took anything away, it's purely because they found what they were searching for. If not,' she paused and sighed, 'there's every likelihood that they'll be back. And if they do return, I for one wouldn't want to be in their way.'

I trusted Eve's judgement implicitly. She was becoming an expert at reading scenes such as this, gauging people and their motives.

'There's more to it than that, though.' She pointed to the desk, where the centre drawer had been prised open and was now little more than kindling, then to the ornaments that had been smashed way beyond repair, and the slashed canvas of the oil painting that hung over the fireplace. 'Whoever did this has a mind filled with hate. Whether it's hatred of Stephen Pengelly, the family, or simply people with money, I can't tell. Alternatively, there could be no motive behind it. Which would mean it's the work of a psychopath.'

'If you've seen enough, I'll show you where you're sleeping.' Robert switched the light off and closed the door. As we followed him up the staircase I thought about what Eve had said, coupled with what I'd seen inside that room. I decided not to tell her what I'd discovered outside. It was bad enough me knowing, without burdening someone else.

It was only as we approached the first floor that I realised the house was designed in a curious way. The grand staircase, as I'd already mentally christened it, split at a half-landing, behind which was the walkway that Mary had referred to as a Minstrel's Gallery. Twin corridors ran from either side of the gallery, which Robert informed us stretched all the way from the front to the rear of the house. These apparently contained enough bedrooms to cope with a large family and a considerable number of guests. The manor house was configured like a letter H, which was a curious method of building in its day. Towards the rear of the first floor, Robert said, a smaller, less ornate staircase led to the upper floor, which I guessed would have contained the servants' quarters in years gone by.

The first floor was in shadow, but as soon as he reached it, Robert went as if by reflex to a switch on the wall. As he depressed it, a gigantic chandelier hanging from the ceiling flooded the centre of the building with warm light from dozens of candle-shaped bulbs.

'I bet that's sent the electric meter into overdrive,' I remarked.

Robert took my flippancy seriously. 'I hadn't thought of it before, but now you mention it, I suppose household bills are part of the things I shall have to consider in future.'

We looked at him, surprised by his remark. 'Does that mean you intend to stay here?' Eve asked.

Robert looked at Alison, and I noticed the couple were holding hands, and realised it was the first sign of intimacy that I'd seen from them. 'I think so,' Robert spoke slowly, hesitantly. 'We talked it over on the train coming here. A lot depends on what Alison wants, and whether she is comfortable living here.'

'I like the house, Robbie,' Alison assured him. 'Or rather, I like what the house could be, if we made it our home. But it isn't as simple as that. It's whether you could be happy here after all the bad memories. And there are other people to consider.'

'I feel sure I can be happy here as long as you are.'

'What did you mean about other people?' Eve asked.

'I think Alison was being tactful and pointing out that I have responsibilities now. Apart from Frank and Mary there are plenty of others who work on the estate, or depend on it for their income. For quite a few of them it not only provides employment, but also somewhere to live. I can't simply walk away and let them down.'

'I'd never given it much thought, but I guess it must be a bit like being the managing director of a company,' Eve commented.

'Anyway, let's sort out the rooms.' Robert turned to Frank who was waiting patiently on the landing. 'Which of them has Mary made up, Frank?'

'All of them on this floor, Mr Robert. She wasn't certain which you'd prefer. There's Mr Stephen's room.' He gestured to the room at the front of the house.

Robert shuddered. 'No fear; definitely not that one. It used to be my father's room. I wouldn't get a wink of sleep in there.'

'How about the one opposite?'

'Yes, I like that room. I believe it used to be where my mother slept and where I was born. Alison and I will be fine there. We could put Adam and Eve in the Rose Room. Is it still called that?'

'Aye, that it is, Mr Robert.'

'Where did you sleep when you were a boy?' Eve asked.

It was an innocuous enough question, but I saw Alison grip Robert's hand tight; saw his expression change and darken. When he spoke, his attempt at humour failed to disguise the bitterness in his voice. 'Oh, I didn't mix with the rabble on the lower floor. I wasn't good enough. The original nursery was even deemed too good for me. No, I occupied what had been servants' quarters on the second floor. When I was allowed to come downstairs I had to be escorted by my nanny. Later, I could come out by myself at strictly controlled times, usually when my father and brother were out. That was so that I didn't "get in the way", as my father so kindly put it.'

We were still coming to terms with this fresh example of the mistreatment Robert had suffered as a child when he opened the door and gestured for us to enter the Rose Room. It was easy to see how it got its name. The amply sized room was decorated in pink and cream, even down to the furniture and the curtains and bedding on the four-poster bed in the centre. The en suite bathroom continued the motif. 'This is beautiful,' Eve said.

'Glad you like it. I'll see you downstairs for dinner.'

I waited until he had closed the door before speaking. 'You tend to think of anyone brought up in a magnificent house like this as being really privileged, but I certainly wouldn't have swapped places with Robert, knowing what I do. He must have been such a sad, lonely child.'

'I agree, and the more I hear of his father and brother, the less I like them. It's remarkable that Robert has grown up to be so well-adjusted.'

When we sat down for dinner, Eve was directly opposite the oil painting I'd noticed earlier. 'That lady looks very much like you, Robert. Is it your mother?'

He looked at the painting, his smile infinitely sad. 'It is, if my brother was telling the truth. He marched me in here on more than one occasion when I was little and made me stand in front of the painting. Then he would tell me about *his* mother and how beautiful and gentle she was, and how much he missed her. Then he would explain that she was dead because of me, that it was all my fault.'

'Knowing that must have made it very difficult for you to sit and eat in this room with the painting in view,' Eve sympathised.

Robert's reply was, if anything, even more shocking than anything we'd heard thus far about his childhood. 'I wouldn't know. Tonight is the first time I've eaten in this room.'

There was a long moment of shocked silence before Alison said, 'Robbie, do you mean that? Didn't you even have one meal in here?'

Robert shook his head. 'No, I was granted the privilege of a private dining room that doubled as my playroom. I had excellent company, because I always dined alone. I usually had exactly the same menu as my father and brother. That was unless they'd eaten it all. The fact that it was re-heated from the previous day didn't matter, though.

It was still fairly edible.'

'You mean they fed you the leftovers from their dinner the night before?'

I think my voice must have reflected my disbelief, because Robert responded sharply. 'Oh, it wasn't just the dinner. I got the breakfast leavings as well. I couldn't eat bacon for years afterwards, because I remembered how tough it is once it's been left for twenty-four hours. Cold toast that has dried out is nearly as bad. And if anyone serves me porridge they'll get it thrown at them.' He smiled at Mary, who had capitulated to Robert's insistence and was seated with Frank at the furthest end of the table. 'Don't worry, though, apart from that my eating habits are normal.'

There was a moment's shocked silence, before he continued, changing the subject abruptly. 'I forgot to mention it earlier, with all the excitement, but we could be getting another house guest soon. Alison's friend Tammy is threatening to descend on us.'

'She's not sure yet,' Alison explained. 'We had planned a visit for her to stay with me and as I'm not going to be at home, Robert suggested she join us here – the more the merrier. Now it could be more a case of safety in numbers. She doesn't know if she'll be able to make it or not. She still has to finish her thesis for submission and she's desperate to get it spot-on because she's relying on a doctorate to further her career.'

'If Alison sounds smug, that's because she has already submitted hers,' Robert commented.

'Just let me know in good time so I can plan the meals,' Mary told them. 'Now, who would like apple pie and custard to finish with? Frank picked the apples for me this morning.'

I looked at Eve. 'Sorry, darling, the wedding's off. I'm running away with Mary.'

Chapter Four

The sadistic treatment meted out to Robert as a child was still on our minds when we retired to the comfort of the four-poster bed.

'I wouldn't blame Robert if he had killed his brother – or his father for that matter,' Eve said. 'If they behaved that way nowadays they'd be in trouble with the authorities.'

I had to agree, and it raised one or two disturbing doubts. 'You don't think that under the amiable facade Robert actually waited all this time to take his revenge, do you?'

'No, all I'm saying is it would be understandable. The fact that he's grown up without any apparent personality defects says a lot for his strength of character. It may well be that in sending him away to school, they actually protected him from becoming warped and twisted.'

I found sleep difficult to come by that night, despite the comfort of our bed. For much of the night I laid awake, waiting and listening for the slightest sound that might betray an intruder's presence in the house. Although Eve slept far better than me, even her rest seemed troubled by dreams, and by her reaction, I guessed these to be less than pleasant.

Next morning, when I opened the curtains, I discovered that the Rose Room commanded an excellent view across the dale and beyond. The first few hundred yards comprised the manicured lawns and well-cultivated flower beds that I'd noticed when we arrived. These were bounded by a large evergreen hedge which divided the private part of the estate from the arable land that I guessed provided much of the manor's income. The fields stretched into the far distance, until the ground began to rise towards the moors. The lower slopes, where the pastures were bisected by a network of dry stone walls, contained sizeable flocks of sheep which would further augment the estate funds. Further up, as the gradient increased dramatically towards the high moor, grassland gave way to bracken and gorse, providing shelter and food for pheasant, partridge, and grouse, but little else, I thought. Faintly, through the mullioned glass, I heard the plaintive cry of a curlew, and swiftly added that to my tally of the moor's inhabitants. When Eve was ready we made our way downstairs.

Alison was alone in the dining room. 'Robbie will be back soon. He insisted on helping Frank clean the grates out, lay the fires, and restock the coal and logs, so he's gone for a shower.' She smiled. 'I think Frank was shocked when Robbie volunteered. It's not what he's used to, but that's Robbie's way.'

Talking of Robert gave Eve chance to bring up the subject she and I had discussed the previous night. 'We were appalled by what he told us about his mistreatment as a child. Adam said he was surprised that Robert has turned out as well as he had, without any of the psychological problems such abuse often causes.'

I didn't remember having expressed it that way, but refrained from comment, being more interested in Alison's response. In addition to explaining much about Robert's poise and level-headed nature, it gave me an insight into how deeply Alison cared for him.

'I admit that Robbie has never been one to show his emotions in the presence of strangers, which I guess could stem from his childhood here. And to outsiders I suppose he must appear as quite a solitary person, but when you get to know him better you find that he's really warm-hearted and generous. I honestly believe he might have turned out very differently had it not been for Paul Markham. He was Robbie's housemaster, and took him under his wing. He mentored Robbie through all his time at school, and I think he became more like a substitute father. I met Paul a few times. He and his wife were extremely nice people, and it was obvious they thought the world of Robbie. They didn't have children of their own, so maybe the parental thing cut two ways. Robbie went to stay with them every school holiday, and they took him away, even when they went abroad.'

Alison paused, and I saw a shadow of sadness cross her face. 'Paul Markham died just over six months ago. I was upset, but Robbie was inconsolable. He shut himself away for days on end after we came back from the funeral. I couldn't comfort him, no matter what I said or did. Strangely, though, after he recovered from the grief, he seemed much stronger; more determined than ever. It was almost as if he knew that from that moment on he would have to stand up for himself, because there was no one else left to rely on. Apart from me,' she added, 'and that has brought us even closer together.'

She thought for a moment, obviously deciding whether to bare her soul even more to relative strangers, then added, 'To be honest, until that point I hadn't been absolutely sure about Robbie and me. When I saw the raw emotion of his grief and how well he coped with it afterwards, and when I appreciated the strength of character he showed at that time, I knew he was the right choice for me.'

Alison's candid account explained a lot. I admired Robert for the way he had come through the nightmares that had beset him, but reflected on how lucky he'd been to have such a wise and understanding mentor.

Having done justice to the splendid breakfast Mary provided, Eve and I set off for Barton-le-Dale and our appointment with DS Holmes. On the way we discussed what we'd learned, and I was pleased that Eve's judgement coincided with mine.

The detective appeared subdued, I thought, as he greeted us and led the way to the cubbyhole he used as an office.

'How did you get on with your bosses?' I asked. I'd have been a great success in the Diplomatic Service.

Holmes winced at the memory. 'Hardy was OK, but the chief superintendent was all for bringing someone with more experience in from another force.'

'Did you manage to persuade him not to?'

'Not really, because he'd already made enquiries and there was nobody else available, so he admitted he's stuck with me, like it or not.'

'Did he actually use those words?' Eve asked. Maybe I wouldn't have been so bad a diplomat after all.

'He did, and a lot more besides. Luckily, the governor intervened. He told the super about your visit, and that you had offered to help. That didn't go down too well either, but when he offered to ring the chief constable, who apparently knows you, things changed. Between them, they cooked up an idea. Obviously you can't be seen to be involved in any sort of official capacity, but given the exceptional circumstances, I'm to be allowed to consult you, as long as I report progress on a daily basis. I hope that's OK with you?'

'I think it's more than fair, and as much as anyone could ask for,' Eve told him.

'When do we start?' I asked. 'Do we have to be sworn in and wear badges?'

Holmes smiled, and I realised it was almost the first time I'd seen him relaxed enough to do so. 'I think that's only in America.'

'So I don't even get to wear a Stetson?'

Holmes shook his head. 'The governor warned me

about you.'

'We'll we have a couple of bits of information that might help,' I told him. 'Shall we start with the burglary at Barton Manor? Go on, Evie, tell him what you suspect.'

'I don't think that theft was the motive,' Eve began, 'or at least, if it was, then the burglar was only after something specific. If the intruder was only there for profit, he would have gone into the rooms where more valuable items were kept. I looked at the mess he created, and it seemed to me that part of it was due to him searching for something in particular.'

'Have you any idea what that might be, or is that too much to hope for?'

'It is at this stage, but there is one other point that disturbs me. The damage in the study suggests a deep level of hatred and a potential for extreme violence. I haven't discussed this with Adam, but I believe that the intruder is highly likely to have been the same person who murdered Stephen Pengelly, and in my opinion he is deeply deranged.'

'Do you think finding out what the intruder broke in to steal will help identify the killer?'

'Yes, I certainly do.'

'There is one other point regarding the intrusion,' I stated. Both Holmes and Eve looked at me questioningly. 'Technically speaking, it wasn't a break-in. Not in the strict sense of the word.'

'I don't understand,' Holmes admitted, and I could see that Eve was also puzzled.

'I mean that the intruder didn't smash the glass in the study window to get into the house.'

My claim left them, if anything, looking yet more baffled. 'I think you're going to have to explain that, Adam,' Eve told me.

'I believe the window pane was smashed purely to lead us to think that the burglar entered that way, whereas in fact they simply unlocked the front door and walked in.'

'What on earth gives you that idea?' Holmes asked.

'When Robert Pengelly and I were helping Frank Jolly with the boarding-up, I shone the torch on the path and flower bed under the window. There was broken glass there.'

Eve caught my meaning immediately. 'If the glass was on the ground outside, not on the carpet, it suggests the window was broken by somebody *inside* the study.'

'That's right.'

'What you're saying is that the intruder had keys to the house, is that it?' Holmes had caught on at last. 'But surely that would have triggered the alarm?'

'There isn't one. Daft as it sounds, Stephen Pengelly never had one fitted. I believe Robert is planning on rectifying that, and having the locks changed and deadbolts fitted.'

'Why didn't you say anything about this last night?' Eve asked.

'I didn't want to scare everyone. It was bad enough me having a sleepless night listening for the noise of an intruder, without wishing that on the rest of the household.'

'So, whoever got in had keys to the house,' Holmes said. 'That would mean there can't be many suspects.'

'Very few,' I agreed. 'And I took the opportunity to check that with Frank Jolly. He only knows of four sets, and three of those have been checked. I think I can even tell you who the missing set were given to.'

'Go on then,' they demanded in chorus.

'Stephen Pengelly's set was in his dressing room. Frank and Mary have their own, which means that the only ones unaccounted for are those Stephen ordered Frank to have cut about six months ago.'

'So who has them?' Holmes was getting quite agitated.

'The only person who visited Barton Manor often

enough to warrant having a key was Stephen's mistress, a woman by the name of Kathy King. She lives here in Barton-le-Dale, but Mary said she spent more time at the manor than she did at her own place. She was the woman we wanted to tell you about a couple of days ago, before you got all officious with us.'

Holmes gave me a slightly shamefaced smile, but asked, 'How did you find out about her?'

We gave him chapter and verse of our conversation at the King's Head, repeating all that Frank and Mary had told us. Holmes listened, and when we'd finished said, 'I need to speak to this woman as a matter of urgency, but I have a problem. Given the serious nature of the crime I ought to take backup before conducting any interviews, and just at the moment there's nobody spare, not even a uniformed man. In fact there ought to be a WPC present too, but that's definitely out of the question. What I certainly can't do is take you along in place of an officer,' he added, forestalling my suggestion.

We were still mulling over the problem when we were treated to one of the fastest examples of wish-fulfilment I have ever encountered. There was a knock on the door, and the desk sergeant entered. 'There's a Constable Pickersgill here to see you. He says the chief constable has sent him to help out.'

'Johnny Pickersgill? That's great news,' I exclaimed. 'Johnny is our local bobby, and he's been involved in a couple of problems we've had to deal with, so he understands how we work.' I leaned forward and added, 'He's also the chief constable's cousin, so the fact that he's been sent here shows your bosses are trying their best to help you.'

'In that case you'd better show him in. Help is what we're most in need of, and it's in desperately short supply.'

Sure enough, when Johnny Pickersgill appeared, he

confirmed what we suspected: the chief constable had been keen to lend what support he could. Johnny masked this by telling Holmes, 'He told me I'd to take care of these two,' he indicated Eve and me, 'because they're forever getting themselves in trouble. They attract danger like magnets. See these grey hairs?' – he pointed to his head – 'Most of them are down to this pair. I've been temporarily assigned to Barton-le-Dale as acting detective constable, but I guess my chief role will be to watch over them. The other thing I should tell you is they tend to collect corpses like some people collect stamps.'

'Great to see you too, Johnny.' I turned to Holmes and added, 'There is one drawback to the arrangement. This is going to cost you a fortune in teabags and milk. Unless you have a huge stock, I'd send out for urgent supplies right now. You might also want to warn local hostelries to buy in a few extra barrels of beer.'

'I feel sure we'll be able to cope,' Holmes smiled. That was twice he'd done that within a few minutes. He was getting to be rather good at it. 'Speaking of tea, I think we should have one while we bring our new recruit up to speed and plan our next move.'

Pickersgill eyed him with approval. 'I think we're going to get along really well.'

Now that tacit official approval for our involvement had been given, Eve and I followed DS Holmes and John Pickersgill on the short drive to the address Frank Jolly had supplied for Kathy King.

'After everything we've heard about Stephen Pengelly's love life, I'm more than a bit curious to see what this woman's like,' Eve told me.

'In the interests of accuracy, I think the correct phrase should be sex life rather than love life. The impression I got was that love certainly didn't enter the equation where he was concerned.'

'You have a point.'

The street Frank had directed us to comprised a long terrace of three-storey Victorian houses on one side and a park on the other. Within the open space I spotted a bowling green and three tennis courts, plus a playground complete with swings, roundabouts, and a climbing frame. The remaining space was wide open, with a couple of tarmac footpaths bisecting the grass. At the farthest corner a pair of goalposts, plus the churned-up surface indicated that a local football team also used the area.

Frustratingly, there was only provision for parking in front of the houses, the opposite side of the road bearing double yellow lines. I managed to secure the last available space, which by a series of careful manoeuvres I was eventually able to squeeze the car into. 'Gosh, that was fun,' I muttered.

We had over fifty yards to walk before we reached the right house. 'Strictly speaking,' Pickersgill greeted us, 'you two shouldn't be here, so we think it would be better if you wait outside and follow us in a few minutes.'

I smiled sweetly at him. 'Has any crime been committed here?'

Pickersgill blinked. 'Not that I'm aware of, why?'

'Apart from your wish to interview Kathy King you have no other reason to be here. No warrant to execute or anything of that nature.'

'No, I guess not. What's your point, Adam?'

'There is nothing to prevent law-abiding citizens from visiting any of the inhabitants of this property, even without prior invitation, so long as they don't break in or do anything illegal.'

'No, I guess not.'

'It would make far more sense for Eve and me to go talk to Kathy King first. That would help us break the news of her lover's murder, and you could follow later. Bear in mind she is likely to be very upset by the news, and it would be better if a woman was present when she hears it.'

Pickersgill looked as if he was about to argue the point, but to my surprise Holmes backed my suggestion. 'That sounds like a good idea. I was worried that we didn't have a WPC available.'

We inspected the plates alongside the door. There were six in number, each bearing a different name. To their right were matching buttons to summon the occupant. Eve pressed the one marked King and we heard the faint sound of a bell ringing in the distance. We waited, but after several minutes with no response, even following Eve's second attempt, I reached forward and tried the door handle. It turned easily. Obviously, it wasn't considered risky to leave the building unlocked during the daytime.

We went inside, where we could just make out the doors to two flats on either side of the hallway, and a flight of stairs leading to the upper floors. The hall was poorly illuminated, with only the light from a grimy fanlight to allay the gloom. There was the persistent odour of over-cooked cabbage, added to by another, faintly unpleasant smell.

Holmes, who along with Pickersgill had followed us inside, flicked a switch and the hall became marginally brighter. At the foot of the stairs was a button, one which would activate a light controlled by a timer. Eve pressed this and I followed her upstairs. We reached the first floor just before the light went out. She pressed a second light button, which gave us chance to identify flat number four, the one occupied by Kathy King.

As we approached I noticed that the cabbage smell was far less noticeable upstairs, being overpowered by the other aroma, a sickly, nauseous odour. I began to feel uneasy. Something, I felt certain, wasn't right. I reached the door ahead of Eve and knocked on it. When I got no response I tried a second time, with no better result.

'Try the handle,' Eve suggested. 'I don't like that smell.'

It obviously wasn't just me who was imagining something bad. Once again, the handle turned easily, and I thrust the door open. The stench hit us with a force that was almost physical. 'Get the others up here, Evie,' I gasped.

I covered my nose and mouth with a handkerchief before entering the flat, moving with extreme caution. The short corridor ran past a kitchen on one side and a bathroom on the other, opening out to a living room beyond. I stopped dead at the end of the corridor, staring down at the body of a woman I assumed to be Kathy King. Stephen Pengelly's mistress wouldn't be telling us anything about his death – or anything else for that matter.

She had died violently, that much was certain. To this day I can't recall what clothes she was wearing, let alone what colour they were supposed to have been. The blood that had gushed from the wound to her ribcage had turned the clothing, the carpet, and the nearby settee to what I guessed had been a uniform red, but was now a dirty russet brown.

In the short space of time before Holmes and Pickersgill pushed past me, I had just sufficient time to glance at the room, before checking out the woman's appearance, concentrating particularly on a brief inspection of the wound that had killed her.

I suppose Kathy King must have been attractive enough, if you went for blondes with large breasts and hourglass figures. However, it was difficult to gauge her looks, as these were marred by the grimace that even the passing of rigor mortis had not eased. It was a measure of the agony she had suffered in her final moments that her features still bore the stamp of her suffering.

I peered closely at the area where she had been stabbed, or shot, or whatever had been done to her. The entry point was about an inch in diameter, and perfectly cylindrical. From the position of her body, lying on her side, I could see that the murder weapon had passed through her body, exiting in the middle of her back. I'd heard police officers in America refer to a 'through and through' where a bullet enters and exits a body, but in such cases, the path is distorted by the obstacles in the body, and the exit wound is always far larger than the hole made on entry.

In Kathy King's case, however, both entry and exit wounds appeared to be the same size and the path taken by the object that had ended her life was perfectly straight. No bullet I knew of could do this, no gun I had ever heard of could deliver such a wound. Indeed, although I had witnessed almost every weapon of violence known to man during my career as a war correspondent, I had never encountered anything that could deliver such a horrific wound.

I remembered the phone call from Jeremy Powell and his statement about the murder of Stephen Pengelly. Like Stephen, Kathy King had been cored.

I was still staring in horror at the corpse when Johnny Pickersgill approached me. He took me by the elbow, gently turning me away from the gruesome sight. 'Adam, take Eve away from here. Take her downstairs. In fact, go sit in your car. I'll come and talk to you when we've sorted out what to do about this.' He gestured behind him.

I did as I was told. Eve went along, but there was no conversation. The appalling sight seemed to have robbed me of both the power of speech and the desire to speak. I was just grateful that Eve hadn't followed me into the flat. After we'd been sitting in the car for a few minutes I saw Holmes and Pickersgill emerge from the building. Holmes stood on the doorstep for a moment, and I saw him take a deep breath, as if trying to free himself from the macabre vision within, before heading off towards his car.

Pickersgill walked over to us, and I wound the window down. 'DS Holmes is contacting the forensics people, plus his bosses and the pathologist, so he'll be a while. We think it would be better if you weren't seen around here. We don't want word of your involvement to get out. Holmes suggested you return to Barton Manor and we'll contact you when we've finished with this. Mind you, that might well be tomorrow.'

We agreed. The last thing Holmes needed was the media attention that news of our involvement in the case would provoke. Keeping the gory details from the press would be hard enough. News of two murders close together in a rural location was sure to be latched onto by any editor or reporter worth their salt. Giving them as little as possible to fan the flames of their curiosity was going to prove a challenging task in itself.

There was little conversation as we drove back to the manor. At one point I said, 'We ought to warn everyone to be on their guard for the possibility of the press descending on the manor.'

'I suppose that's inevitable in the circumstances.'

'Given time, yes, but if Holmes and his senior officers can muzzle their men it will delay things.'

Chapter Five

As we walked across the gravel to the front door, I noticed that the glaziers were already at work repairing the broken study window. Obviously, Robert had wasted no time rectifying the damage. Inside, we headed instinctively for the kitchen, where we found Robert and Alison seated at the table. Mrs Jolly appeared from the adjacent utility room as we entered.

'How did the meeting with Holmes go?' Robert asked. 'Has he agreed …'

He stopped in mid-sentence. Clearly, our expressions told him something was wrong. 'What's happened?'

'Kathy King is dead. We found the body. She had a hole through her chest. Right the way through.' The description, though short, was brutally graphic.

All three of them looked shocked beyond measure, a reflection perhaps of how we'd looked earlier. Like us, they seemed too shock to respond. 'By the look of it,' I told them, 'I'd say the weapon was the same as the one used to kill Stephen. I've seen more than my share of bullet holes, shrapnel wounds, sword cuts, and stabbings, but this was totally unlike anything I've ever come across.'

As they still seemed reluctant to take in what we'd said, Eve explained why we'd gone to Kathy King's flat, and what we'd found. 'We wanted to ask her about the missing set of keys for the manor, but someone beat us to it.'

'It looked as if she'd been dead a couple of days at least,' I added. 'The blood had congealed and dried by the time we got there. It may well be that her keys were taken when she was murdered. We'll know more when DS

Holmes reports his findings. In the meantime I think it would be prudent to have the locks changed and to invest in an alarm system. Apart from the killer on the loose it would make sense anyway. There appear to be some extremely valuable antiques in the house, which would make it a prime target for thieves,' I tried to lighten the mood slightly by adding, 'not to mention you'll probably get a substantial discount on your contents insurance.'

'Actually, that's already in hand,' Robert told us. 'Even before your news, I wasn't happy about the lack of security, so Frank and I had a word with the glaziers. They recommended a reputable local company. We rang them and they're sending someone out to change the locks and give us an estimate for fitting the alarms. The problem is, it'll be a few days before they can get to us.'

I glanced around. 'Where's Frank?'

'He's gone to Barton-le-Dale to collect my friend Tammy,' Alison explained. 'She rang me this morning soon after you'd left. She's handed her dissertation in and caught the train from Leeds. We rang the police station to ask if you'd mind picking her up but they told us you'd already left.'

Mary, who had been waiting patiently, asked if we'd like a cup of tea. We accepted gratefully. As she poured it, Alison told us, 'We were trying to sort out the mess in the study but when the glaziers removed the plywood and the broken window pane it got too cold. We plan to start again when they've left.'

'We'll give you a hand if you like,' Eve volunteered. 'We might get an idea about what Stephen Pengelly was up to that got him killed. Of course it could have been someone who was jealous because of his affair with Kathy King.'

We made a start on rectifying the damage to the study, which principally involved trying to sort papers into some semblance of order, plus collecting fragments of broken glass from the paintings, ceramics from the smashed ornaments, and splintered wood from the desk drawer and a couple of side tables that had been wrecked.

'It would be useful to know what this was originally,' Robert said. He was staring at an untidy heap of broken china I had swept to one edge of the carpet with a stiff brush I'd borrowed from Mary.

'I'm not sure, but they look a bit like vases, and fairly old ones at that,' I replied.

Eve, who along with Alison was on her hands and knees collating paperwork, looked up. 'If that's the best you can do, Adam, I wouldn't apply for a job as an expert on *The Antiques Roadshow.*'

'At least they have whole objects to value,' I retorted, 'not a twenty-four-piece dining set that's been turned into a three-hundred-piece jigsaw.'

'Do you two always go on like that?' Alison asked.

'Not always,' I told her. 'Sometimes Eve is asleep.'

'Hah! At least I don't talk in my sleep, like some people around here.'

I was still trying to think up a suitably witty response when the crunch of gravel outside heralded the arrival of a car. I wondered briefly if the detectives had left the crime scene to visit us, but when the vehicle came into sight I recognised it. Even senior police officers didn't get to ride around in a Mercedes, let alone detective sergeants.

'That'll be Frank with Tammy,' Alison said. She jumped to her feet and hastened out into the hall, closely followed by Robert. We heard the indistinct greetings being exchanged before the couple reappeared with the latest house guest. Alison performed the introductions.

'This is my friend Tamara Watson, but everyone calls her Tammy.'

She explained who we were and then took the new arrival off to show her the rest of the house and the bedroom she had been allocated. I resumed my rather depressing task, but was interrupted almost immediately by Eve. 'This might be of some help to Robert,' she said, holding a large piece of paper. It was crumpled but intact, unlike a lot of the contents of the room.

'What might help me?' Robert asked as he appeared in the doorway.

Eve handed it to him. 'It looks like an inventory of some of the house contents,' she explained.

Robert ran his eye down the list. 'There's one way to find out. I'll ask Mary if she recognises the items.'

He returned from the kitchen a few minutes later, a puzzled frown on his face. 'I don't know where these are from, but they're not part of the manor contents. Mary says she's never seen any of the things on here.'

'Hang on, I've had an idea.' Eve began flicking through one of the piles of paperwork on the floor around her. After a moment she extracted a page which looked, from where I was standing, like an invoice. She passed it to Robert. 'See if any of the items on that list match what's on here.'

He compared the two and after a moment said, 'Yes, there's one item, a vase, that appears on both.' He frowned, then added, 'I'm sure it's the same, because the description is identical, but the value is a whole lot different. On Stephen's list the vase is valued at three-hundred pounds, but according to the invoice he only paid twenty-five for it.'

'That's a huge difference. Perhaps the seller didn't know what it was worth.'

'I doubt that, Adam,' Eve told me. 'The vendor is an antiques dealer, who must surely have had a good idea of what it was worth. Maybe we should look for more invoices. There are lots more items on that inventory.'

When Alison and Tammy joined us a few minutes later they found all three of us on our hands and knees. The neat stacks of paper were no more, having been transformed into a haphazard mess as we searched for invoices. Robert explained what we were doing, and the girls joined in, which shortened the search time considerably. Nevertheless it was almost half an hour before we had gone through all the papers, by which time we had extracted a sheaf of invoices. We compared their contents with the items on the inventory, and managed to match all but two of them. Robert tallied the figures up.

'The total price Stephen paid for the goods on those invoices was just short of four thousand pounds. The sum for the same items on that sheet' – he indicated the inventory – 'is nearer nineteen thousand.'

'That's some bargain,' Tammy exclaimed.

'Maybe so, but it doesn't make sense. Why would an antiques dealer, who presumably knows the value of these things to within a few pounds, sell them for a fraction of what they're worth? I could understand it if there was only one item, and it was outside his field of expertise, but there are pieces of furniture, ceramics, and an oil painting among the stuff Stephen bought, so the vendor must have known the value of most of them.'

'Perhaps the business was strapped for cash, or was closing down,' Alison suggested.

'The other puzzle is what happened to these things. They're not in the house, that's for certain. Mary could have overlooked a couple of vases, although I doubt it, but she certainly wouldn't have missed the furniture. She didn't recognise any of them, which means that not only are they not in the house now, but they've never been here.'

'If your brother didn't keep them, perhaps he gave them to his girlfriend, Kathy King,' Alison said.

I shook my head. 'No chance. I didn't have time to look closely at the contents of her flat, but most of what I did see looked as if it had come straight out of a Habitat catalogue.' There was one notable exception to this, but it didn't seem at all relevant. It certainly wasn't an antique. I thought for a moment, before adding, 'This might have no bearing on why Stephen and his mistress were killed, but it might be worth mentioning to DS Holmes. He could check out the business better than us. Where is it based?'

Robert read the details aloud. 'Graeme Fletcher Antiques, The Old Coach House, Market Place, Barton-le-Dale. I could ring Holmes and tell him, I suppose.'

'Why not leave it until he comes here. He'll want to take statements from Eve and me at some stage.'

That evening, over dinner, Eve suggested that our efforts that afternoon had been pretty much in vain.

'I think we've already worked that out,' I replied. My flippant remark earned me a high-wattage glare.

'What's more,' Eve continued as if I hadn't spoken, 'I think the intruder here was also risking arrest for nothing.'

'How do you work that out, Eve?' Alison asked the question quickly, obviously attempting to forestall another remark from me.

'The study is vulnerable. It has three large windows that face out onto the grounds at the front of the house. No more than fifty or so yards away on the left is dense woodland. To the right there are those huge shrubs. Either of those could conceal someone. If they wanted to, they could stand there in perfect safety and with a half-decent pair of binoculars read the newspaper at the same time as anyone in that study.'

I smiled at Eve's analogy, but remained silent. I thought I could tell where Eve was heading and wanted to give her chance to develop her theory. Obviously, Robert hadn't followed Eve's line of reasoning. 'That may be true, but what would be the point?'

'I know you detested your brother, and by what we've heard so far, that opinion was shared by most of the people who live around here, but nothing I've heard so far suggests he was either dim-witted or naive.'

'I'll grant you that.'

'Only a fool or someone incredibly trusting would keep anything of great value in a room without defences of any sort. The study had no alarms, its contents were highly visible, and it offered a thief easy access, even without front door keys. It stands to reason that he'd choose somewhere far safer to keep anything worth stealing.'

'That's an extremely good point,' Robert said. He turned to Alison. 'I think your brother Jeremy was right to recommend Adam and Eve. They work together so well.'

'Perhaps we should test Eve's theory out on Frank and Mary,' I suggested. 'I'm sure there must be a secure place, and they'll know where it is if anyone does.'

'Oh, good, if they don't know then we can have a treasure hunt,' Tammy said. 'I could enjoy my stay here.'

When Frank appeared a few minutes later bearing coffee, Robert put the question to him. 'Of course there is, Mr Robert. There's a large safe in the wine cellar. Mr Stephen often went down there.'

I nudged Eve's leg under the table, giving it quite a hefty shove. Even that failed to remove the complacent grin from her face. Tammy however looked quite disappointed.

After breakfast next morning the five of us followed Frank Jolly to the wine cellar, which filled only one room of the basement. 'The other part is only used for storage nowadays,' Frank explained. 'I believe in the past it was where they hung game and meat, but Mr Stephen wasn't interested in shooting – or in farming for that matter.'

'More fool him,' Robert said. 'That will certainly change.'

Frank Jolly smiled approval. 'Tony Bishop, the estate manager, will be glad to hear that. He despaired of getting your brother to show more interest in managing the farms.

As for the pheasant shooting, he allowed Tony to let the rights out on a season-by-season basis, but wouldn't pay for a stocking or breeding programme. Nor would he allow stalking or vermin control on the land. That also used to irritate Tony, especially when your brother complained that crop yields were below expectations. Bishop told him straight out a month or so ago, "What do you expect when the place is overrun with deer, rabbits, pigeons, and lots more besides, all helping themselves to free meals on a daily basis?" To be honest, I think Tony was close to handing his notice in.'

'Where is he?' Robert asked. 'Why haven't I met him?'

'He's away on holiday.' Jolly smiled. 'He and Emma, his girlfriend, have gone to Scotland. He had an invitation to a grouse shoot there, and he's also been promised a few days' deer stalking.'

We had passed long rows of wine racks, which stretched from floor to ceiling. I noticed that they seemed well-stocked. One thing Stephen Pengelly obviously wasn't against was alcohol. We paused in front of a large cupboard, about the size of a wardrobe. 'Is that it?' Alison asked, 'It doesn't look very secure.'

Jolly smiled, and by way of explanation, opened the twin doors. The cupboard housed a large, heavy-gauge steel safe, the sort that would not have looked out of place in the vault of a bank or building society. 'There you are, Mr Robert. I'll leave you to it.'

Frank turned to walk away, but Robert stopped him. 'Hang on, Frank, what about a key?'

'I'm sorry, Mr Robert, I can't help you there. I thought you had it.'

'Perhaps it's on your brother's bunch, along with the house keys,' I suggested.

'Good idea. Would you fetch them, please, Frank? They're on the desk.'

Frank returned several minutes later and passed the

bunch of keys to Robert. One glance was sufficient to tell me that a large safe key was not amongst those on the ring. Robert had obviously reached the same conclusion. He stared at the collection, his expression one of dismay..

We all trooped dispiritedly back upstairs, our hopes of discovering something meaningful dashed, and sought solace in the kitchen. Mary, who was soaring in everyone's esteem with every passing day, had baked a batch of scones and these, washed down with tea, were devoured by all. As solace for our disappointment, they were spot on. We had just finished eating when the doorbell rang.

Robert went to answer it, accompanied by Frank. A few seconds later, Frank returned. 'Mr Robert has asked you to join him in the drawing room,' he announced, taking on the temporary role of a butler. 'Detective Sergeant Holmes has arrived.'

We filed into the large, airy room, which I think was probably my favourite part of the ground floor. It came as no surprise to learn later that it had been decorated and furnished to the wishes of Robert's mother. Holmes was seated on one of the twin Chesterfield sofas with his new sidekick Johnny Pickersgill alongside him.

Alison introduced her friend Tammy, who shook hands with both officers. I saw Holmes' eyes light up as he looked at Tammy. That's more than professional interest, I thought. Tammy wasn't exactly pretty, rather more pleasant-looking than a raving beauty. If I'd had to choose a word to describe her, I think it would have been wholesome.

In turn, Eve made Johnny Pickersgill known to everyone, explaining that he was a good friend as well as our local bobby. As I glanced from Holmes to Pickersgill, I noticed that they seemed well pleased with themselves, and ready to impart what they thought would be good news to us.

Holmes' opening words confirmed this. In fact it exceeded it by a country mile. 'We believe we have identified the man who killed your brother and Miss King,' he told Robert. If Holmes was trying to learn the art of shocking an audience to silence, he still had some way to go.

'Really?' Robert responded immediately, 'That is quick work. Can you tell us who the suspect is, or is it *sub judice* or whatever the expression is?'

'I can tell you our suspicions, but that's as far as it goes for the moment. The man we believe committed the murders isn't in custody, unfortunately. However, we have a considerable amount of circumstantial evidence and we believe we have established the motive for the crimes.'

'What might that be?' I asked.

'We think the suspect was seeing Miss King, and was jealous when he found out she was also sleeping with Stephen Pengelly. We talked to the other tenants of the building where Miss King lived, and they were most helpful. The lady who occupies the other first floor flat across the landing from Miss King's told us she encountered a man on the stairs a couple of times. The lady was able to describe him in some detail. She also told us that Miss King sometimes had a visitor who stayed overnight, although she was unable to confirm that it was the same man.'

Holmes allowed us to ponder that for a moment before continuing. 'One of the ground-floor tenants also provided some very useful information. He recognised Miss King's visitor as the owner of a shop in Barton-le-Dale marketplace where she worked. We visited the premises this morning but the shop was closed. We spoke to the manageress of the launderette next door and she told us the shop has been closed all week. She thought the owner might be on holiday. Her description of the shop owner matches that given by the tenant in Miss King's building.'

He paused again, and if his intention was to provide a dramatic revelation, Eve stole his thunder. 'Was it an antique shop, and was the owner a man called Graeme Fletcher?'

Holmes and Pickersgill stared at Eve, plainly astounded by her question. They didn't answer; their silent amazement confirmed the accuracy of Eve's guess.

'How on earth did you know that, Eve?' Johnny Pickersgill asked eventually.

We explained what we'd found in the study, and when we finished, Holmes had recovered sufficiently to tell us more. 'When we couldn't find Fletcher at the shop we visited his house. That was also locked up. A neighbour told us they'd seen Fletcher load his car with suitcases a couple of days ago and drive off. They remembered thinking it was a strange time of year to be taking a holiday. Fletcher hasn't returned. We've put a nationwide alert out to all forces, warning them that this man could be armed and highly dangerous. We've also applied for a search warrant for Fletcher's house and the shop. There's no way he could have carried out those crimes without getting covered in blood.' Holmes looked at me. 'You saw the Kathy King crime scene.'

'Thank you so much for reminding me. That was an image I was trying to forget.'

Holmes smiled, but with little evidence of humour. 'I'd really like to get my hands on that weapon. I've already seen the damage that thing can do on two occasions. I certainly don't want to see it again.'

'You think Fletcher's motive was simply jealousy?' Robert asked.

'We do, going from what Miss King's neighbour told us about the visitor who stayed overnight at the flat. If that was Fletcher, and he thought he was the only man in Miss King's life, he could well have been enraged when he found out about her affair with your brother.'

'There may be more to it than simply a love triangle,' I told them. 'Kathy King worked for Fletcher and if she was the person who sold those antiques to Stephen Pengelly at knock-down prices, Fletcher might have been angry about that as well as the affair.'

'We won't know until we've had chance to arrest Fletcher. Hopefully that won't be long. The neighbour told us Fletcher had recently bought a new car, a BMW, so we spoke to the local dealer. He gave us the registration number, so we've been able to pass that to other forces as well.'

We remained in the drawing room after Holmes and Pickersgill left. Robert voiced the general consensus by saying, 'I think we can afford to relax now. The threat from an unknown killer seems to have gone and I can't imagine this guy Fletcher coming here to the manor while he's on the run, not with every police force in the land on the lookout for him.'

I saw Eve look at me and could tell by her expression that she shared my reservations. 'I wish that was so,' I told Robert, 'but I'm by no means convinced it's as clear-cut as Holmes suggested. I'm not saying that they're chasing the wrong man, but I certainly don't believe the jealousy motive as the overriding reason for the murders. Even if Fletcher did kill your brother and Kathy King, there has to be more to it than a jilted lover taking revenge.'

'Are you saying that Detective Sergeant Holmes got it wrong?' Tammy asked. 'That's a bit presumptive, isn't it? After all, he is a police officer, not an amateur detective.'

I found her defence of Holmes, and the tone she expressed it in, quite intriguing. 'No, I'm not saying he's wrong, but what nobody seems to have taken into account is the break-in here. That happened after Stephen Pengelly and Kathy King were murdered. Unless you believe that the burglary was committed by someone other than the killer, why did it take place at all? Why would the killer have risked arrest by breaking into the manor if his only motive was jealousy? He'd already exacted his revenge, according to the police theory. It doesn't make sense. Whether Fletcher is the killer or not, there has to be more to it. I believe we should search for that safe key.'

'That's going to be like looking for a very small needle in a very large haystack,' Alison pointed out.

I agreed, and so too, judging by their glum expressions, did the others. Fortunately, Eve came up with an idea for narrowing the search parameters. 'Perhaps if we were to ask the right questions of the right people we might get a clue as to where Stephen Pengelly kept the key,' she suggested. 'We know Frank can't help but Mary might have an idea.'

Following Eve like a flock of sheep with a devoted shepherdess, we went in search of Mary. She wasn't too hard to locate, being seated at the kitchen table along with Frank.

'Did either of you ever see Stephen Pengelly as he was on his way to the cellar?' Eve asked. 'I don't mean when he was on his way to collect a bottle of Mouton Rothschild, I mean when he was going to put something in the safe. We need to find the safe key.'

Frank shook his head. 'Sorry, most of my time is spent outside.'

'I did,' Mary's response was instantaneous, 'on one or two occasions. He must have been going to the safe because he was carrying documents from his study when he went downstairs, and when he returned he was empty-handed.'

'In that case,' Eve told us, 'I think we ought to concentrate our effort in the study. That seems the most logical place. Thank you, Mary; you might just have saved us a lot of wasted time and frustration.'

Chapter Six

It was one thing deciding to concentrate on the study, but where to start was another matter. Tammy opted out, saying she wanted to take a walk. Alison watched her friend leave, an air of mild concern on her face. 'Something wrong?' Eve asked her. She was getting to be as good as me at stating the obvious.

'No, but Tammy occasionally suffers with migraines, I hope she isn't going to have an attack.'

We split the task in two. Robert and I were given the task of emptying the trio of filing cabinets that were situated on the side wall, while Alison and Eve concentrated on Stephen Pengelly's desk. 'I don't know much about Stephen, apart from what I've been told,' Eve said, 'but I'd guess that his desk would be the obvious place.'

I glanced across the room. Eve had a point, where else would Pengelly have secreted the key? As I worked, I checked the tabs on the suspended files, in the faint hope that I would find something of interest. As we reached the lower levels, that hope receded.

Our luck changed when Alison, who had been reaching into the cavity where the bottom drawer of the desk had been, feeling for the missing key, decided to stand up. As she rose from her kneeling position, she put out one hand to steady herself against the desk. As she pushed against the desk top for leverage, the whole top section moved slightly, swivelling. Her surprised cry of, 'What happened there?' caused us to look round. She pushed a second time, then again, harder, and to everyone's surprise, the top section of the desk swivelled open, to lock in place at ninety degrees to the rest of the frame.

We crowded round to look. At first glance it seemed that all she had done was to reveal the divider between the two parts of the framework, but then Robert noticed finger-marks close to a knot in the wood. He pressed it, and half of the section sprang open, and we could see that the flap was controlled by tiny concealed hinges.

'Well, well, well, a secret compartment. How like my brother, or my father,' Robert commented.

The open section contained a folder marked 'Pengelly Family Tree, Part One,' which Robert put on the desk top and ignored. Our attention was taken with the contents of the small compartment to the left of it. There were three keys inside. A large steel one, with a bunch containing half a dozen slightly smaller brass keys alongside it. Eve pointed at the larger key. 'At a guess I'd say that's the safe key.'

'I agree,' Robert replied, 'but what are those other ones? I've never seen keys like them.'

I picked them up and inspected them. 'You may not, but I have. You need to check with Frank, but I'm fairly certain these are the keys to gun cabinets. Which is extremely interesting, because if your brother was against shooting, why would he keep gun cabinet keys so close at hand? All right to keep them secure, but I hardly think he'd want them in his desk.'

Nobody seemed particularly interested in my theory, preferring to concentrate on the possibilities raised by gaining access to the safe. That was a shame, as things turned out, but I shelved the idea rather than discarding it altogether.

We left the study as Tammy returned from her brief walk. 'Too cold to stay outside for long,' she commented. 'Any luck?'

Robert held up the key by way of a reply.

'We're off to try the safe. Do you want to come along?' Alison asked.

Excitement and curiosity won, and she willingly tagged along, which turned out to be a blessing.

Mary Jolly was obviously of an easy-going nature, otherwise I feel sure she would have commented as a party of five traipsed to and fro through her kitchen with irritating regularity. As we entered her sanctum yet again she was rolling pastry, which augured well for the evening meal. She looked up and saw the key in Robert's hand. 'Oh good, you've found it. That looks like the one I saw Mr Stephen carrying.'

'We'll let you know soon, Mary. If it is, then perhaps we'll stop disturbing you.' It seemed that Robert Pengelly was as good as me at making rash statements. 'Do you know what these fit?' he asked, showing Mary the brass keys. 'Adam seems to think they might be for gun cabinets.'

'They could be, Mr Robert. Frank may know. Shall I call him? He's out chopping wood at the moment. He says we need extra for the drawing room, the hall, and the dining room. We hadn't bargained for guests.'

'No, don't disturb him, it can wait. It's not urgent.'

In the cellar Robert paused briefly alongside the wine racks. 'I'll have to ask Frank about these,' he told me. 'I think we ought to sample one or two and see how good Stephen's taste was.'

Having opened the cupboard door, Robert offered the key up to the lock. It entered the chamber smoothly and as he turned it we could hear the tumblers clicking, signalling his success. He grasped the handle and turned it to horizontal, and with some effort pulled the heavy door open. We crowded round to peer inside.

Much of the space was taken up with ledgers and file folders. The ledgers were marked on their spines with dates, and the contents, which, according to the writing, were nothing more exciting than the estate accounts. These might have been of value to the Pengelly family, but I could not imagine them being of the slightest interest to a burglar. The only other item in there was what appeared to be a photo album.

Robert turned his attention to the twin drawers at the base of the safe. The one on the left yielded up a jewellery box covered in deep crimson velvet. He opened it to reveal a magnificent necklace, with matching bracelet and earrings. The settings were gold, and there was little doubt in my mind that the stones were diamonds, not paste. Something in the way they winked and sparkled as they reflected the light suggested that these were far more than mere costume jewellery. To one side of the box were two rings, one of diamonds, the other a plain gold band, obviously engagement and wedding rings.

'Those are absolutely beautiful,' Alison breathed, 'I wonder who they belonged to?'

'They were my mother's,' Robert told her. 'If you examine her portrait in the dining room, you'll see she's wearing these.'

He returned the box to the safe and opened the second drawer. The only item inside was, at first sight, much less valuable. It was a small notebook of the type sold in any high street stationers. Robert opened it and stared at the top page uncomprehendingly. 'What do you think this might be?'

Eve and Alison peered over his shoulder. Both of them shook their heads. Robert passed it to me. At first glance, the crude lines reminded me of the matchstick figures drawn by LS Lowry. 'I've absolutely no idea. It looks just like a load of random lines, as if somebody was doodling. But if that's the case, why would you lock them away in a safe?'

'May I have a look, please?' We'd almost forgotten

Tammy. She scanned the page quickly. 'There's nothing random about these marks. I'm surprised you didn't recognise them, Alison, but then you concentrated on the medieval period. If you'd studied earlier times, you'd have spotted what they were at once. They're runes.'

'Does that mean they're Viking?' Robert asked.

Tammy shook her head. 'Not necessarily. Vikings did use runic script, but runes go back way before them. These look more Celtic in origin.'

'You mean they're from Scotland?' Eve asked.

'It's possible. However, runic script is just as likely to hail from Wales, Ireland, anywhere in England, or even Brittany. There are examples of runic carving all over Europe. The Celtic tribes covered much of the Continent at one time.' She glanced down at the page again. 'There's something odd about these characters, though. They don't seem to match any of the examples I've seen before.'

'That means we're going to have a problem finding someone who can translate them.' Alison commented.

Tammy looked at her friend and shook her head in mock sorrow. 'Come on, Alison, where's your brain gone? Have you forgotten Old Mother Riley?'

Alison gasped, 'Of course, I never gave her a thought.'

'Apart from a music hall act, who is Old Mother Riley?' Robert looked puzzled.

Tammy smiled at him. 'When Alison and I were in our first year we had a superb tutor, a woman called Victoria Riley. Sadly for us she retired at the end of that year and we got lumbered with that dickhead, Professor Locke, who was appointed to replace her. He's a waste of space.'

'What's the point about Professor Riley?' Robert was still staring at the pages as he spoke.

'One of her specialities is ancient languages and alphabets. If anyone can translate those runes she can.'

'How do we go about getting hold of her?' Eve asked.

Alison and Tammy looked at one another. 'Can you

remember where she retired to?' Tammy asked.

'Somewhere around here, wasn't it? In the Dales, I think.'

'Would the university know?' Robert asked.

The girls exchanged another glance and said in unison, 'Jackie!'

Robert and Eve's chorus was almost as good, 'Who's Jackie?'

'A friend of ours, she works in the university offices.'

'So what are you wasting time for? Get on the phone and see if you can locate this Professor Riley,' Robert said.

'I'll phone Jackie, you can tackle Old Mother Riley,' Tammy said.

'I don't mind that,' Alison agreed.

We returned upstairs, and while Eve and I continued to examine the notebook's mysterious contents, Tammy obtained the phone number from the university. She passed this to Alison, who began planning her approach to her former tutor. 'Robert, Professor Riley is a connoisseur and will do almost anything for a top-class wine. Do you think I could mention the wine cellar?'

'Why not explain to her that I've recently inherited the house and I need some advice about what's in the wine cellar and what to choose for restocking it?'

'That's a great idea! I'm sure she'd go for that, even without the runes to look at.' Alison picked the phone up and began to dial.

While we studied the book, I began to feel we were at a dead end. Without some clue as to why Stephen had saved the notebook with the runes drawn inside, we were no closer to guessing what relevance, if any, they might have had in why he was murdered. Whatever the others might think, I had all but discarded jealousy as a motive for the crimes. It seemed to me they were too cold-blooded to have been the actions of a jilted lover. At the same time, I couldn't think of any reason for Stephen Pengelly to have acquired the rune drawings, let alone secrete them in a safe.

Robert looked at us and smiled ruefully. 'Saying that about the inheritance has reminded me that I ought to contact the solicitor who handled Stephen's affairs. Everyone has assumed that the estate will come to me, but there's nothing to say that Stephen didn't will it elsewhere.'

'Wouldn't you be able to challenge the will if he left it to someone other than his immediate family?' Eve asked.

'I've no idea, and there's nothing to say that he did so. He might have thought of doing it, but whether he would go ahead with it is another matter. I suppose it depends on whether he still hated me. I think family pride would outweigh that, though. In his more amenable moments, which admittedly were few and far between, he used to tell me about all the different ancestors whose paintings hang from the walls hereabouts. To be honest, from what I can remember they seemed a disreputable mob, but Stephen was obviously very proud of them, and his heritage.'

'If he thought that way, I guess he wouldn't have risked dragging the family name through the courts and attracting the unsavoury publicity a legal battle over the estate would provoke,' Eve pointed out.

I re-focused Robert's attention on the more immediate problem. 'Do you know the name of the solicitor?'

'No. I do remember a man coming to visit my father who I believe was the solicitor, but I've no idea what he was called. In any case, he was quite elderly, so he'll have retired long since, even if he isn't pushing up daisies.'

I looked around. 'I suppose there must be correspondence from them somewhere.'

Robert eyed the piles of paperwork and winced. 'I don't fancy going through that lot. Maybe there will be a file in the cabinets.'

Even that might be tricky to find without a name, I

thought, but decided not to mention it. 'Why not ask Frank or Mary?' Eve suggested, 'If the solicitor visited the house, they might recall his name.'

'And if they know that,' I added, 'Alison's brother would be able to find out the name of the law practice via the Law Society.'

Robert was about to go to the kitchen to ask the question, but at that point Alison put the phone down. 'Professor Riley would be delighted to help on both the runes and the wine, but she's leaving for London later today and won't be back until Sunday. There's an exhibition she's keen not to miss. After that she's available, so I said I'd talk to you with a view to her coming to stay for a few days. Would that be all right?'

Robert smiled. 'Of course it would. I feel better here when there are people about. I don't think I could have crossed the threshold if I'd been alone, so as long as it doesn't cause Mary too many problems.'

'I'll ring her back and confirm that.'

Before Alison had chance to lift the receiver, the phone rang. Robert answered it, and I saw a look of astonishment on his face as the caller identified themselves. 'Yes,' he said after a moment, 'this is Robert Pengelly speaking. Sorry, what did you say your name is? This is an unbelievable coincidence, I was about to try and find out about you so I could phone you.' He listened for a moment, then said, 'No, don't worry about that. No, from my point of view that's ideal, couldn't be better. Yes, OK, when? Yes that'll be fine, what time? No, no problem, see you then.'

Robert looked up. He saw the questioning look on our faces and grinned. 'That was the Pengelly family solicitor,' he explained, 'from a firm called Alderson & Co. His name is Nigel Alderson, only a young bloke by the sound of it. He's just read about Stephen's death. Apparently his father used to deal with the account but he's semi-retired and Nigel was asking if I minded him handling things. I told him that suited me. I'd rather have somebody I don't associate with the past. He's coming the day after tomorrow.'

'One thing I should say,' I said, looking at Robert. 'Until Professor Riley arrives to translate them, I think you should return the notebook to the safe. If it was important enough for Stephen to put it there, that would be the best place for it.'

Robert agreed, but quite naturally he had other things on his mind right then. 'I'm more concerned about what this chap Alderson has to say,' he told us. 'There's no certainty that I actually have inherited the estate until he confirms it; I'm not counting on it.' He looked at Alison. 'Will you sit in with me when he comes? I'd rather you were there to hold my hand.'

'Of course I will, Robbie. What time is he coming?'

'He said he'd be here just after lunch.' Robert looked at Alison and smiled. It was a tender expression, unlike any I'd seen from him before. 'If he does confirm that I own Barton Manor, I have lots of decisions to make, and I want you alongside me when I make them.'

Eve got hold of me by one hand, gesturing to Tammy with the other. We exited the study and left them alone.

As we retreated to the kitchen, which was rapidly becoming my favourite haunt, I thought about Robert, and how he rarely displayed signs of emotion. Was that, I wondered, a by-product of his upbringing. I reckoned the only person who could answer that was Alison, and I certainly wasn't about to ask her.

That evening, before dinner, Robert asked Frank and Mary to join us all in the drawing room, where he and Alison formally announced their engagement. After everyone had congratulated them, with plenty of hugging and handshaking, Robert explained to Frank and Mary about the solicitor's impending visit. 'If he confirms that I *do* own the manor, I hope you will feel comfortable with the new arrangement, and continue here. I may want to make some changes, but if and when I do, you will be consulted beforehand. One thing I can say, and Alison agrees, is that I will definitely not be selling the manor, nor any part of the estate. We want to live here, and hopefully raise our family here. What do you say, will you work with us?'

They didn't even need to glance at one another, and their response was both immediate and enthusiastic. 'We'd be more than happy to, Mr Robert,' Mary said.

Later, after we had consumed another of Mary's excellent dinners, Frank asked Robert if he would be needed the following day. 'No, I don't think so.'

'There's some dead trees and broken branches in Home Wood I want to move before we get severe gales or heavy snow.'

'That's fine by me.'

That night, Eve and I slept much better, no doubt because we no longer felt the threat of an intrusion at the manor. Next morning, as we prepared to go down for breakfast, Eve suggested that we should go for a walk. 'Apart from driving to Barton-le-Dale and back we've hardly set foot outside the house since we arrived. It would be nice to explore the grounds, don't you think?'

Last night's news of Robert and Alison's engagement reminded me that Eve also wore a ring, my mother's ring. Maybe while we were out I could take the opportunity to remind her there was a wedding to plan, I mused. I glanced out of our bedroom window before agreeing to her idea. The sun was shining, and although the trees were bending in the wind, it looked like a nice morning for a walk. Besides which, as I told Eve, 'If Mary continues feeding us the way she has been doing we're going to need lots of exercise to burn off the calories.'

'It might help if you decline the extra portion of apple pie once in a while.'

'I don't like good cooking to go to waste.'

Eve's scornful laugh left me in no doubt as to her opinion of my remark.

After breakfast we made our preparations, with guidance from Mary Jolly. 'If you turn right when you leave the kitchen, the corridor leading to the laundry room has lots of coats and boots for you to choose from. You'll need to wrap up well. It might look nice from inside, but there's a sneaky cold wind blowing.'

The corridor had a row of coat hooks mounted on one wall, from which a wide variety of garments hung. I saw tweed shooting jackets, waxed Barbour coats, long riding cloaks, and even sets of waterproof leggings and waders. There were also scarves and hats, and below, a row of wellingtons, plus walking and riding boots of all shapes and sizes. Nothing, it seemed, had been unaccounted for.

'There seems to be an awful lot of clothing here for a man living alone,' Eve said as she tried on a waxed coat.

'I suspect by the look of them that most of the coats have been here since long before Stephen's time. The styles are mostly pre-war, I'd say. That was the heyday of big shooting parties and country house gatherings. In addition to the family and their guests there would be the servants to cater for. They would need access to outdoor clothing too.'

'Would they be allowed to use the family's clothing?'

'I think the domestic arrangements were far more democratic than portrayed in books and films. It stands to reason that if you have to send one of the servants to the outbuildings in a snowstorm, to say, fetch logs for all the fires in a house this size, you'd want to ensure they were adequately protected.'

'I didn't think estate owners were so considerate.'

'They weren't; this was down to self-interest. If your

servant caught a chill they might take a long time to recover and be fit for work again. That meant you'd have to keep them without getting any work out of them.'

'And there was me thinking you were becoming romantic, when you were merely being your cynical self.'

We were about to set off when Mary came bustling along the corridor, a plastic carrier bag in one hand. 'Would you mind doing me a favour?' she asked. 'Frank went and forgot his flask and sandwiches. If you could give them to him it would save me a job.'

'That's no problem,' Eve told her, 'but where will we find him? Home Wood is pretty big, and we don't know our way round. Did he tell you whereabouts he was going to be working?'

'No, but you should be able to locate him easily enough. Just listen for the sound of his chainsaw.'

Having taken possession of the carrier bag, we opened the door and stepped outside. The walls of Barton Manor are almost a foot thick, and it was only when we exited the house that we realised the extent to which they protected the occupants from the weather. The wind must have been close to gale force, buffeting us, even where we were standing, in the lee of the building. Out in the open it would be even worse. As we made our way to the corner of the house and began to walk across the courtyard towards Home Wood, we discovered that even making headway against that wind was difficult, and when it was blowing at its fiercest, we had to make a conscious effort to avoid being blown over.

Another potential problem occurred to me. The sound made by the wind was bad enough where we were. Inside the wood the noise was probably going to be greatly magnified. Unless we happened to be downwind of Frank Jolly, hearing the sound of his chainsaw would be nigh on impossible. I was also concerned from a safety point of view. Being in dense woodland in high winds was hardly the most sensible thing to do. Nevertheless, we had promised to deliver Jolly's lunch, so we made our way slowly towards the edge of the wood, walking hand in hand to brace each other against the worst of the blasts, our ears straining for the buzz of the chainsaw.

When we reached the trees we struck lucky, finding a well-beaten path almost at once. 'Who walks through here often enough to create this path?' Eve asked, her voice raised against the moaning of the wind.

'Not who, what,' I replied in a muted bellow. I pointed to the ground, where the imprints of dozens of small cloven hooves were clearly visible. 'Those are deer prints. Slots, they're called. Remember Frank telling us the estate was overrun with them? Looks like he wasn't exaggerating.'

We made our way along the deer path, our progress slow. Although the dense woodland protected us from the worst of the wind, new problems were provided by the brambles and briars that tugged at our feet and ankles with almost every stride, threatening to trip us. We also had to duck or move sideways from time to time to avoid overhanging branches or parts of shrubs. All along, we were accompanied by a wailing instrumental played by the wind in the topmost branches of the larger trees. It sounded a little like a totally inept player trying out an Aeolian harp, or pan pipes.

As I held up a trailing overhang of bramble to allow Eve to pass without scratching her face, I noticed movement in the periphery of my vision. I turned swiftly, startled by what I thought I'd seen, and remained standing, rooted to the spot, long after Eve was clear of the obstruction. Whatever I'd seen, or thought I'd seen was no longer there – even if it had been there in the first place. I followed Eve along the trail, trying to convince myself that if I had actually seen something, it had only been a deer, and that the animal had moved so quickly that I'd only caught a glimpse of its hind quarters, perhaps. I almost succeeded, but at the back of my mind doubt remained. The vision I retained was unlike a deer. It had been larger, and darker. Or had it been nothing more than a figment of my over-active imagination?

Chapter Seven

Five minutes later, we found Frank Jolly. Or at least, we found his chainsaw. It hadn't only been the wind that had prevented us hearing the motor. The machine wasn't switched on. In fact, one look told me the machine would never run again. It was lying beneath the trunk of a fallen ash tree, and from what we could see, the chainsaw appeared to be smashed beyond repair.

Seconds later, as we rounded the obstacle with considerable difficulty, scrambling over the trunk, we found Frank himself. At first sight, he appeared to be in no better shape than his chainsaw. Luckily, though, it seemed that he had avoided being struck by the main trunk. Had that been so, the outcome would have been fatal – instantaneous death caused by the crushing weight of countless tons of timber.

Frank was unconscious, but a quick check revealed his pulse was strong. Nevertheless, there was no cause for celebration. He was lying face down, pinned by a branch of the ash tree that had almost ended his life. We couldn't be sure what injuries, either external or internal, he might have suffered, but one thing was certain. We had to risk potential damage by removing him from under that branch as quickly as possible. There was a real danger that with his mouth and nose pressed so close to the ground, he might suffocate or choke if we couldn't move him.

I looked at the branch, and was relieved to see that it had snapped, either by contact with the limbs of another tree, or when it had hit the ground. The break was a few feet from where Frank was lying, and with luck, I thought, this would give us chance to extricate him. 'If I manage to lift the branch for a few seconds, do you think you'll be able to drag him clear?' I asked.

Eve looked at me, her face a mask of concern. Then I saw the look of determination in her eyes. That's my girl, I thought. Indomitable. 'I'll do my best,' she promised. 'Shout when you're ready to lift.'

I wriggled and pushed until I was in position, bending and breaking a host of smaller branches and twigs until I succeeded in getting my shoulder under the one that was trapping Frank. I dug my heels into the soft earth, striving for every bit of purchase, then shouted, 'I'm ready.'

I heaved, and as the branch lifted, I felt the strain on the muscles of my shoulders, back, and thighs, even my calves. I continued to push until I was upright. I wasn't sure how long I'd be able to maintain this position. The ache was already close to intolerable. I gritted my teeth, closed my eyes and concentrated every scrap of my attention on holding steady.

Then, just as I was thinking I couldn't bear it any longer, I heard Eve shout, 'He's clear.' The relief was immense. I lowered the branch until I was bent almost double, then scrambled clear. Eve called out again. 'He's coming round, I think.'

I walked slowly over to where she was kneeling alongside Frank. I waited for the ache in my muscles to ease. It showed little sign of doing so. As I reached them, Eve said, 'Frank, Frank, can you hear me? Can you open your eyes?'

He did so, and immediately looked from right to left, before concentrating on us. I wasn't sure what other injuries he might have sustained, but I was reasonably certain he was suffering from some form of concussion. In that brief moment, as he'd first looked round, it seemed as if he was expecting to see something else. And that something terrified him. The expression on his face had been one of pure, naked fear.

'Where is it?' he asked.

'Frank,' Eve's voice was low and soft, soothing and speaking slowly, as if to an infant, 'Frank, you were hit by a falling tree. We had to drag you from under it. Where does it hurt? Have you banged your head?'

'I remember.' His face cleared. 'Aye, it was the tree. No, I think I'm OK.' He made as if to move, but then winced. 'My arm hurts.'

'Don't try and sit up. Lie still until I can fetch help. Adam will stay with you.'

'I'll be as fast as I can,' she told me. 'He seems all right, but there could be internal injuries, so don't let him sit up. The ambulance people will know how to move him without risking further problems.'

'Fetch blankets,' I suggested, 'and possibly a hot water bottle. The ambulance could be a while. In this weather there might be a lot of calls on them.'

Once Eve left I sat alongside the injured man and explained why he shouldn't try to move. He agreed to lie still, and to help pass the time, I asked him what he could remember about the accident. I was keen to see how clear his mind was.

As soon as I asked, I saw that look of fear return, and his eyes went beyond me, as if searching for something he expected to see there. It was a long time before he spoke, and when he did, his words chilled me to the bone.

'I was standing under that big ash tree,' his voice was little louder than a whisper, almost as if he was scared he might be overheard. 'I was trying to decide whether to make a start or wait until the weather cleared. The wind was making a hell of a racket, so much so that it almost sounded like a huge animal roaring.'

He stopped suddenly, licked his lips nervously and once again his eyes traversed what bit of the woodland he could see beyond me. I still had no idea what he expected to see. Then, when he told me, I couldn't believe it. What's more, I didn't want to believe it.

'I'm not sure how long I stood there before I saw it. Or at least I thought I'd seen it. But I couldn't have, could I?' He looked at me, his expression pleading for reassurance. But I had none to give. I was half expecting him to tell me he'd seen a ghost, of Stephen Pengelly perhaps, or even of Kathy King. But he hadn't. What he'd seen was even stranger, even more incredible.

'What was it, Frank? What did you think you'd seen?' I kept my voice soft, emotionless, trying to coax the answer from him.

'It was over there. Over to the right of the big holly bush. No more than twenty yards away. I could see it as plain as I can see you. It was just standing there; staring straight at me. I've never been so frightened in all my life. I dropped the chainsaw and ran. I'd only gone a few yards when I heard this crashing sound. At first I thought the thing was coming after me, then something hit me in the middle of my back and I felt this bang on the head and that's the last I remember until Miss Samuels spoke to me.'

'And what was it, Frank? What did you see?' I thought I knew the answer, but I didn't want to believe it.

'I thought … it looked like … I thought it was … a bear. But there aren't any, are there? Not in this country?'

'No, Frank, there haven't been any bears in Britain for hundreds and hundreds of years. I think what you saw was probably nothing more than a trick of the light, perhaps, or a deer.'

I paused for a moment, allowing him time to respond, and when he didn't, added, 'I think it would be wise not to mention this to anyone. They might think the bump on the head has sent you doolally tap.'

'You don't believe me, do you?'

'Actually, you're wrong, Frank. That's the problem. I

86

do believe you.'

I didn't tell him that only moments before we found him, as I'd been helping Eve through the undergrowth; I thought I'd seen the very same thing. Nor did I tell him that Detective Inspector Hardy had thought he'd seen a bear in the split second before his car crash. It was bad enough me knowing, without anyone else being saddled with the knowledge.

Later, my decision to remain silent extended to Eve. I wasn't in the habit of keeping things from her, but, as with the intruder's mode of entry to Barton Manor, I judged it better for her peace of mind to remain in ignorance. It made for an uncomfortable time, as Eve naturally wanted to know what Frank had said. I told her that Frank had described the accident as best he could, and that I'd reassured him. Eve must have sensed that I wasn't giving her the full story, but unusually she didn't press me for further details.

As it happened, the truth soon emerged, in a further strange twist.

We weren't alone for long. Having raised the alarm, Eve returned with Mary while Robert, who'd called for an ambulance, followed hard on their heels. 'Alison and Tammy are waiting to guide them here,' he told me. 'How is he?'

'I'm no expert, but I believe his arm is broken, and he could be suffering from mild concussion. All we can do is keep him comfortable until we can hand him over to the professionals.'

Mary had already seen to that, placing a cushion carefully under his head, and wrapping a hot water bottle in a towel before putting it alongside him. Robert and I draped the blanket she had brought over the injured man, and retired, leaving Mary talking to him, gently soothing him. I couldn't make out what she was saying, but I could tell Frank looked more relaxed than at any time since we'd found him.

'They'll probably want to keep him in hospital overnight,' Eve told us. 'That's standard procedure, I believe, when they suspect someone might be suffering from concussion.'

'Yes, but that's only half the problem,' Robert replied. 'Even when Frank comes out of hospital, it would be grossly unfair to expect Mary to spend her time dashing between the manor and the lodge, attending to Frank and catering for us. We'll have to fend for ourselves for a while. That's not a problem. The important thing is getting Frank fit again. Between us, we should be able to take care of the household chores easily enough.' He paused and looked from me to Eve. 'Sorry, I'm presuming you'll be staying for the time being. I forgot you might have other plans.'

'There's nothing that can't wait,' Eve told him. She glanced at me and saw my nod of confirmation. 'Adam and I wouldn't dream of deserting you. Apart from anything else, unless you or Alison or Tammy has a licence we're the only qualified drivers.'

'Good heavens, I'd not thought of that. Alison and I certainly haven't taken our tests. Neither has Tammy as far as I know. There didn't seem the need, living in Leeds. Anyway, that can wait. I'm going to talk to Frank and Mary, to stop them worrying.'

'The better I get to know Robert, the more I like him,' Eve told me, her tone quiet enough so that Robert couldn't hear. 'It makes his father and brother's behaviour even more inexcusable.'

I agreed, and was about to add something, but at that moment we heard the bells signalling the approach of the emergency vehicle. The fact that we were able to hear it, implied that the wind had slackened from its earlier ferocity.

Half an hour later, having assisted the ambulance men in their task of extricating Frank from Home Wood and placing him securely in the back of their vehicle, we returned to the manor kitchen. 'I told Mary not to worry about us,' Robert said to Alison and Tammy, 'which means we're going to be self-catering for the time being. First off, I need to find out how to get Adam and Eve onto the car insurance policy. It's unfair to expect them to drive us everywhere in their own car, using their petrol. Have either of you seen any paperwork about insurance when you were tidying up the study?'

'That might not be necessary,' Eve told him. 'If you look inside the car, you'll probably find either a policy or cover note in there.'

Eve's confident prediction was proved correct, and when we found the cover note, it had a compliments slip from a local broker attached. Robert phoned them and was put through to the director. After Eve and I had answered questions regarding our ages and driving record, we were covered to drive the Mercedes , and the confirmation of our addition to the policy would be sent in the post.

When Robert ended the call he told us, 'He wanted to discuss the other estate insurances, but I had to tell him I can't commit to anything at the moment until I've met with the solicitor. It was strange, but he said I don't need to worry too much about everything. What do you think he meant by that?'

'It may be that he's only playing safe, and doesn't want to risk upsetting a potentially valuable client,' I pointed out. Nevertheless, I was left wondering what it could be that the broker knew, or might know. Even one of my wildest guesses couldn't have got close to the truth, and it was only after the solicitor's visit that some of the truth began to emerge.

Later that afternoon, Robert and I left the girls in charge of culinary arrangements and set off for the hospital to visit Frank. In my new capacity as chauffeur, I had to familiarise myself with the Mercedes, no easy task on the country lanes. However, once I got used to it, I found the car a joy to drive. As we travelled to Thorsby, Robert confided in me, which I found mildly surprising, as I'd thought of him as reserved, self-contained, up to that point.

'This business is far more complicated than I imagined,' he said. 'Handling the estate, I mean, not the murders and so forth. Not that I ever actually did imagine owning it. I thought Stephen would have amassed a crowd of heirs by now. Of course, I still might not own it. He might have left it to the RSPCA or something.'

'I doubt it, Robert. For one thing, the solicitor wouldn't be coming to see you unless he had something to tell you. And that insurance broker seemed confident that you were the new owner of Barton Manor. If that's the case, what's your problem?'

'There are all sorts of things, little ones when you take them individually, but when you put them together, it looks as if managing the estate is going to be a full-time job. I have no idea how we go on about paying household bills, wages, and so forth. Nor do I know what we do about things such as Frank's accident.'

He looked out of the window, and as I glanced at him, I saw his expression was sombre. 'I have no idea what sort of state the manor finances are in. For all I know the estate could have a whacking great overdraft and the house could be mortgaged to the hilt. Then there are death duties to worry about. They could be an enormous burden. I don't fancy reaching retirement age and still having to pay back huge sums because we've had to shell out to the Inland Revenue.'

'You might get a clue as to the finances via bank statements,' I suggested. 'Wouldn't your brother have kept them in the study?'

'I didn't see any sign of them when we were tidying up.

They might be in the safe, or perhaps they're in the estate office.'

'Where's that?'

'Over on the other side of Home Wood. It's attached to Tony Bishop's house, according to what Frank told me. It's a bit inconvenient Bishop being away, to put it mildly, but I suppose he couldn't have foreseen anything so dramatic happening during his holiday.'

I'd had time to think further about it. 'You could always phone the bank,' I suggested. 'However, I'd be tempted to wait until after you've seen the solicitor. He's going to be handling probate, I assume, so why not get him to earn his money by arranging things for you. The bank will need specimen signatures and so forth.'

'That is an extremely good idea, Adam. I'm afraid all this has caught me unawares, and I'm really grateful to you. And to Alison's brother for asking you to help me.'

We returned in the early evening, and after housing the car, made our way to the kitchen entrance. 'Now let's see what the witches have brewed up for us,' I said as Robert opened the door. Fortunately, we were out of earshot of the chefs.

Robert's report was brief, and was mostly good news. 'Frank has a broken arm, which they've set, but they don't think he's got concussion, which is a blessing. They're keeping him in overnight. Mary will stay until the end of visiting time, and I've given her money for a taxi back to the manor. I've told her to report here, rather than stay at the lodge for the time being.'

'He was very lucky,' Alison said. 'If he'd been directly under that tree when it fell, the outcome would have been far worse.' She shivered. 'I saw what happened to his chainsaw. I dread to think what a state he'd have been in if he'd been next to it.'

I was about to respond, but changed my mind,

remembering what Frank had told, me, and my promise to him to keep quiet. If the apparition hadn't scared him, he *would* have been under that tree. It might have scared him into running from it, but in so doing it had undoubtedly saved his life, just as it could well have saved DI Hardy from hitting the black ice that had caused the death of the van driver.

Although none of the others noticed my preoccupation, Eve knew me too well. She looked at me intently, but didn't speak, for which I was grateful.

I'd half-expected Eve to question me further about Frank's accident when we were alone in the Rose Room, but when I'd finished in the bathroom she was already in bed and fast asleep. I climbed carefully in alongside her, managing to achieve a comfortable position without disturbing her. The day had been both stressful and tiring, and I too was soon asleep.

I'm not sure what time it was when I woke up, or rather when I was awakened, but it was still dark outside. It was Eve who had awoken me, by talking in her sleep. I listened for several minutes, but was unable to make any sense of the sounds she was uttering. I was intrigued and amused at first, but then, without warning, she turned and gripped my arm, shaking it as if trying to wake me, or point my attention to something only she could see.

'What is it, Eve? What's wrong? Are you awake, or still dreaming?'

'There,' she said, her voice loud and clear. 'Can't you see it? There, by the tree.'

I couldn't see anything. Not in the darkness of the room, and I certainly couldn't see any trees. I'd have been convinced she was awake but for that. 'Go back to sleep, Evie,' I told her, and slipped my arm across her waist, hoping to comfort her. It had the opposite effect. She writhed and threw my arm off. I waited, and slowly, her breathing eased, and I knew she had dropped into deep slumber once more. I was curious as to what she had been dreaming about. It seemed the dream was ongoing, for, after some time, she began muttering again, her words indecipherable. She continued to sleep until early morning, but that sleep was restless, and at around six thirty I decided enough was enough and got out of bed. The room was cold, so I put on my dressing gown and slippers, and went across to the armchair alongside the small electric fire. I switched this on, and after angling the reading lamp away from the bed, began to read a book I'd brought from home. On a whim, I'd chosen a favourite from my early teenage years, Sir Thomas Malory's *Le Morte d'Arthur*. The tales of chivalry and adventure had appealed to my romantic young mind. Quite why I'd chosen to reacquaint myself with it, I'd no idea.

I'd been reading for around half an hour when I heard Eve say my name. I looked over at the bed, and saw that she was awake. She sat up and peered at me. 'Is something wrong, Adam? Why are you sitting over there? What time is it?'

'Just gone seven o'clock, and I'm waiting for you to tell me the result of the match.'

'What match? What are you talking about?' Eve can get a bit testy if she doesn't get a good night's sleep.

'The football match you were playing. It must have been exciting, but I got a bit fed up of being used as the ball.'

Her face changed abruptly and she sat bolt upright. The bedclothes fell away, which did my concentration no good. 'You were dreaming,' I said, which was a pretty obvious statement. 'What was it about?'

I'm not sure what I expected by way of a reply. However, if I'd had to make a list of possible answers, the one she gave wouldn't have been on it. 'We were being chased through Home Wood,' she told me. She paused, before adding, 'I know it sounds daft, but I dreamed we were being chased by ... by a bear.'

My face must have reflected my shock, because Eve noticed the change in my expression immediately. 'I thought it was just a silly dream,' she said, 'but something tells me it wasn't all that silly. Come on, Adam, out with it.'

I couldn't keep it to myself any longer, even had I wanted to. I walked over to the bed and sat alongside her as I explained what Frank had told me as we'd waited for help to arrive, and what I thought I'd seen before we found him. 'Add that to what DI Hardy told us, and your dream, and see what you can make of it, because I have absolutely no idea what's going on.'

Eve thought about it for a long time before speaking. 'I don't understand it either, Adam, but one crumb of comfort is that whatever is causing it doesn't seem ill-disposed. If we're to believe what people thought they'd seen, two men would probably have died had it not been for this thing, be it real or imagined.'

We talked for a little while longer, then I climbed back into bed. The shared knowledge had left us both shaken, and as was our custom, we comforted one another in the best way possible.

When we went downstairs, Robert greeted us with good news. 'I've spoken to the hospital, and the report on Frank is positive. The ward sister told me the doctor has seen him and is happy to discharge him when someone can collect him. Apart from a little discomfort from his broken arm, he's as fit as a fiddle.'

It was a relief to know that Frank had suffered no lasting ill-effects from his encounter with the ash tree, so, soon after breakfast, in my new role as chauffeur, I drove Mary to Thorsby to collect him. While I was waiting for her to return from the ward, I enquired about one of the other patients. DI Hardy, I was told, had been taken to the operating theatre to have his leg re-set, because the surgeon was unhappy with the way it was responding.

Later, having installed Frank and Mary in the back of the Mercedes, I drove to Barton-le-Moors. On arrival, I swung into the drive and past the lodge, ignoring my passenger's protests. 'Sorry,' I told them, 'boss's orders. You're staying at the manor for the time being. You want to argue, take it up with Mr Pengelly. It's more than my job's worth to disobey his instructions.'

As we approached the house, I resisted the temptation to take them to the front of the building. That was just as well, for everyone was awaiting our arrival by the back door. There had been a development, it seemed, while I'd been away, and a major one at that. Eve told me, as I helped Mary assist Frank to exit the car. 'DS Holmes rang Robert half an hour ago. They've arrested Graeme Fletcher. Even better news, he's confessed to having killed Stephen Pengelly and Kathy King.'

'That's right,' Robert agreed, 'and according to Holmes, the motive was jealousy. He sounded cock-a-hoop.'

'That's only natural,' I replied. 'This is his first big case, and to get a result this quickly will be a real feather in his cap. I only hope he manages to tie up all the loose ends.'

Curiously, what should have been cause for celebration gave me a sense of anti-climax, in addition to which, something didn't seem right. It all seemed too easy. And it still didn't explain the break-in at the manor, or the mysterious weapon used. Neither of those questions had been answered, and that was two too many for my liking.

With Robert on edge, awaiting the solicitor's visit, I commandeered the phone, hoping to resolve at least one of my queries. I rang Barton-le-Dale police station and managed to get hold of Johnny Pickersgill.

'We're about to begin questioning Fletcher,' he told

me, 'so I can't talk for long.'

'It's about that interview I wanted a word. I'm not suggesting you've got the wrong man, but I think there's more to this than simply jealousy. Do you mind if I make a suggestion?'

'Why not? You normally do, whether you're asked to or not.'

'Very droll. Have you thought of a stage career? As a juggler, perhaps. Anyway, here's what I have in mind.'

Pickersgill listened to my idea, and agreed it made sense. 'I'll put it to Holmes. I'm sure he'll agree. All joking apart, Adam, we both reckon Fletcher is lying, but we can't work out why.'

Chapter Eight

Whatever Nigel Alderson might have expected when he arrived at Barton Manor, I doubt whether he could have foreseen that he would be met by a welcoming party clustered in the entrance hall. Robert greeted him, inspected his visiting card and introduced Alderson to everyone, before he and Alison ushered the solicitor into the study.

Once the door closed behind them, the rest of us wandered back into the kitchen. Eve and Tammy insisted on helping Mary prepare the evening meal, despite her protests. She was, she told us, behind with her work as she was being hampered by Frank, who was proving to be a very impatient patient. He looked at me, a plea for help in his eyes.

'Why don't we go to the wood store, Frank? We're going to need more logs. The ones Robert and I brought in yesterday were still a bit green. If you point out which are dry enough to use, I'll bring them in.'

I'm not sure which of them looked more relieved, Mary or Frank. The task took some time, but as I was stacking the final load in the basket alongside the hall fireplace, Alison emerged from the study. 'I'm on a mission,' she told me. 'My lord and master-to-be has commanded me to fetch tea and biscuits. He also wants everyone to join him in the study.'

'They're all in the kitchen.'

Ten minutes later, supplied with refreshments, we listened to Robert and Alderson explain the situation. Robert began the surprising account. 'I was quite prepared for Nigel to tell me that Stephen had died intestate, or even that he had willed the property elsewhere, but it seems that neither of those facts is correct. I'll let Nigel tell you in detail, but I think you will find it more than a little interesting. In view of my previous history with my brother, some of what we're going to tell you is startling, to put it mildly.'

Alderson took up the story. 'I think part of what Robert has just referred to relates to the letter I have just handed him, but I'll leave him to explain that. For my part, you must know that I only took over handling the Barton Manor estate a few months ago, when my father went into semi-retirement. He told me he was more than a little exasperated by Stephen Pengelly's reluctance to make suitable provision for anything that might happen to him. Apparently, he'd always fobbed my father off, telling him that he was far too young and healthy to worry about that sort of thing.'

Alderson paused and sipped his tea. 'Naturally, having taken over the account, I also tried, and got a similar response. That was how matters stood until about three months ago, when I got a phone call from Stephen, demanding an urgent appointment. By that, he said he wanted to come into our offices in Barton-le-Dale at the first available opportunity in order to make a will, have it witnessed, and to lodge a letter with us for safe keeping. He asked if it would be possible to do it the following day, but as my diary was full, I had to make it for two days later, and I could tell he was uncomfortable even with that short delay.'

He took another sip of his tea, eyed a biscuit longingly, then resumed. 'That in itself was a first. Before then, we had always conducted estate business here. I asked my father, and he was astonished. He said that as far as he could remember, neither Stephen nor his father had ever set foot in our premises. Add to that the urgency behind

Stephen's request, and I was naturally more than a little curious. Once the paperwork was complete, I asked him what had caused his sudden change of mind about making a will. In view of what has happened since then, I think his reply is … interesting, to put it mildly.'

Robert interjected, 'This is the bit I particularly wanted you to hear.'

'I didn't think Stephen was going to reply,' Alderson continued, 'and he didn't for some time. Then he told me, "I've come to realise how fragile and uncertain life can be. Who knows what might happen tomorrow, the next day, or even as I cross the road after leaving here. Things that I've learned recently make me concerned as to what might be around the next corner, both figuratively and literally". Naturally, at the time I didn't think there was any reason for his fears, but now I wonder if he had some sort of foreboding.'

'Either that,' Eve said, 'or he had become aware of a specific and very real threat, which in the circumstances seems far more likely.'

I agreed, and so, it seemed, did all the others.

'Do you think it worth telling Sergeant Holmes about this?' Alison asked.

Everyone agreed with that too, but I had more questions in mind. 'What were the provisions of the will, and what about that letter he lodged with you, what happened to that?'

Robert held up a sheet of paper. 'I'll tell you about that in a few minutes, when Nigel has finished.'

'Was there anything unusual in the terms of the will?' I asked.

Alderson looked surprised, and I could tell my guess was correct.

'Adam's like that,' Eve told him with a touch of pride, 'he spots things that everyone else misses.'

'Eve does too,' Alison told the solicitor. 'They're very

99

astute.'

'Well, you'll be pleased to learn that you were right. The will is curiously phrased. Not in the bequests themselves, those are relatively straightforward. There are only four beneficiaries. Mr and Mrs Jolly will each receive £1,000 for every year of their service, as will Tony Bishop.'

Frank and Mary looked stunned at the news. Not surprising, I thought, as they had just become £20,000 better off. 'Apart from that, the estate goes to Robert Pengelly. It is in the wording surrounding that bequest that the odd part comes.' He glanced down at the document. 'It reads, *the residue of my estate, comprising that property entitled Barton Manor and all my other properties, assets, and holdings, I give and bequeath to my brother Robert Pengelly, and in so doing I deny and exclude any other claimants to any part of my estate whatsoever. This bequest acknowledges the great hurt and suffering I have caused to Robert Pengelly, and is in part an apology for that mistreatment.'*

'That exclusion clause seems a bit belt-and-braces,' I commented. 'Did he give any reason for that wording?'

'No, and although I told him it was unnecessary, he insisted it remain in.' Alderson shrugged. 'He was paying the piper, so I allowed him to call the tune.'

'Do you have any idea what the estate is worth?' Eve asked.

'You can always rely on Eve to take the mercenary point of view,' I told him. 'She only agreed to marry me because of my immense fortune.'

'Hah! I got that wrong.'

'Ignore them,' Robert told him, 'they always go on like that. It's quite harmless.'

'I can't give you a precise sum, or even an approximation, because there's still a lot of work to do before we even think of applying for probate. We haven't even got the land valuation yet, but taking the manor, the other houses on the estate, and even the land alone, you'd be looking at a sum in excess of seven figures, I guess. It could be more, depending on bank balances, shareholdings, insurances and so forth.'

'I suppose that means Robert will face a huge bill for death duties,' I said. I can always be relied upon to cheer folk up.

'Actually, that isn't so. Stephen took out an insurance policy covering the potential liability. It even covers events such as death by violent means, which is highly unusual. The only exclusion is suicide, and of course that does not apply.'

By now I was convinced that Stephen Pengelly had become aware of a threat against his life. I could tell that Eve was of the same mind, but neither of us thought it wise to mention that. The contents of the letter Stephen had lodged with the solicitor simply reinforced our point of view.

Alderson looked across at Robert, who lifted the single piece of paper he was still clutching and began to read. The knowledge that the writer was dead, and in such horrific circumstances, lent extra poignancy to the message.

'*Dear Robert,*

I am handing this letter to our solicitor in the knowledge that when you receive it, I will be dead. Whether that death is from natural causes or otherwise is anyone's guess. Either way, I know my time is short, and although I have tried every means I can think of to defer my demise, those efforts have ended in failure.

I am writing this, not because I have left Barton Manor to you; that is yours by right, now that I am gone. The reason for this letter is to tender a much belated and abject apology for the mistreatment I handed out to you as a child.

Please believe me; the guilt I felt at the time, the guilt I still feel to this day, has been a heavy burden, but no greater than I deserve. My only excuse, and I know it is a poor one; is that I was influenced by our father, who used it as a vehicle to expiate his own self-hatred. His only way of avoiding the guilt and shame he felt over the way he misbehaved and caused such distress to our mother, was to heap the blame on you for her death.

I understand that you might find it hard to excuse my conduct, but to help you appreciate the way I felt, I have to explain that I was overwhelmed with grief at Mother's death, a grief that has not abated, even with the passage of years. It cannot be easy for you, because you did not have the luxury of knowing her, and that is another cause for much regret. Had you done so, it might possibly have helped you gauge the extent of the loss I felt.

She was such a radiant person, with a bright, bubbly personality which was only surpassed by her gentle, loving nature, her tolerance and understanding. She graced any company with her presence in a way no other person I have ever encountered could do.

I have written enough, and yet all the words I can think of are insufficient to make amends for my behaviour. I have also come to realise how important our family is, and I urge you to seek out that importance for yourself. If you should doubt either my sincerity or my sanity; a detailed scrutiny of the Barton Manor estate records will prove my point.

I will close this wretched letter now, but before I do, I hope and trust you will find it in you to enjoy Barton Manor. In this respect, I commend Frank and Mary Jolly, and also Tony Bishop, who are steadfast and loyal. I hope you will be able to dismiss the bad memories; to make the manor your home; to settle there and, perhaps with Miss Powell alongside you, raise a family there. For that is what the manor needs. To have the laughter of children, their voices echoing as they run along the corridors, is something the old house has lacked for far too long.

I wish you all the best for the future, your future, and hope that it may be filled with peace and contentment.

Your brother,

Stephen.'

There was a long silence after Robert finished. 'That is some apology,' Tammy said eventually, 'but how did he know about Alison?'

'I think I can explain that,' the answer came from Alderson. 'My father was commissioned to employ a private detective and a credit reference agency to keep track of Robert on an annual basis since the time Stephen's guardianship ceased.' He turned to Robert and added, 'It seems that even back then, your brother was sorry for your treatment, and anxious to see how you were faring.'

'What do you make of it, Robbie?' Alison asked him.

It was clear that the letter had affected him deeply. 'I just wish I could have spoken to him,' he said at last. He shrugged and sighed. 'But it wasn't to be.'

Later, when we were alone, Eve and I discussed the contents of the letter. Whereas the others had been more affected by the emotional tone of the contents, Eve, like me had noticed the less personal aspects.

'It sounds to me as if Stephen knew he was in danger,' Eve commented. 'That bit about natural causes or otherwise seems to show he was aware of a specific threat.'

'I agree, but it was obvious he didn't believe that danger extended to Robert, because he didn't warn him that there might be someone out there determined to do him harm. That's only half of it, though. There was something else. We need to ask Holmes if he has the post-mortem findings. It sounds to me as if Stephen was aware he had some terminal illness or other. Something untreatable, by the sound of it, going from the way he wrote about his life being over.'

'What do you make about that bit about the importance of family?'

I shrugged. 'Simply part of the regret he felt, I guess.'

Which just shows how wrong I can be.

Later that afternoon, Johnny Pickersgill called me. 'I'm not sure if this is good news or not. Graeme Fletcher says he knows nothing about a break-in at Barton Manor. To be honest, that's about all he has said, about that or anything else. Apart from telling us that he killed Stephen Pengelly and Kathy King because of jealousy, he refused to elaborate. Holmes pressed him time and again, but his stock reply was "no comment". However, we believe we have the right man, because when we executed the search warrant at his house we found a bloodstained pair of trainers in his bedroom wardrobe, and there are stains inside his BMW, on the driver's floor mat, that look like blood.'

'I don't suppose you found the weapon, did you?'

'No such luck. There was no trace of it, either in his house, the shop, or his car, but nobody suggested that this detection lark was easy.'

'Well, I have some interesting news for you.' I repeated what we'd learned from Alderson and gave him the solicitor's details should he require confirmation. 'One other thing, Johnny: can you get your hands on the post-mortem findings regarding Stephen Pengelly?'

'Why do you want those? I'd have thought the cause of death was obvious.'

'Yes, but that's not what I'm after.' I explained what I was looking for.

'OK, but it'll have to be tomorrow. The files are all locked away now. I'll call you back when I've taken a look.'

I'd just finished talking to Johnny when Robert entered

the study. 'One good thing that's come out of Alderson's visit is that he's agreed to your suggestion about the finances. For the time being he's handling everything, so all the bills can be directed to him. Wages and so forth are all dealt with either by standing order, apparently, or by Tony Bishop via the petty cash account, so that's another worry less. About all I have to do is go into the bank and provide signatures plus proof of ID. Luckily, I have my passport with me. I thought it best not to leave it in my flat in Leeds.' He paused and smiled wryly. 'There have been a few burglaries near there recently.'

Next morning, after breakfast, everyone was pondering how to spend the day. Eve and I came up with ideas simultaneously, which quite often happens. They were connected too, which is also not rare.

'I was thinking about the desk in the study,' Eve told the others, 'and in particular the contents of the hidden compartment.'

'That's interesting, I was also thinking about that,' I said.

'What's your idea?'

'I wondered why Stephen kept those keys in there. If he had no interest in guns and shooting, why bother hiding the keys away?'

'My thoughts were on that folder. The one that's labelled "Pengelly Family Tree, Part One". I thought it might be worth looking inside it, and also trying to find the other part or parts to it.'

'I think Adam and I ought to investigate the gun cabinets,' Robert suggested.

'That's fine, but where should we start?' I asked. Sometimes I have a knack of asking the obvious.

'I think the gunroom would be the place, don't you? Unless Stephen had it converted into a sauna or Turkish bath.'

We smiled at the absurdity of Robert's remark. 'We'll let you boys go play with guns,' Alison told us, 'Tammy and I will help Eve search for the dodgy Pengelly ancestors.'

'From memory of the past few generations you'll have plenty to choose from. Finding some that aren't dodgy might be a harder task.'

Robert and I left the girls studying the first page of the papers inside the folder. We found Frank in the kitchen, attempting to dice carrots one handed. 'I've been put to work,' he told us. 'I'm just glad the oven isn't an old-fashioned spit, otherwise I think Mary would possibly have me turning on it.'

Robert asked him about the gunroom, and was relieved to hear that it still served that purpose.

'I don't think anyone has been in there for years,' Frank told us. 'The key is hanging up there.' He pointed to the set of hooks alongside the kitchen door.

'Not exactly security-conscious,' Robert remarked.

'Possibly, but if intruders didn't know it was a gunroom, they wouldn't have bothered about breaking in there,' I pointed out.

Ten minutes later we were inside the room, which was situated in the corridor leading from the kitchen to the back door. I half expected the light bulb to be broken, but it came on as soon as Robert pressed the switch. I looked at the far wall, which had three identical cabinets bolted to it. 'Bingo!' he breathed.

Having opened the first one, Robert swung the door open. I whistled with surprise and admiration. 'Those are absolutely beautiful.'

'They're shotguns, Adam. What's special about them?'

I lifted one of them clear. 'These aren't just any old shotguns, Robert. This one and the one alongside it are Purdeys. Unless I'm very much mistaken the other pair in the cabinet was manufactured by Holland and Holland.

What you have here are the Rolls-Royce and Bentley of twelve-bore shotguns. I can't say how much they're worth, but I'd check with your insurance broker. If they're not listed on the policy, they should be. And you will also need a certificate if you intend keeping them.'

'Could you make a guess? At the value, I mean?'

'Not really, but if it was into six figures I wouldn't be at all surprised.'

The second cabinet yielded a smaller .410 shotgun plus a pair of stalking rifles, which, although I was no expert, also looked expensive. 'If your father bought these, he had good taste,' I told Robert. 'Let's see what treasures the third cabinet has to offer.'

At first sight, the final cabinet seemed only to have ammunition inside. One box in particular caught my attention. I lifted it out and stared at it in surprise.

'Something wrong?' Robert asked.

'This is odd.' I showed him the label. It clearly meant nothing to him.

'I don't understand. It's ammunition, isn't it? And it's in the right place.'

'It might be in the right place, Robert, but the ammunition is wrong.'

'I still don't get you.'

'This ammunition doesn't fit any of the guns in these cabinets. These are Parabellum 9mm rounds. They are for a handgun, not a rifle or shotgun. These are the standard issue NATO ammunition.'

I peered inside the cabinet, and after a second, noticed a dark case at the bottom, almost obscured by the boxes of shotgun cartridges stacked in front of it. I lifted it clear, opened the lid and stared at the contents. My jaw dropped as I stared in open-mouthed amazement. 'What the heck is that doing in here?' I muttered.

'It's a pistol, isn't it? Maybe my father was into pistol shooting, although I don't remember him doing any. He was forever off shooting pheasant or grouse, or deerstalking, but I don't recall him doing any target shooting.'

'You don't understand, Robert. Your father didn't buy this. The only member of your family who could have purchased this was your brother. The gun has only been on the market a couple of years. I read an article about it a year or so back. This is a revolutionary design. It's made by an Austrian company called Glock.' I lifted the automatic from the case and handed it to Robert.

He looked at it. 'Are you sure this isn't a toy? It feels too light.'

'That's the revolutionary bit. It's made from some sort of cast polymer, I believe. What I want to know is why Stephen bought such a gun as this. I wasn't even aware they were widely available. The other question you might like an answer to is: what happened to the other one?'

'The other one?'

I nodded, and turned the case round so that Robert could see the inside. The inner part of the container had been moulded so that two guns could fit alongside one another. Coupled with Stephen's statement in his letter, the sudden urge to make his will, and the life insurance policy clauses regarding violent death, I was now more convinced than ever that Stephen Pengelly had known he was in imminent danger. The only unresolved issue was, if that threat was as lethal as he believed, why had he opened the door to the manor, and what's more, done so unarmed.

The only reason I could think of didn't make sense. It was almost as if he'd ceased to care whether he was in danger or not. The answer to the riddle, or part of it, became clear almost immediately after we left the gun room. As Robert was locking the door, Alison came in search of us. 'Your friend the policeman is on the phone,' she told me.

I'd forgotten that Johnny Pickersgill had promised to

call me back. 'I'm beginning to think you're psychic. I've got the post-mortem findings here. Your theory was correct. The pathologist reported that Stephen Pengelly was suffering from the early stages of cirrhosis of the liver. That is untreatable, isn't it?'

'It is, and if Stephen Pengelly knew that diagnosis, it would explain his comment in the letter to Robert, and why he was so careless about answering the door to his killer.'

I told the others what Pickersgill had said. However, having answered one question, another remained. If Stephen knew he had cirrhosis, the specialist would have told him it was untreatable. However, in his letter, he had written that he had tried every means possible to find a remedy. What other methods could he have used to try and cure his illness, if medicine couldn't provide a solution?

While I'd been speaking to Johnny, Robert told the girls what we'd found in the gun room, which explained why I was brandishing a wicked-looking automatic pistol. He didn't mention that the second gun was missing, which I thought was sensible. The sight of just one had made Tammy and Alison nervous, to judge by their expressions.

Changing the subject, he asked what they'd found. 'Nothing dramatic, if you discount the fact that your great-grandfather was christened Horatio Algonquin Amadeus Pengelly, which you kept a closely guarded secret from me,' Alison replied.

'I didn't know that. If I'd been aware of it, I'd have kept it secret from everyone,' Robert retorted. 'Anything else, apart from my ancestors' lamentable choice when naming their offspring?'

'We've read through that folder, which as you know is labelled "part one". It takes us back to Norman times. After we'd looked through that we began searching the filing cabinets in case we came across more, but without luck.'

'It may well be that there isn't anything else,' Robert suggested. 'I'm not sure how far back it's possible to go.'

'Much earlier than that,' Tammy told him. 'I believe there are descendants of Irish chieftains living in Spain who can trace their ancestral line back to around 3000BC.'

'Wow,' Eve said, 'that's before even Adam was born.'

'Another thing it proves is that Tammy wasn't asleep during all our lectures,' Alison said hastily. 'I remember Old Mother Riley telling us about that.'

Tammy snorted derisively. 'You'd have to wait a long time for Locke to tell you it.'

'You've referred to someone called Locke before in rather derogatory terms,' Eve said. 'I take it you don't think much of him.'

'He's our Professor of Ancient History now that Riley has retired. He's all right, I suppose, and I grant you he certainly knows his stuff on most of the subjects, but he has some weird theories regarding others. It might help if he was to attend more often. It's supposed to be the students who skip lectures, not the tutors.'

'That's not fair, Tammy, and you know it,' Alison reprimanded her. 'You're well aware that Professor Locke is ill. It's hardly his fault if he's too poorly to go to work.'

'Yes, OK, I suppose you're right, and if I didn't have Professor Riley to compare him to, I probably wouldn't have commented – but once you've had gold, it's far from easy to put up with brass.'

'Going back to your family tree,' Alison told Robert, 'the earliest entry in that folder is dated 1141AD.'

'Who was on the throne then?' Robert asked.

'Was it Henry I?' Alison suggested, looking at Tammy.

'No,' I told them, 'it was too late for Henry. If my memory's correct, 1141 would have been in the middle of King Stephen's reign. Stephen was on the throne from 1135 to 1154, I believe.'

'He'll be right,' Eve said. 'Adam likes to get his facts

correct, which I admit must seem strange, considering he was a reporter and therefore more used to making things up. Also, he's lived through more history than most of us.'

I was still looking around for something to throw at Eve when Tammy said, 'Adam is correct. It was King Stephen. Anyway, that wasn't what we thought was significant. Alison noticed it.'

'I don't know if it's unusual, but there seem to have been a lot of twins in your family, Robert. It isn't one set every generation, but it's not far short of it,' Alison told him. 'I might not have thought about it had you not been a twin.'

It was an interesting fact, but none of us thought it was either relevant or important at the time. What did intrigue us was the point Eve brought up. 'Talking of family,' she began, 'reminds me of something.' She had that little frown of concentration on her face that I found endearing. 'Robert, would you describe your brother as a sentimental person?'

'If you'd asked me a couple of weeks ago, I'd have said most definitely not.' He smiled. 'In fact I might have added one or two colourful adjectives to emphasise that. However, since I read the letter he left for me with the solicitor, I'm beginning to revise my opinion of Stephen. Why do you ask?'

'I was puzzled by something we saw,' she said, 'but nobody seemed to think anything of it at the time. It was when you opened the safe. In the main compartment there were the estate ledgers and one or two other files. We never looked to see what they contained. There was also a photograph album. I just wondered why Stephen thought it necessary to take such precautions over a set of family photos.'

Eve was dead right, and it was something we had all overlooked. However, before we had chance to rectify the omission, we were summoned through for dinner. We decided the second, closer examination of the safe's contents could wait for another day. That was a really wise decision, although we weren't to know it at the time.

Chapter Nine

The following morning, as we were finishing breakfast; Frank appeared in the dining room. He looked a little sheepish, the reason for which was explained when he spoke. 'Mary needs to go into Barton-le-Dale,' he told Robert. 'She hadn't reckoned on there being so many people to cater for and she's running short on a lot of things. Normally, she'd send me off into town, but as things are, that's out of the question.'

He lifted his arm as he spoke, and we saw him wince.

'Is that causing you a lot of pain?' Robert asked.

'Aye, it is, a bit.'

'Didn't the doctor say you should go back if it was painful, in case it wasn't set correctly?' I asked.

'Aye, he did,' Frank admitted reluctantly.

'I think we could combine a shopping expedition with a trip to the hospital,' Eve suggested. She looked at me, and I nodded confirmation. 'If I take Frank across to Thorsby in our car, it will give me chance to pop home and collect more clothing for Adam and me while Frank is being seen to.'

'And I can take Mary into Barton-le-Dale in the Mercedes to sort out the shopping,' I added.

'If we go with you, between us we could make the job easier,' Alison suggested.

'I'm going to give Nigel Alderson a call,' Robert told us. 'If he can get me an appointment at the bank I can introduce myself to the manager.'

The plan was readily accepted by all concerned, with

the exception of Tammy, who thought she might be developing a migraine, and decided spending the day in a darkened room was preferable to a trip into town.

Before we set off, Mary asked if Robert had any specific likes or dislikes that she could include or omit from her list. 'Nothing that I can think of,' he told her, 'but if that policeman friend of Adam's is going to be a regular visitor, I think you should ensure we have plenty of tea in the house.'

I smiled at the notion that Johnny's reputation was beginning to spread. Another adjustment to our plans was agreed when we were about to set off. 'Why don't we meet up in Daleside Tea Rooms,' Robert suggested. 'When Eve comes back from Thorsby, hopefully we'll have finished the shopping, and I for one will be ready for a cuppa.'

'Ready for another chunk of their Black Forest Gateau, you mean,' Alison retorted. She turned to the rest of us and explained. 'He had some when we were staying at the King's Head, and the portion was so big I'm surprised the waitress was able to lift it. That didn't stop greedy guts here demolishing it. The way he wolfed it down I thought he was trying for an entry in the *Guinness Book of Records*.'

'That settles it,' Eve said, 'wild horses wouldn't keep Adam away after hearing that.'

I smiled benignly at my beloved. 'I'll even eat your share if you're on a diet, or fasting. Not that I've seen much evidence of that recently.'

The only reply I got was a two-fingered gesture similar to the one that had got a famous showjumper into bother a few years previously.

Having completed the shopping, which tested even the ample capacity of the Mercedes' boot, we met up with Eve and Frank at Daleside Tea Rooms. Frank reported that the doctor had insisted on new X-rays, and on seeing them had re-set the arm and instructed him to report back in a week's time. We did justice to various items from the sweet trolley, washed down with considerable quantities of tea. It was late afternoon, almost dark, before we set off back to Barton Manor.

The house was in darkness as we approached down the long drive, but Alison didn't seem concerned. 'If Tammy has one of her more severe migraines she could be out of it for a day, maybe longer. With luck, she might be fast asleep. It seems to be the only thing that does any good.'

I parked the Mercedes close to the kitchen entrance to make unloading the shopping easier, and a few seconds later Eve pulled our Range Rover to a halt behind us. 'Robert and I will carry the goods inside,' I volunteered, 'just tell us where you want everything, Mary.'

She opened the back door and went inside. As we delved into the boot for the first of the bags we heard Mary scream. We abandoned the shopping and hurried inside, with Alison, Eve, and Frank close behind. In the kitchen Tammy was tied to a chair, her arms behind her back; a handkerchief across her mouth as a gag and a tea towel fastened across her eyes. We hastened to untie her, and loosened the gag, which provoked a stream of rich invective.

'What happened?' Alison managed to ask when Tammy eventually paused for breath.

'You'd only been gone a few minutes. I decided I'd have a cup of tea before I went for a lie down. I came in here to put the kettle on. I looked across towards the back door and there was a man standing there. I was about to ask who he was, and what he was doing here, but before I could say anything, somebody grabbed me from behind. I struggled and bumped my head on the cupboard before I was tied up like you found me. I've been here ever since.'

'Did you see the man who attacked you?'

'No, I barely saw the other one. I certainly didn't get a

proper look at him, just a momentary glance.' Tammy began to rub the ugly bruise on her forehead. 'He was young, I think, slim, not tall. That's about all I remember. Except that he smelt, or one of them did.'

'Smelt? As in body odour?'

'Not exactly. It was more like an animal scent. Not very nice.'

'How do you know that?'

'It was as they were tying me up.' Tammy shuddered. 'That was when I was really scared. I thought they were going to … well, you know … what happened to Robert's brother and the woman. But they didn't. I heard them leaving, that was around two o'clock.' She pointed in the direction of the hall to the grandfather clock. 'It chimed not long after they left.'

'I think we ought to call the police before we do anything else,' I suggested. 'They'll probably want to check the house over.'

Eve had been talking to Mary, who was searching one of the kitchen cupboards. 'This will help with the bruise,' Mary said, and began to bathe Tammy's forehead with a piece of cotton wool soaked in something. 'This is arnica,' she explained. 'It's very good.'

'Mary says the rope used to tie Tammy up was cut from her washing line,' Eve told us. 'By the sound of it, the attackers expected the house to be empty. They certainly don't appear to have come prepared.'

'That's true, and perhaps Tammy was lucky.' I pointed to the discarded gag. In one corner of the handkerchief were the initials SP. 'They obviously used what was close to hand.'

We were still standing around, indecisive, when Robert returned from his abortive attempt to phone the police. 'Neither Holmes nor Pickersgill are available, not even a constable,' he told us, 'nor can they tell us when they will be. I left a message, explaining what had happened, but whatever they're doing, it seems to be more important than a break-in and assault.'

'Well, we know how short-handed they are. I think we should have a look around, making sure we don't touch anything.'

'I think they were wearing gloves, but I can't be sure,' Tammy told us.

The study had again been the focus of the intruders' attention.

'They mustn't have found what they were looking for the first time,' Eve said. 'But look at the mess!'

One glance was enough to realise that they had emptied every drawer of the desk, every folder in the filing cabinet. Whether they had found what they were searching for or not, it was impossible to gauge. The result was an untidy heap that stretched across much of the floor space. This time, however, there looked to have been little or no damage to the contents of the room. In the drawing room, and upstairs, there was evidence that the intruders had been intent on finding something, but as with the study, no damage appeared to have been done. This was no random act; this was a mission to obtain something specific. Whereas the others concentrated on the rest of the house, I volunteered to inspect Stephen Pengelly's room. I found the contents undisturbed, and in his dressing room discovered something of great interest, but decided not to reveal my findings at that stage.

It was almost eight o'clock before DS Holmes phoned. Robert explained what had happened, and when he ended the call, reported that the detectives were on their way, and would ask for a forensics team, should one be available.

'That sounds a bit odd,' Eve commented. 'I'd have thought they would always have someone on standby.'

'Possibly they're tied up with something else. Holmes did say there had been another development. He wouldn't tell me what it was, not over the phone, but by his tone of voice, I guess it isn't going to be good news.'

That, as we soon discovered, was a strong contender for understatement of the year.

Thankfully, the kitchen and dining room had not been disturbed and we felt able to use the rooms. We had just finished eating when the doorbell rang. Robert got up to go and answer it, but Alison stopped him. 'Hang on, Robbie. No way are you going alone.' He looked surprised, until she added, 'Think what happened today, when Tammy was alone, and what happened to your brother.'

'Alison's right,' I added, 'I'll go with you.'

'You be careful, Adam,' Eve cautioned me.

'Don't worry, Evie.' I patted my jacket pocket. 'I've got my insurance policy with me, and it's bang up to date.'

I'm not sure if the others got my meaning, but Eve certainly did. 'Well, don't hesitate to make a claim if you need to.'

I waited to one side as Robert unlocked the door. As he went to turn the handle I took my hand from my pocket. Whatever the detectives might have expected when the door opened, I doubt if their wildest imagination could have prepared them to be greeted by a man pointing an automatic pistol at them.

I lowered the Glock and smiled apologetically. 'Sorry, gentlemen, but we're a bit on edge here, and we're not taking any chances.'

'Very wise, Adam,' Pickersgill replied. 'Now can we come in?'

He and Holmes watched approvingly as Robert ensured the door was securely locked, before showing them into the drawing room. 'I'll fetch the others,' he told me, 'you explain about the hardware.'

I'd just finished telling them about the discovery in the gunroom when the others walked in. 'I assume you don't have a firearms licence for it, so we'll have to confiscate the gun,' Holmes told me.

I unloaded the Glock and passed it to him without comment. I glanced sideways and saw Eve's look of surprise at my meek compliance with the request. Holmes turned to Tammy and asked her what had taken place. He listened carefully to her account, his sympathetic attitude seeming to increase her distress rather than alleviating it. Or perhaps, I thought cynically, she was playing up to his obvious interest.

'We'll need a formal statement,' he said eventually. He looked at Pickersgill. 'Will you see it gets typed up, Johnny, and I'll pop back and get Miss Watson to sign it?'

He turned to the rest of us. 'I'm afraid it will be tomorrow before we can get fingerprint officers here. If you can avoid using the rooms they targeted until after then that would be helpful. The reason they can't get here earlier is because, as I told Mr Pengelly on the phone, there has been a development. A very serious development, I'm sorry to say. This morning, we were called to the house of a local solicitor, a man by the name of Arnold Wharton, whose professional reputation was somewhat dubious. His cleaning lady found his body in the bedroom. He had been murdered.' Holmes paused, before adding, 'The wound to Wharton's body was identical to those suffered by Stephen Pengelly and Kathy King.'

'How long had he been dead?' Eve asked.

'According to the pathologist, time of death was somewhere between six o'clock yesterday evening and around midnight. Certainly no earlier than that.'

'Which means,' Johnny Pickersgill told us, 'that the man we have in custody, Graeme Fletcher, who had confessed to the two previous murders, could not have been responsible for Wharton's death. So either he passed this strange weapon to someone else, or he was lying when he admitted to the killings.'

Holmes grimaced. 'We were certain we had the right

man. The blood found on shoes in his house was of the same type as Kathy King's. It's possible that he might have an accomplice, as Johnny suggested, but neither of us are sure about that.'

'I think you're right to be suspicious,' Eve told them. 'There might be another reason for him making a false confession. Let's suppose that Fletcher heard about Stephen Pengelly's murder and went to see Kathy King, knowing of her association with Stephen. If he found her lying in a pool of blood, that would explain his shoes. If he thought that because of his connection with the two of them he might be next on the killer's shopping list, that would explain his hasty departure. And, once you'd detained him, he might have thought the safest place for him would be inside a police cell. The best way to stay there would be to own up to a crime he hadn't committed, and hope that the real killer would be apprehended while he was still in custody.'

There was a long silence as Holmes digested what Eve had said. He smiled at her, before responding. 'I have to say that is a very plausible theory, and I think it well worth taking up with Fletcher. Whether we'll be able to get him to talk is another matter.'

'Why not threaten him?' I suggested. 'Tell Fletcher the killer has struck again, then ask him about his association with this man Wharton, if there is one, and finally explain that in view of the latest murder, you will have to release him without charge. If Eve's theory is correct, that should panic him enough to loosen his tongue and give you the truth.'

'I think that's a good idea, and one we'll try on him tomorrow. For the meantime, I want you to be on your guard, and take all sensible precautions. I thought it important that everyone should know this killer is still on the loose.'

'That's all very well,' Eve objected, 'but taking away

the gun Adam found isn't going to help us stay safe.'

'I'm sorry, but there's nothing I can do about that.'

Eve looked at me for support, but with no success. 'I guess not,' I told him, 'I understand though. Regulations have to be obeyed.'

Eve and Johnny Pickersgill both looked at me with deep suspicion. My innocent smile did little to lessen this. Once the officers had gone, Eve asked why I'd capitulated. 'Why did you hand over the pistol you found in the gunroom? It's so unlike you to give in as tamely as that.'

'I didn't.'

'How do you mean you didn't?'

'I didn't hand over the pistol from the gunroom. I gave Holmes the one I found in Stephen Pengelly's dressing room, hidden inside a cigar box under a pile of sweaters. I couldn't understand why he had a cigar box. There are no ashtrays anywhere, so it seems obvious that he isn't a smoker.' I reached into my pocket and pulled out the other Glock. 'This is the one from the gunroom.'

Robert's concern over the news that Holmes and Pickersgill had brought reflected the fears of the others. As he spoke I could tell by their faces how troubled they were. 'How are we going to keep ourselves safe in here if that killer can walk in and out of the front door with the key?'

There is a way,' I told him. 'All I need is some wood, a hammer, and nails. It won't look very good when I've finished, but it will serve its purpose.'

It was ten o'clock at night by the time, having outlined my plan, Frank Jolly escorted Robert, Eve, and me to the workshop at the rear of the manor. Within minutes I had what I needed, and we returned inside. One curious thing, I told Robert, was that the house had bolts on the back door, but not on the front, the main entrance to the building.

'It does seem odd, I agree.' He shrugged. 'But then, many things about my family seem strange, even to me.'

Anyone standing outside the manor that night would probably have agreed with Robert's statement. The sound of hammering as I constructed simple bolts for the front door would have left passers-by scratching their heads. Having fixed two blocks of wood to the frame on either side, I then screwed two more to them, to form blunt letter L shapes. The sturdy longer sections of wood I had selected were then dropped into position to form an effective, if less than decorative, barrier.

I managed the whole operation without hitting my thumb with the hammer or cutting myself with the saw, which I was pleased about, especially as I was working before an audience, which was a little unnerving. The relief on their faces, especially those of the four women, was reward enough.

Eve masked her pride at my handiwork well. 'I don't think Chippendale or Sheraton would feel challenged by your carpentry skills.'

'I did say it wouldn't look good, but it will act as a deterrent. If an intruder is determined enough, they'll find some other way in, even if it means breaking a window,' I told them. I could see by their changed expressions that my talent for cheering folk up hadn't diminished.

Eve was obviously of the same mind. 'I think Adam's right. It would be wise to have someone on guard throughout the night.'

Robert agreed, but with a proviso. 'I don't think it would be fair to ask one person to do it on their own. For one thing, they might fall asleep, or they could be easily overpowered.'

'That's true, and I think it would be preferable not to expect anyone to go without sleep all night.'

In the end, we decided that a rota system should operate. Eve and I would take the first shift, and at 2 a.m. we would hand over to Robert and Alison. When their stint ended at 5 a.m., they would awaken Frank and Tammy, who would see us safe until after daybreak.

'What about me?' Mary objected, 'I ought to take a turn.'

'No way,' Robert told her, 'you have more than enough to do already. Besides which,' he added with a smile, 'who'll cook breakfast if you're asleep?'

Before the rest of the household retired, Robert and I visited the gunroom, where we supplemented the security measures with one extra item. As we returned, he collected a gong which had been standing in the corner of the dining room. It was an impressively large brass cylinder, suspended from a sturdy frame, and reminded me of the one used to introduce Rank films. He set it down near the foot of the staircase. 'I thought it would be useful as an alarm If you hear this you'll know we've either got intruders or you've overslept and breakfast is ready.'

When the others had bidden us goodnight and retired upstairs, I handed the Glock to Eve, with instructions on how to use it, and a warning about recoil. I lifted the shotgun, after opening it. 'Unless you'd be happier with this?'

Eve shook her head. 'No fear, this is more than enough.'

We alternated between sitting on the armchairs alongside the log fire and patrolling the ground floor. The night was all but silent, apart from the nocturnal creatures we heard occasionally. The hoot of a hunting owl and the screech of a vixen were all that disturbed the peace. On each of our forays we ended in the kitchen, where coffee provided the stimulant to keep us awake and alert. On our third patrol, as we reached the door leading to the wine cellar, Eve stopped; then muttered in disgust. 'I knew there was something I'd forgotten. Everything that's happened drove it right out of my mind.'

'What are you on about, Evie?'

'The safe, Adam. Don't you remember, I mentioned to

Robert about the photo album?'

'You really think it might contain something important, don't you?'

'I'm not sure, but perhaps what's inside there might be what the intruder is so desperate to get his hands on.'

'We'd better make it our first priority tomorrow, then, if only for your peace of mind.'

Chapter Ten

Our shift passed without incident, and after handing over to the next pair of sentinels, we retired for the night. Our sleep was undisturbed by the sound of intruders, gunshots or the clamour of a gong being beaten. Next morning, members of the household appeared at irregular intervals, roughly corresponding to the order of their tour of duty. It was almost lunchtime before everyone was assembled in the dining room, where coffee had been the number one priority for most of us. It was then that Eve pitched her idea of the photo album to the assembly.

'I can't think why Stephen kept it locked away,' Robert replied. 'I wouldn't have thought it was the kind of sentimentality he would go in for. In fact, I don't recall either him or my father using or owning a camera, and there were never any photographs on display. There was the portrait my father commissioned of my mother,' he gestured to the painting, 'but that was soon after they were married, I believe. It's the only image I can remember of her, or any of the other members of the family.' He paused and added with a smile, 'Unless you count that gloomy, debauched-looking set of ancestors whose paintings are hanging in the Minstrels' Gallery. I'll go fetch the album and we can have a look through it.'

It took only a few minutes before we began to examine the contents, crowding around him in a small huddle. The image on the first page stopped us for several minutes. It was a head and shoulders shot of Robert's mother, taken, I guessed, at around the same time as the portrait had been painted. 'I must say the painter hasn't done her justice,'

Eve commented. 'It's good, but this is even better.'

The next three pages were filled with wedding photos of Robert's parents plus their guests. Looking at the pictures of his father, I failed to trace any similarity between Robert and Pengelly senior. An uncharitable thought crossed my mind, but I reserved it until much later, when Eve and I were alone. Had Robert's mother got sick and fed up of her husband gallivanting off, conducting a string of affairs with other women and sought solace in her own extra-marital affair, and had Robert been the result of such a liaison? That would also explain his father's dislike of the boy.

Eve would have none of it, and upbraided me for even thinking along those lines. 'Sometimes, Adam Bailey, you revert to your muckraking, scandal-mongering reporter persona. Shame on you for even entertaining the idea.' Eve has a way of putting me in my place. When she uses my surname, I know I've offended her.

For the most part, the album contained pictures from an earlier generation, many of them in black and white, and some from the twenties and thirties, to judge by the hairstyles and fashions. 'I have absolutely no idea who these people are,' Robert admitted. 'I guess they must be members of my family and friends, but I don't recognise them.' He pointed to one ferocious-looking elderly man. The gentleman in the photo looked less than happy to have been caught on camera. 'That could well be my grandfather. He has the same cheerful expression as my father, and I remember Stephen telling me he was a cantankerous old sod. Luckily he kicked the bucket long before I was born.'

He turned a couple more pages without finding anything remarkable, and after that, the rest of the album was blank. 'That's it,' he told us, 'nothing there to get excited about.'

That seemed true, but there was equally nothing in

what we'd seen to warrant keeping the album under lock and key. He closed the album, looking apologetically at Eve. 'Sorry, it seems your theory was a bit off beam.'

As he was shutting the book, I noticed something. 'Could I have a look, Robert?'

He passed me the album and I began to inspect it closely. On the cover I'd seen a tiny blob which appeared to be dried glue. I was about to pass it off, dismissing it as residue from when the photos had been fixed in place, when I noticed that the back cover appeared to be out of alignment. The album was too well-made for this to have been done during the manufacturing process. I opened the back cover and inspected it. Along the edge of the leather binding was more dried glue.

'What have you found, Adam?'

'I'm not sure, Evie, but it looks as if someone has tampered with the back cover. I assume that must have been Stephen, but why? Unless he wanted to hide something.'

The discovery had rekindled everyone's interest. 'We need to prise the glue loose and see if there's anything under the cover,' I said, which was rather stating the obvious.

Alison passed me a knife, one that hadn't been used for spreading marmalade or butter, I was glad to note. As gently as possible, trying not to damage either the card of the cover or the leather facing, I eased the edge of the binding away. After several minutes I had it clear, and eased it back.

Inside was a small, flat wallet, bearing the name of a famous high street pharmacy chain that also specialised in developing customers' photos. In addition, there was a folded sheet of notepaper which I handed to Robert.

He eyed it curiously and read the handwritten content. I watch his expression change.

'Gosh,' he said, after a moment, 'that's a bit saucy!'

and passed it round.

The note to Stephen was in an almost childlike hand and signed 'Annie', obviously from one of his conquests. 'Whoever she is, she doesn't leave much to the imagination does she?' I remarked.

'Who is it, Robert?' Alison asked. 'Do you remember a girl called Annie?'

'I've absolutely no idea.'

I remembered something Robert had told us about Stephen. 'Do you think this might have been the girl who caused the row between Stephen and your father?'

'It could have been, I suppose, but from what I remember there could have been lots of contenders for that role.'

'What about the photos in the wallet?' Alison asked. 'They might give us more clues.'

However, there was nothing inside apart from several sets of negatives. We were unable to discern the subjects, even when we held them up to the light, but one thing was certain, they weren't photos of girls, or any animate object.

'All I can make out,' Robert told us, 'is what look like flat stones or rocks. I haven't a clue why Stephen would have hidden them away.'

'They must have some importance, though, and for that reason I suggest you return everything to the safe for the time being. Perhaps we should take the negatives for developing next time we go into town.'

Robert agreed, and had just returned from the wine cellar when we saw a car approaching. The increased tension was immediate, and we only relaxed when it pulled to a halt and DS Holmes got out. 'I need Miss Watson to read and sign her statement,' he told Robert.

This process had apparently to be conducted without anyone else present, and it took so long I wondered if he had spelled every word out letter by letter. Eve entertained similar suspicions about Holmes' motives as I did, it seemed. 'I'm sure a uniformed constable could have performed such a menial task as obtaining a signature, don't you? I'm beginning to think our young detective has a more than passing interest in Tammy,' she suggested.

'That would be nice,' Alison agreed. 'Tammy is a bit shy when it comes to men, and someone like Holmes would be good for her.'

'It would help solve the murders quickly too, if they got together,' I told them, straight-faced.

'How do you work that out?' Robert asked.

'It can't fail, if Holmes and Watson are working together.'

Robert waited for the collection of groans to die down before speaking. 'I'll hold him if you hit him, Eve,' he offered.

DS Holmes had only been gone a few minutes, and Tammy was resisting Alison's attempts to ask why the interview had taken so long, when the phone rang. Robert went into the study to take the call, and emerged a few minutes later looking puzzled. 'That was Nigel Alderson,' he told us. 'Apparently the estate finances are in good shape, which is a huge relief. However, he's unearthed something in Stephen's personal finances that has baffled him, so he rang me to ask about it, and now I'm baffled too. It appears that Stephen made several large payments to a company I've never heard of, and Alderson can't work out what those payments were for. He says the company sounds like one of those off-the-shelf ready registered jobs. Apparently they give them all weird names and then after they're sold, the new owners rename them.'

'What is the name?'

'It was called Overtring Ltd, but who they are and what they do is a mystery, but it must have been something special to get Stephen to part with so much cash. Alderson reckons he shelled out somewhere in the region of

£200,000.'

'What did you say the name of the company is?' Tammy asked.

Robert repeated it. Tammy smiled triumphantly. 'I don't think it was a ready-registered company name, although why they chose it, I've no idea, but Overtring is an anagram for Vortigern.'

'Who or what is Vortigern?'

'Didn't you learn anything about British history, Robert? Vortigern was a Celtic king, before the time of Arthur. He wasn't a very pleasant character; in fact there seems little he wasn't capable of. He betrayed the Celtic cause, sold out to the Saxons, and according to later accounts came to a very bad end.'

'What on earth can that have to do with Stephen?' Alison wondered.

'Maybe it has some connection to those runes in the notebook we found in the safe,' Eve suggested.

Robert continued, 'Nigel said he requested a company search and should have the results today. That might give us more of a clue.'

Alderson rang midway through the afternoon. Robert reported the conversation immediately. 'Apparently, Overtring Ltd was incorporated eighteen months ago as Casper 3712 Ltd. The company changed its name immediately and at the same time appointed two directors and a company secretary to replace the nominees listed for registration purposes.' Robert paused for a moment before adding, 'The new directors were Arnold Wharton and Graeme Fletcher; with Kathy King as the secretary. The issued share capital was one thousand pounds, which apparently is fairly normal in such cases. Wharton and Fletcher each owned forty per cent of the shares and Kathy King owned the rest.'

Discussion regarding the mysterious company was suspended when the phone rang again. This time it was for

Alison. She listened to the caller for a few moments, then asked them to hold. 'It's Professor Riley. She's travelling back to Yorkshire tomorrow, and can come straight here if we want. Shall I say we'll collect her from the station, or ask her to get a taxi?'

'We'll pick her up,' I said immediately. 'In fact, we can kill two birds with one stone. If we take those negatives with us we can leave them to be developed before we collect the professor. All we need to know is what time her train gets into Thorsby.'

Eve and I decided we needed a breath of fresh air. It was a cold, clear, crisp afternoon, with the promise of frost later. I took her hand as we meandered down the steps and across the extensive lawn. I still got a thrill from that highly personal contact. 'Did I do right volunteering us to collect the professor?' I asked, noticing that Eve had barely spoken since then, and still looked preoccupied.

'What? Oh, yes, of course you did. In fact, I think the sooner she gets here, the better.'

'Because of the runes? Is that what you mean?'

'I don't know, to be honest. I think it might be far more than merely translating those runes. Don't ask me to explain, Adam, because I can't. I just have this feeling that Professor Riley might hold the key to the whole mystery, and why I should think that is beyond me. I could be completely wrong in this, but I've been having strange thoughts ever since we got here, and I'm not sure what any of it means.'

'Do you want us to leave?'

'No, certainly not. I didn't mean that I was upset by them, or that they were bad thoughts. It's simply that my imagination seems to be working overtime, and more often than not it turns out to be accurate. Like with checking that photo album, for example.'

'That wasn't your imagination, Evie darling; that was

sheer deductive brilliance. They say that brains and beauty don't mix, but you prove that to be completely wrong.'

Eve squeezed my hand. 'The album might have been deduction, but I have a feeling the safe hasn't yielded all its secrets up yet, and that is certainly my imagination.'

It might well have been, but if it was, as I explained to her, my imagination and hers were in tune, for I had also thought exactly the same.

The following day, Eve and I set off in the Mercedes, along with Alison. Before we left, I warned Robert to keep his guard up. 'Remember, there's only you and Frank, plus Tammy and Mary.' I handed him the pistol. 'Don't hesitate to use it. This killer has struck three times. Another body or two isn't going to faze him.'

'You really have a way of cheering people up.'

Once we'd dropped the negatives in the photographic store, we parked outside Thorsby station to await the professor's train. Anyone less like the music hall character that had inspired her nickname would be difficult to imagine. Victoria Riley was slim, elegant, and handsome, with fine-boned features framed by superbly groomed hair. It seemed incongruous to think that she had retired on the grounds of her age. She appeared little more than fifty, I thought. I wondered flippantly if, like Dorian Gray in Oscar Wilde's story, she had a rapidly ageing portrait in her attic.

After Alison had performed the introductions we returned to Barton Manor. To be honest, I was glad to get back there, and relieved to find that nothing untoward had happened during our brief absence. As Alison and Tammy were showing the professor to her room, Robert covertly returned the Glock to me, admitting that he didn't feel comfortable carrying a handgun.

'It's their purpose that disturbs me,' he said. 'I'd be perfectly content wandering the estate with a shotgun, knowing that I was after pheasant or other game, or even carrying a stalking rifle, but a pistol is only designed with one target in mind, and that's to take another human's life.'

I shook my head in mock sorrow. 'With an attitude like that, Robert, you wouldn't have lasted five minutes in Tombstone or Dodge City.'

When we took our places for dinner I noticed that Robert ensured he had Professor Riley next to him. Conversation was light for the most part. Robert began by asking the professor how she was occupying her time since retirement.

'I've written a couple of books on Ancient Britain that missed the best seller list by a wide margin and I'm busy with a third book at the moment dealing with the Celtic age.'

'You shouldn't have retired at all, then we wouldn't have that dickhead Locke to contend with,' Tammy muttered.

'I'm afraid the University authorities didn't consult me about my successor,' Victoria told her dryly. 'If I had been consulted, I certainly wouldn't have opted for Professor Locke. That, I might add, is a strictly private opinion I'll deny having passed if challenged.'

'I know Alison and Tammy have a fairly low opinion of him, but why do you say that?' Robert asked.

'History, my dear Robert, is based on sound research and accurate interpretation. It is no part of the historian's duty to write ostensibly authoritative conclusions based on shaky evidence and supposition presented as hard fact. Nor should a serious historian suppress information that doesn't fit with their own theories. An even worse crime is to manufacture evidence to bolster their position. All those devices are the province of the novelist, not the historian.' Victoria smiled wryly. 'Perhaps that is why novels outsell history textbooks by such a wide margin. I'm afraid

Professor Locke stepped over the boundary between factual reportage and fiction a long time ago. His approach to teaching the subject does not appear to reflect well on his tutelage at Bristol University, but a teacher cannot instil talent, all they can do is nurture it, so it would be totally unfair to blame the deficiencies he now exhibits on the way he was taught. However I believe the poor man is seriously ill, so perhaps it is unfair of me to judge him too harshly, despite my strong feelings on the matter.'

'I heard that too, what's wrong with him, do you know?'

'According to what I was told, I believe he has cancer. It's both inoperable and terminal. He has only a few months to live. However, enough of Professor Locke, I'm really looking forward to getting to work on your runic inscriptions tomorrow. Tell me where you found the text.'

By the time Eve and I went down for breakfast next morning, Professor Riley was already ensconced in the study working on the runic inscriptions in the notebook. Later, when Alison took her a coffee, she emerged with disturbing news. 'There's a lot of bad language flying around in there,' she told us, pointing to the study door. 'The runes may be Celtic, but what Victoria says about them is pure Anglo-Saxon.'

'I take it from that she's having problems,' Eve said. Sometimes, Evie is almost as perceptive as me.

'That's the polite way of putting it,' Alison agreed, 'but nowhere near as colourful as Victoria's description.'

'What's the problem?'

Alison smiled. 'The problem is that she doesn't know what the problem is. That sounds weird, but it's true. She can't work out what language the runes have been transcribed in, for one thing. She says it's either one she hasn't come across before, or the person who wrote them in that notebook encoded them beforehand. A lot of the symbols are ones she has never encountered. That's the situation in a nutshell, or in other words, with the expletives omitted.'

It was disappointing, to say the least. We had pinned our hopes on the runes to provide, at least in part, a motive for the murders. They might still do that, but for the moment, their secret remained hidden.

Victoria had been no more successful by the time we assembled for dinner. We were gathered in the entrance hall, where the huge log fire was countering the severe frost outside, and were about to make our way into the dining room when Johnny Pickersgill phoned. He wanted to update me about their prime suspect. I chatted to him for some time, and when I emerged from the study, found the hall deserted. Everyone had moved to the dining room and taken their seats around the table.

'The police have decided to release Graeme Fletcher,' I told them. They only have circumstantial evidence against him regarding the first two murders, and he has a very good alibi for the third one. Added to which they still haven't found or identified the mystery weapon.'

'What murders, and what weapon?' Professor Riley asked.

'Didn't Alison tell you when she asked you to decipher the runes?' Robert asked.

'No, she mentioned something about your brother's papers, but that was all.'

'I didn't want to scare her by explaining that Stephen had been murdered,' Alison said, 'or that his mistress had been killed as well.'

'That wouldn't have scared me, Alison; history is littered with the corpses of murder victims. However, I had no idea your brother had been murdered, Robert. What happened? Was he shot, or stabbed, or poisoned?'

'That's just the problem, we're not sure,' Eve told her. 'We can rule out poisoning, though.'

'It sounds like the plot of one of those films by Mr Hitchcock, or a rather lurid mystery novel.' She accompanied the final remark with an accusing glance in my direction.

'It's certainly a mystery,' I agreed, 'and a rather singular one indeed. I'm afraid even my lurid imagination couldn't dream up a weapon that inflicts wounds such as this one, though.'

Riley frowned. 'I don't understand. What was so special about the wounds?'

Robert took over the tale. 'Adam's right, it is difficult to grasp. Imagine some sort of a blade that leaves a surface wound similar to a bullet hole, but then goes in a perfectly straight line to reach the heart. During its passage, the weapon removes skin, tissue, flesh, blood vessels and bone, everything in its path. A weapon that has literally extracted a core from the victim's body.'

As he was speaking I saw Victoria's expression change. All the colour drained from her face, her eyes widened with shock, and suddenly, for the first time, she looked her true age. She pushed her chair back, stood up, then swayed and crumpled towards the floor, striking her head against the corner of the table as she fell, to remain, eyes closed.

We watched as the ambulance crew stretchered Professor Riley into the emergency vehicle for the dash to Thorsby Hospital. Despite their anxiety, we managed to dissuade Alison and Tammy from going with their former tutor. Instead, they agreed to my suggestion that Eve should drive them, with Robert, to the hospital. 'That means you'll be guarding the manor on your own,' Eve objected. 'I thought we agreed that nobody should be left to do that.'

'I won't be alone. I'll have Frank and Mary with me, plus my guardian angel.' I patted the pocket of my coat, which contained the pistol.

'Just make sure you don't open the door to anyone

except us.'

'Yes, Evie, but you must phone to tell me when you're setting off back. Then I'll know not to shoot you.'

My fear that Victoria had suffered a heart attack had not been assuaged by the ambulance crew's reassurances. 'We don't believe it was a heart attack or stroke,' they told us. That was a long way from stating it with certainty, I reflected. My concern was heightened by the thought, implanted by Eve, that the manor might be subjected to another assault during the absence of most of the inhabitants. In the event, the evening was trouble-free, but nevertheless I was immensely relieved when the phone rang shortly after 10.30. I heard the bleep that preceded the coins being inserted and knew this would be Eve's promised call.

'How is she?' I asked immediately.

'She's conscious at last, but extremely confused, according to what the staff nurse told us. They're going to keep her in for a couple of days at least. It sounds as if they're erring on the side of caution, because the doctor who examined her doesn't think she had either a heart attack or a stroke. Having said which, once we told them how it happened they said they wouldn't take any chances. They've scheduled a barrage of tests for tomorrow, and until they're satisfied with the results, she's not going anywhere. Unlike us, because we're setting off for the manor shortly. They've allowed Alison and Tammy to see Victoria for a few minutes, and then we'll be on our way. How are things there? Is everything OK?'

'It is indeed. The roast lamb was delicious, and the apple crumble and custard absolutely divine.'

'Adam Bailey, I hate you, I really do.' Eve rang off then, as her money ran out, and I went through to the kitchen to warn Mary when to expect the delayed diners, and to collect a mug of coffee.

Later, when the travellers had returned unscathed from their expedition and claimed their delayed meal, Eve and I resumed our night patrol. There was no shortage of a conversational topic, our discussion centring mainly around Victoria's dramatic collapse.

'I'm beginning to think this house is jinxed,' Eve said. 'Even without the murders there have been a lot of nasty incidents. First there was Inspector Hardy's car crash, which happened as he was travelling to get here. Then Frank Jolly's broken arm. They were both freak accidents. Tammy was tied up, and now Professor Riley has such a dramatic fall, or faint, whatever you want to call it.'

'I agree there does seem to have been a chain of mishaps, but I don't think you can blame a curse on the house for the latest incident.'

'Why not?'

'Because I was watching Victoria's face as Robert was speaking. She looked absolutely fine until he began to describe the wounds made by that weapon. The effect of hearing the details was truly dramatic. She went as white as a sheet, and when she tried to stand up I could see she was trembling, then she seemed to faint. I can't prove this, but I am absolutely certain in my own mind that our worthy professor of history knows something about that weapon, and whatever it is, it scared the living daylights out of her.'

'I'm not sure I go along with that, Adam. What is it that she could possibly know?'

'That's just the problem, I can't imagine what it might be. I certainly don't think a woman of Professor Riley's standing would have any guilty knowledge. All we can hope is that she makes a full recovery and will tell us what she does know. The other thought that crossed my mind was regarding something you said before Victoria arrived here. You told me that the professor might hold the key to the whole mystery, but that might have been your wild imagination. I don't think it was at all wild, and if she can help identify that mysterious weapon, it will be a huge step forward.'

The dramatic events had caused me to omit telling the others about the rest of my conversation with Johnny Pickersgill. It wasn't until he called me again that I rectified the omission. 'I forgot to say that I told Pickersgill about Fletcher's involvement with Wharton and Kathy King in that company Stephen paid so much money to,' I explained.

'He and DS Holmes paid Fletcher a visit this morning. That man must be sick of the sight of police officers. The upshot was that Fletcher claims that Overtring is a genuine company, used by Stephen to conduct historical research and when Holmes asked what that research entailed, Fletcher said it was mainly to do with Pengelly family history from before the Norman invasion. He claimed that because the period covered is shrouded in mystery, the cost was huge, which explains the large sums of money involved. Apparently, when Holmes asked Fletcher for paperwork to back up his story, Fletcher told him that Wharton kept copies of it all, but handed the originals to Stephen.'

'That sounds very iffy to me, Adam,' Robert told me.

'I agree, but as everyone else connected to that company is now dead, I don't see how we're going to be able to prove it.'

'Maybe the historical-cum-family research thing is simply the tale they cooked up in case anyone started asking awkward questions,' Eve suggested. 'People such as Stephen's accountants, for example.'

'And they used that as a cover story in the event, you mean?' Alison interjected.

'If that's true, what was Stephen really paying the money for?' I asked.

'What do you think it might be?' Robert asked.

'I don't think it was trafficking in drugs, or stolen property. Not with what we do know. If that had been the case, Stephen's accounts would have shown a correspondingly larger income. My best guess would be that they were blackmailing him, but over what I'm not sure. If Stephen had a guilty secret, he might have been prepared to pay out large sums, given his position in local society. However, if Fletcher won't talk, unless we can think of some other way to get at the truth, the only way we could hope to find out would be by the use of a medium.'

Chapter Eleven

'I'm beginning to develop a hearty dislike for this road,' Eve said.

We were passing the point where Hardy had crashed his car, on our way to Thorsby hospital to collect Victoria. When Alison had enquired that morning, the ward sister had told her that as the test results had shown no permanent damage, Victoria could safely be released from medical care.

'What has the road done to upset you?' I joked.

'It isn't the road itself, but every time we travel along it, something weird happens soon afterwards.'

Eve had a point, but I don't think either of us could have foreseen the outcome of our trip to collect the professor, or what she would reveal. We called at the shop in Thorsby and picked up the prints developed from the negatives we had left there days earlier. Eve stuffed them in her handbag and promptly forgot about them.

Professor Riley was extremely quiet during the journey back to Barton Manor, and seemed on edge. At first, I put this down to the effects of her fall, and it was only later that I realised the true reason. When we arrived at the manor, she responded to the greetings and enquiries after her health by pleading a headache. There was ample evidence to support this, via a large, unsightly, multi-coloured bruise on her cheekbone. She asked if she could go to her room until the headache wore off.

Her condition seemed to have improved by dinner time, because she responded to Alison's summons and joined us for the meal. As we were awaiting her arrival, Robert and I had a private conversation regarding Professor Riley. I was surprised to discover that Robert shared my suspicions regarding the cause of Victoria's collapse.

'I'll leave you to try and find out what she knows,' Robert said. 'You're the expert, after all. However, I do want answers, and if Victoria has something to tell us, I want to hear it, especially if it impacts on Stephen's death. I know we had been estranged for years, but it's only now, when I have no family left, that I realise how much I missed having one.'

I waited until after dinner before bringing the subject up. By that time, with no further uncomfortable questions, I could tell that Victoria had relaxed, and was savouring the red wine Robert had poured for her. Once Alison and Tammy had assisted Frank to clear the table and serve coffee, I judged it to be time to make my move. I tried to keep my voice relaxed, reassuring. 'Victoria, we were interrupted a couple of nights ago, just as I was about to ask you a very important question. Would you please tell us what you know about the murder weapon Robert described?'

There was a long silence. Victoria's face went deathly pale. For a moment I thought she was going to faint again. Eventually she gasped, 'The murder weapon?'

'Yes, Victoria, the murder weapon.' There was nothing casual or reassuring in my voice or demeanour now, and I hoped my determination to get the truth showed. 'Tell us what you know about it.'

'What makes you think I know anything about it?' The denial was unconvincing.

'We hoped you would tell us that,' I persisted. 'Have you seen it, perhaps?'

'No, no I haven't.'

'If you haven't seen it there's no harm in telling us about it.'

The silence that followed was oppressive with tension.

'Very well, I'll tell you what I know.' There was a world of reluctance in Victoria's voice. 'Although *know* is too strong a word. *Rumour* would be better, and even that's a wild exaggeration. You will have to suspend judgement and cast away any pre-conceived notions about the subject. And you will have them,' she added, 'everyone does. What I'm about to tell you is a story I have spent the better part of my life dismissing as a fable; a fairy tale that came from an old man's fevered imagination. That was until Robert told me a story that seemed to indicate there could be more substance to the fantastic tale I had heard long ago than just an old man's ramblings.'

She sat back, and I thought she looked relieved to be given the opportunity to share the burden of her knowledge. After I heard what she had to tell us, I could readily understand how great that burden was. 'I must take you back over forty years, to when I was about your age, Alison. I went on an archaeological dig in the summer. A lot of students did, they still do. It was fun, it was interesting to anyone keen on history, and one got fed, housed, and paid a small amount. This particular site was in the West Country. The head of the team was a brilliant historian called Professor Gladstone.' Victoria smiled. 'He was also a lecherous old soak, who was forever chasing female students. He managed to get astride at least one every summer. They became known as "The Gladstone Bags".'

I saw Victoria look across at Alison, and noticed the quizzical expression on the younger woman's face. It appeared that Victoria had also seen it. 'No, Alison,' she told her dryly, 'I wasn't one of them. My taste has always been for younger men. Anyway,' she continued, 'when Gladstone wasn't screwing a student he was usually unscrewing a bottle, or uncorking one. That wasn't to say he was bad at his job. Edwin Gladstone was one of the finest historians of his era. His knowledge of Britain prior to the Anglo-Saxon era was unrivalled then and now, despite the many discoveries that have been unearthed since his death.

'The incident occurred one evening after a highly successful day on the site. One or two very significant specimens had been unearthed and the dig team was in the mood to celebrate. So we trooped off to the local village pub, which had a good menu, an excellent wine cellar, and a very relaxed attitude to the licensing laws. We ordered a meal and proceeded to get sloshed. After dinner we decided to play a game. It involved selecting an event from history, one that had never been explained satisfactorily, and giving a new version. One of the students named it *Mystery from History*, I remember, and we were drunk enough to find that amusing. I chose the Princes in the Tower, the only other I can clearly recall was the *Marie Celeste*, because there was some argument whether it counted, because it was a sea mystery really.

'Everyone bar Gladstone had told their tale. Some of them were good, most were poor. By then it had got to one o'clock and we were about as drunk as we could get. One or two had fallen asleep when Gladstone started to speak. They soon woke up though. If he hadn't opted for an academic career Gladstone would have a made a damned good actor. He had a magnificent, compelling voice. He stood up, not even swaying, although he'd consumed the best part of two bottles of claret. "I want," he began, "to tell you the true story of King Arthur."

'There was a howl of derision, "Not that old chestnut. You'll be quoting Tennyson or Malory at us next," someone called out. Gladstone raised one hand and said, "No!" Or rather he boomed it. That one word was enough to silence the objectors. Then he went on. I was drunk, yet I can still recall every word of that story as if it had been last night.

'"You will not find this in any book or poem, play or

144

film. Not in Gildas or Bede, Nennius, the Black Book, the Red Book, or any of the Welsh legends. It is a story to put flight to myth and legend, or perhaps to create another one. Towards the end of the fifth century AD the Celtic tribes that had lived under the uneasy protection of the Roman armies occupying Britain were oppressed from all sides. The collapse of Roman rule left Britain prey to all sorts of acquisitive aggressors. From the North, the Picts and Scots came marauding unchallenged over the now deserted Hadrian's Wall. Raiders from Ireland came looting, carrying off women, cattle and slaves, but the greatest threat of all came from the Continent, where Angles, Jutes, and Saxons queued to invade.

"'These were desperate and dangerous times. What the Celtic tribes needed was a warlord, a hero, a man they could trust to lead them and wield them into a fighting force worth the name. There had been one, Vortigern by name, but he had betrayed them, sold them out to the Saxons. In answer to their prayers they got not one man, not one leader, but two.

"'Celts were masters of metal. Celtic metalwork is still greatly admired to this day; and rightly so. Yet there was one man who took this further, took it to a fine art form. He used his unrivalled knowledge of science to great effect. Some said he was a magician, so great was his skill. No doubt he did little to discourage the notion. Of his character let's say he was no better and no worse than others of his age. Among his misdeeds he had fathered two illegitimate sons, probably twins. In order to escape the wrath of the kinfolk of the woman he had wronged and fearful for the fate of his babies he fled with them to Brittany where the boys were raised and taught many of his skills and arts.

"'When they had become young men they judged it time to return to their native land. Accompanied by their father they set sail for England. Before they left, their father used all his knowledge and some say his magical powers to forge a mighty weapon each for the sons, weapons he knew would render them all but invincible in battle.

"'And so it proved. So great was the prowess of these two warriors that their fame spread and with it the reputation of the weapons. One of the sons, with a small band of followers, established himself as warlord along the southern coast of Britain, with a territory stretching to the Thames estuary. The other, with his cohorts, struck further west and soon became leader over the people dwelling in the West Country and the Marches. His campaigns even took him to the north of England.

"'But the Anglo-Saxon menace was growing all the time. The two brothers joined forces and with their armies routed the invaders in a mighty battle, at Mount Badon, also known by the Latin name of Mons Badonicus. So overwhelming was their victory that the Saxon advance was halted for almost a century.

"'One of these brothers, wise and cunning as his father, foresaw that the Celtic age was passing and that the Saxons would eventually hold sway. He married a Saxon princess and from his offspring came the dynasty that ruled the Kingdom of Wessex until the Norman invasion. Among his many illustrious descendants, the most famous was Alfred the Great. The founder of this dynasty was Cerdic. Most historians will state categorically that Cerdic was Saxon. Not true, for Cerdic is not a Saxon name. It is a Celtic name, meaning *strong arm*.

"'Further to the west, his twin had also become ruler, but his life was beset with more battles and campaigns until after fighting his last campaign he slips from out of the pages of history books to reappear as one of the most legendary figures the world has ever known. The curious thing is that although much has been made of one brother, to the extent that even the weapon he wielded has become world famous, little has been made of his equally illustrious twin except to acknowledge his existence as the founder of a dynasty.

"'The weapons they carried were totally different, equally deadly. One was a sword whose blade was so sharp to receive a wound from it would inevitably prove fatal. The other was a dagger that would tear out the victim's heart with the ease of a needle passing through silken fabric.

"'The western king was Arthur, his mighty sword Excalibur, kept sharp by the scabbard wrought for him by the boy's father. The Wessex king was Cerdic, his weapon, longer than a knife, shorter than a sword, bore a cylindrical blade so sharp it would cut through skin and flesh, sinew and bone alike all the way to the heart and remove the flesh from a man's body. The weapon wrought for Cerdic was named Excoria.

"'That is the true story of King Arthur, his twin brother King Cerdic and their weapons Excalibur and Excoria, forged for them by their father. The father has been ascribed many names, but you know him best as Merlin. I could tell you more, had you the wit to appreciate it, greater legends even than the Arthurian one could spring to life here, but I will not. Some things are better left unsaid; some things are better left as myths for the world to speculate on.'"

Victoria Riley stopped. She was trembling and pale, and for a moment I was concerned, but she recovered and took a gulp of her wine. After a few minutes, she licked her lips and added, 'Gladstone said no more, but everyone in that room believed him, for a time at least. I was more persistent. Something told me that there was more in that story than a drunken interpretation by a clever historian, and then there was that cryptic ending. What myth was it, I wondered, that was so great it would put even the legend of King Arthur into the shade? I was sure Gladstone had something to back up his wild tale, some evidence that none other had seen. I pursued him until he was dying, but without success. Nor was I the only one, as he remarked the last time I saw him. He told me, "I believed the secret was safe for all time, but recent developments make me wonder and worry if that might not be so."

'I asked him what he meant, and he said, "There are others seeking the same information as you, and they are equally determined to try and get it, which is one reason I have no regrets about what is happening to me. To be honest, Victoria, I tremble to think what might happen if the truth came out. If you have the bad luck to be the one to find it, the wit to decipher it, and the wisdom to interpret it you will know all I do, and I trust that you will interpret the danger and act accordingly." I thought that was all he was going to say, but then he added something even more cryptic, "I hope for your sake, Victoria that you never find it. I hope it stays lost in the mists of time, where it belongs. If, by some evil mischance it should come to light, I hope you, or whoever finds it has the strength, the wisdom, and the courage to do what I have done and leave it for the past. Let the dead bury their dead. One resurrection is enough." Then he burst out laughing.'

'What do you think he meant by that?' Robert asked quietly.

Victoria shook her head. 'I've absolutely no idea. I have racked my brains ever since then to try and work out what else he might have concealed from me, but I cannot claim any success.'

'Do you believe his tale has any merit to it?' Alison pressed her.

'I've wondered that too, ever since I heard it. The problem has always been evidential. Recently one or two theorists have suggested a link between Arthur and Cerdic. The popular misconception that Cerdic was Saxon arose because he ruled a Saxon people, his Celtic name said to have been given to him by his mother, who may have been a Celt. That is entirely possible, but look at the names he gave his own offspring. For the next three generations these were all Celtic. How much more likely that Cerdic himself was a Celt and ruled over the Saxon kingdom of Wessex because he was both the most powerful man of his time and had married well. As to whether I believe it, I might have gone to my grave not knowing, or classing it as yet another Arthurian legend and God knows we don't need any more of them, until I sat there and listened to Adam and Robert telling the story of the murders. I was little more than mildly interested in what they had to say, and then, suddenly, from out of the blue, Robert described wounds that could only have made by a weapon from a time fifteen hundred years ago, a weapon of fable at most.

'It was then that I realised that evidence might exist that pointed to the existence of Arthur, Merlin, and Cerdic, beyond the pages of fiction, or doubtful factual accounts written many centuries later; proof that could lead to the complete re-writing of the history of that period. Can you wonder that I fainted?'

Discussion of Victoria's extraordinary tale took up the remainder of the evening. I could tell the others were having as much difficulty as me in believing what she had told us, and I mentioned this. 'I think we have a huge problem here, Victoria. Let's be honest, how often do you hear of myths and legends being brought to life without huge scepticism from those who witness it? Having said that, I must admit that you have provided the only indication yet as to how those wounds were inflicted, and the only weapon that might have been used, improbable as it might sound.'

'Where does it leave us, though?' Robert asked. 'Should we go to the police with this story?'

Eve counselled against that idea. 'I have to say, I did

wonder whether we ought to, but then I tried to imagine what their reaction would be, and I don't think the time is right to involve them with something they would consider as far-fetched as this.'

'Eve's right,' I added. 'They would probably consider that the bump on the head had affected Victoria and have her carted off to the funny farm and then search the manor for the hallucinogenic drugs they thought we'd been taking.'

My absurd remark made everyone smile, even Victoria, who I could tell was still affected by the story she had recounted. I guessed that the tale was something she had kept to herself for a long time, never imagining that she would share it with anyone.

'Apart from Adam's suggestion,' Eve told them, 'looking at it from a practical point of view, as far as the police are concerned hearing what Victoria has told us wouldn't take them any further forward in solving the murders. We may have a clue as to the nature of the weapon, but that gets us no closer to identifying the killer or their motive. Whether you choose to believe the story of Arthur and Cerdic or not, we need something else, something that will lead us to whoever wielded the weapon that inflicted the wounds. Only when we get that will we be on our way to solving the mystery.'

It was Alison who had the final word on the matter. 'I agree with everything Adam and Eve have said. Their advice is spot-on. It is far too early to go to the police, not unless we have something far more credible. Having said that, the prospect of discovering anything that would prove the existence of King Arthur beyond the pages of fiction is immensely exciting.'

There was total agreement on that score, and yet, as I pointed out to Eve in the privacy of the Rose Room, everyone had seemingly ignored or missed the possibility of something even more intriguing in Victoria's story;

something she had only hinted at.

'You don't think she was holding something back, do you? I thought she told us everything she knows. It didn't seem to me that she was hiding anything.'

'I'm not suggesting she withheld anything, Evie, but at one point she admitted that Gladstone hadn't told her everything. The way she told it, there was the hint of an even greater mystery, and yet I can't think of anything that might surpass the Arthurian legend as a sensational revelation.'

I found sleep hard to come by that night, which was hardly surprising given what we'd heard. Eve was luckier it seemed, having dozed off even before I got into bed alongside her. However, her rest was uneasy, and seemed troubled by dreams once again. From time to time she spoke, or rather she uttered sounds, but they were unintelligible. Not only that, but her voice changed, the tone deeper and more guttural.

Hours passed and I was still awake. I was aware that Eve's dream was causing her to become more agitated. Concerned by this, I reached over and put my arm around her, my sole object being to console her; to provide comfort. At first she stiffened, resisting my embrace, but then I felt her body relax, and she sighed contentedly. Her breathing eased and she turned to face me, returning my embrace. 'Sorry,' she murmured, 'I was dreaming again, wasn't I?'

'You were a bit. Are you OK?'

'I'm fine, absolutely fine.' She began to caress me, and her voice dropped to a whisper, 'Or rather, I will be if you make love to me.'

I couldn't see a problem with that idea.

Next morning I was awake before Eve, but I didn't move, not wanting to disturb her. I wondered what her dream had been about. Whatever it was, it obviously hadn't upset her. Not if the outcome was anything to go by. I smiled at the memory of the passion that had preceded our falling asleep in each other's arms. Almost immediately, however, as if she sensed that I was no longer asleep, she stretched and opened her eyes, her expression one of drowsy content. And as if she had read my mind said, 'Good morning, lover, would you like to hear about my dream?'

'Yes please,' I replied. 'I enjoyed the effect too much not to.'

'It was the bear, like before, but this time he was showing me things.'

'What sort of things?'

'I don't know, that's the weird part, I couldn't really make sense of a lot of it. I do remember some bits, though. There was an old cottage, one that was in a very dilapidated state, and a marsh, with reeds and an open expanse of water, and a baby's cot, but I couldn't see inside it, so I don't know if it was empty or not. It was all very confusing and jumbled up, and I've no idea what it meant, if anything.'

'Dreams are like that.'

'One thing I do know, that when I woke up it was important that you were with me, and that we should be together. I knew I had to show you how much I love you.'

'You do that all the time, Evie darling.'

'Perhaps I do, but I'm not always sure you understand that, and it is so very important.' She snuggled closer and whispered, 'Just to be on the safe side, I think I should show you again, don't you?'

I couldn't see a problem with that, either.

Chapter Twelve

It was after 9.30 when we headed down for breakfast. We had almost reached the end of the Minstrel's Gallery when a thought struck me, one so powerful that I stopped dead. Eve also had to stop, because we were holding hands. 'What's wrong, Adam?'

'That letter of Stephen's; the one he left with the solicitor for Robert.'

'What about it?'

'I've just had a thought. We were all so surprised by it, and by the sentimental tone, that I believe we missed the point he was trying to get across.'

'And that was?'

'I think Stephen wanted to direct Robert's attention to something important that he wanted him to look at. If I remember correctly, he referred to the importance of the Pengelly family. And the need to inspect the estate records, or something of that nature.'

'I'm not sure you've got the wording exactly right, though that sounds pretty much as I remember it. But what of it? Where's the significance in that, except to highlight Stephen Pengelly's change of heart? He knew he was dying, remember, so you can't fault him for having regrets and harking back to the past. The poor man knew he had little future to look forward to, and he wanted to make amends as best he could before it was too late. That's all. I don't think there was anything more to it than that.'

'And that's exactly my point. I think Stephen Pengelly was far cleverer than we've been led to believe. He might have been weak and gullible in certain areas, but I think that letter was a masterpiece of coded writing. I believe he was afraid it might fall into the wrong hands, and if it did so, he wanted it to seem to be nothing more than the sentimental ramblings of a dying man. Whereas, in fact, he was actually giving Robert strict instructions as to where to look for something. And whatever that something is, Stephen regarded it as highly important. He disguised those instructions astutely enough to fool anyone who took the wording at face value, as you did; as we all did for that matter. However, we have one definite advantage over others who might have read the letter had circumstances been different.'

'And what might that be? We've looked in the safe and there's nothing more in there.' Eve stared at me, and from her concerned expression I guessed she thought I'd gone mad.

'Think about it, Evie, and imagine that you are Stephen Pengelly. You're seated at your desk in the study when Tony Bishop brings in the milk yields for the month of August, or the lambing statistics from the spring, or the crop returns from the wheat fields. Your first thought would be to compare them with the figures for the previous year. Well, that would be my reaction, anyway.'

'OK, what of it?'

'In order to do that, he'd have to take the key, go through the house and down to the safe, to get the ledger. Why? Why not keep them at hand in the study, where he could reach out and check the figures instantly? It isn't as if they contain anything secret, I'd have thought. Unless, of course, what's on the label isn't what's inside the jar.'

'Sorry, you've lost me.'

'On the spine of the ledgers it says, "Barton Manor Estate Accounts", followed by the year they refer to. But, we didn't open the ledgers to look inside and prove that was what they contained.'

'I take your point, but if that was what happened, why

do you believe Stephen went to all that trouble?'

'Because something within those ledgers could provide the motive for his murder, or those books have absolutely nothing to do with estate records. And if you think about it, even the labelling on the spine is a bit suspicious. Why go into so much detail? Why write that they were "Barton Manor Estate Accounts"? He knew what was inside the books, or what was supposed to be in them, so why not simply write the year?'

'I get your point, Adam, and you could well be right, but if you're going to try and convince Robert, I wouldn't go into as much detail as you gave me. He might view it a bit like we did Victoria's tale last night.'

'Is that your tactful way of telling me you think this is one of my wild ideas, Evie?'

She smiled and took my hand again. 'Something of the sort; now, can we please go for some breakfast? All that exercise has left me ravenous.'

We entered the dining room to be greeted by the rest of the party. 'My word, you both look well this morning,' Robert told us. 'I take it you slept well?'

I felt Eve squeeze my hand, which I took to be a signal for me to remain silent. 'We did indeed,' Eve responded, 'the bed in the Rose Room is so comfortable.'

As she was speaking, I noticed Alison nudge Robert, who promptly changed the subject and asked what we would like for breakfast. As we were sampling the delicious kedgeree Mary had made, Eve informed Robert that I'd had a bright idea. 'At least, Adam thinks it's a bright idea, but I'll let you be the judge.'

I gave Robert the outline of my theory.

'I suppose it might be worth taking a look,' he said, eventually. His distinct lack of enthusiasm told me I hadn't convinced him, and neither, judging from their reaction, had my other listeners bought into the idea of a secret in the ledgers.

Victoria was the first to display her disinterest. 'If you don't need the study, Robert, I'm going to take another crack at those runes. Hopefully I'll have more success this time. Let's face it, I couldn't have any less.' With that, she stood up and went into the kitchen to thank Mary for breakfast. As she passed through on her return journey, Alison promised to deliver coffee to the study later. Then she and Tammy announced their intention of getting some fresh air and exercise.

'Don't stray too far from the house,' Robert cautioned them. 'Would you like me to come with you?'

I almost detected a hint of an appeal in his voice, indicating a desire to be anywhere but in the cellar examining musty old tomes, but they told him they'd be fine. With no allies left, Robert reluctantly agreed to open the safe for us. As we passed through the kitchen, Frank asked if there was anything we required.

'No thanks,' Robert told him. 'Adam is keen for me to open the safe so he can inspect the estate ledgers.'

Frank stared at him, his surprise patently obvious. 'Nay, they're not in the safe, Mr Robert.'

'Sorry, Frank, but you're wrong. I distinctly saw them when we were down there.'

'I don't know what you thought they were, but I do know for a fact that all the estate books are kept in Tony Bishop's office. Mr Stephen used to spend hours over there with Tony every month going through the figures. I distinctly remember Mr Stephen saying, "You need access to them far more frequently than I do, Tony, so the best place for them is in the estate office". Then he instructed me to take all the books across there. So whatever *is* in the safe, I don't think it's the estate accounts.'

I got a dig in the ribs at that point. Eve has extremely sharp elbows – and at times, a tongue to match. 'Take that extremely smug grin off your face, Bailey. Nobody likes a Smart Alec.'

As were passing the wine racks, Eve stopped suddenly. 'Adam, lend me your handkerchief, please.'

I passed it to her. She unfolded it and gave me it back. 'Now wrap it around my wrist and tie a knot in it, will you?'

'Certainly, but why?'

'To remind me that I'm an idiot. Robert, please accept my apologies. When we collected Victoria from the hospital we also called in and picked up those photos. I stuck them in my handbag and forgot all about them.' This,' – she pointed to the handkerchief – 'is to prompt me to get them when we return upstairs, otherwise I might forget again.'

'Can I borrow your handkerchief, Robert?' I asked, 'because I also forgot all about them.'

'I think we can manage with just one. And it really doesn't matter. I don't suppose a few hours here or there will make much difference.'

In saying that, Robert was wrong. Had we remembered the photos earlier, we would have saved Victoria several hours of fruitless toil. How easy it is to be wise after the event.

Once we had secured Eve's memory tag, Robert opened the safe. The fact that there were only four volumes of accounts should have been a clue, I told Robert as we stared inside the cavernous chamber of the safe. 'From memory, I believe the Inland Revenue requires people and businesses to retain records for at least six years. I certainly think they can revisit the returns for longer than four years, so retaining only four sets would be imprudent.'

'I get that. Which one should we try first?'

'Why not go for the earliest dated one,' Eve suggested.

He removed the volume and opened it at the first page. We saw his face change, from an expression of mild curiosity to one of total bewilderment.

'What does it say?' I asked. 'Read it out for us.'

'That's just the problem. I can't.'

'Not more runes,' I suggested, half-jokingly.

'No, but it might as well be as far as I'm concerned. I can't be sure, but I think it's written in Latin. What's more, the handwriting is very difficult to decipher.'

'Give it to Adam, he's the best linguist around.'

I waited for a dig, but for once it seemed that my beloved was paying me a genuine compliment. The first thing I noticed was that the script within the book had been pasted inside, and from the look of it the original had been a much smaller volume. I was also aware that this was not the original. Despite the obvious age of the manuscript, there was no yellowing at the edges of the pages or crease marks. It was in such good condition that it must be a photocopy. Whoever had copied the original had been both painstaking and committed to their task, given the amount of work involved. To have completed the job and then pasted the contents into another book to hide them must have required hours of work.

'Can you tell what it's about?' Eve asked. 'Read it for us.'

I began to read the script aloud. '*Mihi nomen est Domenico, cognomen Gaetano et acta haes letatio, et comites. Haec scripsi in Anno Domini MCXCII.*'

'OK, now translate it, for those of us too young to have learned Latin at our mother's knee,' Eve told me.

'The opening sentence is the writer's name. *My Christian name is Domenico, surname Gaetano.* Then he goes on to explain what the book is. *This is the journal of my mission, and that of my comrades. I am writing this in the year of our Lord, 1192.*'

I looked from Robert to Eve and then back again. 'This obviously has nothing to do with the runic inscriptions, or anything earlier than Norman times. Why Stephen would have a journal that was supposedly written at the end of the twelfth century locked away in his safe beats me. I could have understood had it been the original, but this is quite clearly a copy. Maybe he was interested in that period of history, but I can't begin to think it will give us any clue as to the motive for his murder. We'd better check the other books.'

Robert lifted the other volumes out in turn. The second and third contained more of the same. If I was going to be asked to translate all of that, I reckoned that, given the fact that my Latin was not so much rusty as almost falling to pieces, it might take me months, if not years. I was filled with apprehension when he removed the last of the four books. His opening words allayed my fears. 'This is in English, and it's what we've been looking for. This is the other part of the family tree. You remember? The first part was hidden in the desk compartment.'

'Why don't we take that and the first part of that journal upstairs so we can show the others?'

'Good idea, Eve, the light in here isn't exactly ideal for reading anyway,' Robert said as he began to close the safe.

'I don't mind having a go at translating that journal,' I told him, 'but I'd rather not attempt the whole lot in one go. I might need a dictionary anyway. Added to that, even when it's translated, I could miss the meaning, with the fact that it's so old.'

'If you want to, but I don't reckon it's of any real importance,' Robert told me. He tapped the ledger containing the family tree. 'I think this is far more likely to be relevant.'

With the benefit of hindsight, I realised that it wasn't only me who was capable of making huge errors. 'It's going to be interesting to see what Stephen discovered about our ancestry,' Robert continued, 'even if it does mean I'm descended from Genghis Khan or Attila the Hun.'

'You'd already know if Genghis Khan was one of your

ancestors,' I pointed out. 'His date of birth was somewhere around 1170, I believe, which would put him in part one of the tree.'

'You know what Robert means, Adam, stop being so bloody pedantic,' Eve told me.

I can always rely on Eve to point out any minor errors or flaws in my character. I suppose the fact that I find it endearing is mildly masochistic.

As we returned upstairs, my intention was to take a further look at the journal, while the others concentrated on the Pengelly ancestral roll. However, that plan was scuppered early on.

Our arrival in the drawing room coincided with the return of Alison and Tammy, who had abandoned their walk. 'It's bloody cold out there,' Tammy explained, 'especially now the sun's gone in. I think it might be cold enough for snow.'

Alison pointed to Eve's wrist. 'Have you injured your arm?'

'Oh, I'd forgotten about that. Back in a minute.'

As Eve darted from the room, I explained that the handkerchief was an aide-memoire. 'Except that she forgot all about it,' I added.

She returned and passed the wallet to Robert. He took the photos out and began to examine them. 'Oh no!' he muttered, 'this is all we need.'

The women crowded round, blocking my view as they stared at the photos. 'What is it?' I asked.

Robert looked at me over Alison's head, his expression one of comic dismay. 'More bloody runes, as if we didn't have enough of the damned things.'

'Why don't we take them and show them to Victoria,' Tammy suggested.

When Victoria looked at them, she pointed out there was a huge difference between these and the ones in the notebook. The photos appeared to show inscriptions that had been carved in stone. It was impossible to tell where they came from, because the camera had been in close-up mode, concentrating on the inscriptions and excluding the surroundings. From the quality of the prints, I guessed that the photographer had been very competent, and had used a top-quality camera.

As I was pondering this, an idea came to me. I left the room unnoticed, returning a few minutes later. It was obvious that they hadn't noticed my absence. 'I've another puzzle for you to work on,' I told them.

Eve looked up and frowned. 'What might that be?'

'Discovering who took those photos.'

'I assume it must have been Stephen,' Eve retorted acidly, 'after all they were in his possession, and he hid the negatives away in the safe. It seems logical to suppose that the man who has the negatives is the person who took the photographs, or is that too simplistic for your convoluted mind?' She has a very sarcastic turn of phrase at times, my Evie.

I smiled sweetly at her, then pointed to the images. 'Would you care to tell me how?'

'How?'

'Yes, how did Stephen take those photos?'

'It's called a camera, Adam, you point it at the target and press the button. The shutter opens and the image is recorded on the film.'

'Thank you, I'm indebted to you for your wisdom. Now show me it.'

'Show you what?'

'Stephen's camera.'

I noticed that as our verbal sparring was continuing, Robert and Victoria were staring fixedly at the photos, while Tammy and Alison had developed a keen interest in what was happening outside, by gazing out of the window at the darkening skies.

Eve looked around the room, as if expecting the camera

to materialise out of thin air. 'It must be upstairs in his room, or in some other part of the house,' she suggested.

'I wouldn't bother looking for it. That would be a waste of time and effort. It doesn't exist. I checked with Frank and Mary. As far as they're aware, Stephen didn't own a camera. They never saw him carrying one, nor have they seen one in the house. Certainly not one capable of taking photos of such high resolution as those. I'm surprised, Evie, that with your deep knowledge of the photographic process, you failed to notice that those were taken by either a professional or a very gifted amateur. So, returning to my initial, naive question, who did take those photos?'

To give Eve her due, she accepted defeat as gracefully as she could, muttering, 'Oh, lovely, just what we need, another mystery.'

We agreed to leave the prints with Professor Riley, while we returned to look through the Pengelly family tree. 'I might give those a try,' Victoria said, 'I might get lucky with them.'

'Now for the gory revelations about my dodgy ancestors,' Robert said when we reached the sitting room. 'I'm dreading what we might find in there.'

'It's a lottery, I grant you,' Eve told him. 'My sister Harriet did our family tree, and discovered we were indirectly descended from Mary Queen of Scots.'

'Shame it wasn't Bloody Mary, that would explain why you both like vodka and tomato juice,' I retorted.

Alison deftly fielded the cushion that was heading my way with all the force Eve could hurl it, and returned the projectile to the sofa. 'Go on, Robert, be brave. Who knows, you might be descended from royalty. Come to think of it, the way you burn things when you're cooking, the most likely candidate would be Alfred the Great.'

Family trees, it seemed, bring out the worst examples of humour. We waited, watching Robert as he pored over the opening pages of the Pengelly family line. 'This is a bit confusing, to say the least. My family speciality seems to be to give their children names that are designed to baffle everyone.' He pointed to the page he was inspecting. 'On this bit alone there's someone called Aelfgar, another called Aelfgifu, and a third one called Aelfnod.'

'Those are Saxon names,' Tammy told him, the prefix "Aelf" means elf, surprisingly enough.'

Robert continued, 'That's not where the confusion ends, though, there's also a Hild and a Hildraed. I don't know how ordinary people are expected to follow this.' He turned the page and smiled. 'Now here's someone I approve of. One of my ancestors was apparently named Wine.'

'That's not quite what you think,' Tammy told him with a smile. 'Wine is the Saxon word for friend. Hence Godwine means a friend of God.'

'It's still appropriate, though,' Robert told her, 'wine and I have been friends for years.'

'How far back does that document go?' Alison asked.

'I'm not sure yet. The names are beginning to change. If anything, these are even more difficult to pronounce.'

'They're probably Celtic, I'd guess, which means you've gone back a heck of a long way,' Tammy observed. 'This is beginning to get really interesting. You probably don't realise how lucky you are, Robert. There aren't many people who can trace their lineage back to the Celtic Age.' Her tone reflected her excitement, but then, this was her specialist subject.

'Go to the end, Robbie,' Alison urged him, 'I can't stand the suspense. See who is at the head of the tree.'

Robert obeyed, skipping a couple of pages to reach the last entries in the book. He began to trace the names with his finger, then stopped suddenly, his expression one of astonishment.

'What is it, Robbie? Who have you found? Julius

Caesar? The Emperor Hadrian?'

He passed the book to Alison and pointed to the entry that had shocked him. 'See for yourself.'

We saw Alison's face change, her reaction mirroring that of Robert a few seconds earlier. 'That can't be correct, Robbie. No way can that be true. It simply isn't possible.'

'Who is it? Come on, tell us, what name have you found?' Tammy and Eve were almost beside themselves with impatience.

'You'd better show them, Ally, they won't believe us if we tell them. To be fair, they won't believe it in any case.'

That was certainly no exaggeration. When we found the name, we didn't believe it. We discounted the entry as fictitious, and the remainder of the family tree was immediately under suspicion. 'Do you honestly believe that your brother thought that this was true?' Eve asked him.

'I don't know,' Robert replied. 'I certainly don't believe it.'

'There must be something else,' I told them.

'What do you mean, Adam? Isn't that enough?' Alison pointed to the ledger.

'No, I mean there must have been some back-up information, some research papers, that led Stephen to even contemplate this being accurate. Just think of our reaction. No matter how naive or gullible Stephen Pengelly might have been it would have taken something truly convincing to persuade him that he and Robert were descended from King Arthur.'

Prompted by the seemingly incredible discovery in what purported to be the Pengelly family tree, my thoughts turned to the likely source of that highly suspicious document, and the only person left alive who could vouch for its authenticity, or, far more likely, confirm that the whole thing was a fabrication, designed to relieve Stephen

Pengelly of a large chunk of money.

I pointed to the ledger. 'I bet that is what Stephen paid all that money to Overtring Ltd for.' I paused and thought for a minute. 'This, together with the accompanying documentation.'

'What accompanying documentation?' Tammy asked.

'There must have been something to back this up, and quite a lot of it, I'd suggest. What's more it must have been extremely convincing to have taken Stephen in so completely. I admit that half the art of a successful confidence trick is to tell the victim what they want to know, but I can't for one minute believe that Stephen Pengelly was gullible enough to pay out a sum that was well into six figures without a huge amount of supporting evidence.'

'It might not have been the family tree he was paying for,' Eve suggested. 'It might have been something entirely different. I admit that the existence of that document and the amount he paid do suggest it was the tree he paid for, but we can't be certain.'

'We can't find out now, can we,' Tammy said. 'The other paperwork hasn't been found, and everyone who might have been able to tell us the truth is dead.'

'That's not strictly correct, there is one person still alive who could tell us the truth, if he can be persuaded or cajoled into talking.'

'You're referring to Graeme Fletcher, aren't you, Adam? What makes you think he would tell us anything when the police couldn't get him to talk?'

'That's a very good question, Evie, and at this precise moment I can't think of a way, unless we were able to tempt him, to offer him something that would persuade him.'

'I'm not happy at the thought of shelling out more money on top of what Stephen paid,' Robert told us.

'I wasn't thinking of a monetary bribe. Perhaps if we

could offer him immunity from prosecution for the fraud in exchange for information and the return of some of that money, he might be tempted to spill a few beans.'

'How do you suggest that approach should be made, and by whom?'

I considered Robert's question for a moment or two. 'It might be worth having a word with DS Holmes before we decide to make a move. Besides, I wondered if he'd had any success looking into the background of the victims. Wharton, Kathy King, and Fletcher didn't simply dream up this fraud overnight. It would have taken a lot of preparation and planning, and that argues that they must be experienced, and therefore that they might be known to police forces elsewhere.'

'Except that Fletcher isn't a victim,' Eve pointed out.

'Now who's being pedantic? I have an idea in mind, and I think it merits further thought before I put it to Holmes.'

'I have this strange sensation that comes over me when Adam utters the words, "I have an idea",' Eve told them. 'I think people usually refer to it as dread.'

Chapter Thirteen

There was only one main topic of conversation when we foregathered in the entrance hall before dinner that evening, and it was the revelation in the family tree. It foreshadowed even Victoria's continuing fruitless struggle to interpret the runes, and the Latin manuscript, if not completely forgotten, certainly didn't rate a mention.

I was particularly interested to hear what Professor Riley, as a professional historian had to make of what the rest of us considered an outlandish claim. On hearing that the Pengelly family tree purported to show a direct line of descent from the legendary King Arthur, her refusal to dismiss the claim out of hand surprised everyone. In defence of her stance, Victoria pointed to the lack of proof, which seemed contrary until she explained. 'It is a historian's job to record only those facts that can be verified in full, and with incontrovertible evidence to back them up. If there is conflicting material, it is also the historian's task to point to that divergence. In the instance of King Arthur, where there is absolutely no evidence either for his existence, or to prove that he did not exist, then a historian cannot prejudge the issue by declaring one or the other to be correct. There are theories enough to support either point of view, but that is all they are, theories.

'If however someone has stumbled across proof that Arthur *did* exist beyond the pages of popular fiction and Hollywood productions, that would bring about a massive change to the way we view the Dark Ages. I would have said that it was impossible after all this time to discover such evidence, were it not for Edwin Gladstone's tale. If Arthur did exist, and if he fathered children, someone, somewhere will be descended from that line, and I can see no reason why it is any less likely to be the Pengelly family than anyone else.'

She paused, before adding with a flash of humour, 'Before you consider calling a press conference to announce the fact to the world's media, though, I suggest you attempt to discover what grounds your brother had for believing such an astonishing claim.'

I found what Victoria had to say fascinating, even though I was left feeling as if I'd just wandered into one of her lectures by mistake. It was only later, when Eve and I were alone in the Rose Room, that she suggested a line of enquiry we might have overlooked.

'We all seem convinced that the motive for the murders must be linked to the historical research, that manuscript, the runic inscriptions, and the family tree, that we've ignored another piece of possible evidence.'

I had to admit that I didn't know where she was leading me until she explained, 'We know that Stephen spent most of his time and energy chasing one woman after another, so isn't it just as likely that the reason Stephen Pengelly was killed was the one the police believed originally?'

'That doesn't explain the other two murders,' I pointed out.

'It would if there was someone else vying for Kathy King's affections, but with no success. Or if it was connected to another female in Stephen's life, one from a much earlier time?'

'You're thinking of the girl in that letter, aren't you?'

'I am, and I think it well worth spending a bit of time trying to discover who she is and what happened to her.'

'You could be right, Evie, but it might not be easy trying to find someone who could identify the girl after all these years; we only have the name Annie.'

'I still think it worth a try, if only to eliminate that line of enquiry.'

It was at that point that I came up with what could be charitably called a radical theory; or, as Eve referred to it, one of my wild ideas. 'What if the reason we're failing to make any headway is that we're thinking in compartments rather than looking at the overview?'

'I don't get you.'

'What if they're all connected; the girl's letter, the family tree, the Latin manuscript, and the runes?'

'How on earth can they be?'

I had absolutely no idea. The clues might all have been there, but attempting to string them together was a bit like Victoria's efforts to decipher the runes. The only result was a headache.

We both slept soundly once our sentry duty was over. This surprised me a little, in view of the startling revelations of the day. When we awoke next morning, we discovered that the weather had taken a dramatic turn for the worse overnight.

For the previous week there had been clear skies, long periods of sunshine, and sharp overnight frosts. Now, with the wind having changed direction, it had picked up and was driving in from the west, bringing with it heavy rain.

The near-gale-force wind was buffeting the old manor house, the rain, almost horizontal, lashing the windows with angry force. Whereas on previous mornings it had been possible to look across the valley, beyond the grounds of the house and the arable fields towards the slopes of Barton Moor, that view was now strictly curtailed. I could see little beyond the lawns, waterlogged already, and even the lower slopes of the hills were shrouded in a curtain of grey.

This wasn't exactly ideal for what I had in mind to do that day. My plan had been for Eve and me to visit Barton-le-Dale to meet up with Holmes and Pickersgill. The only positive thought induced by the weather was that it might persuade the villains to remain indoors.

When we joined the others, Robert had good news for us. 'I had a call from the locksmith a few minutes ago. He's hoping to get here this morning and will change the locks on all the outer doors, plus see what he can do towards fitting an alarm. The only proviso is that he's unsure what time he'll be able to get here. Apparently there's a big tree blown down the far side of Barton-le-Dale and the Dinsdale road is completely blocked. He thinks it should be cleared before lunchtime though.'

'That's excellent,' Eve responded, 'if only because we might be able to get a full night's sleep now.'

'I also got a phone call from DS Holmes. He and your friend Constable Pickersgill are visiting us this morning. They should be here in an hour or so. He told me there have been developments he wants to discuss, but he wouldn't go into detail. I told him Alison and I would be busy, but he seemed more interested in talking to you two.'

'That saves us a job,' I told him. 'Eve's been having ideas she wants to put to Holmes.'

'It isn't just me,' she protested, 'you wanted to talk to them too.'

'Yes, but mine was just a standard procedural thing, whereas yours was a really constructive theory.'

She eyed me with deep suspicion, but eventually seemed satisfied that I wasn't being sarcastic. Instead she asked Robert what he and Alison were going to be busy with.

He grimaced slightly. 'There was a third phone call. I thought at one point we might have to get a second line installed. The caller was Nigel Alderson. He needs an inventory of the house contents before applying for probate, and it's fairly urgent, so Ally and I are making a start this morning. It's going to take a few days, I reckon, given the size of the place. He turned to Eve and smiled. 'So if you walk into the Rose Room and find a strange man in there, don't worry, it'll only be me.'

'That won't be a problem,' Eve smiled at me sweetly, 'I'm used to having a strange man in my room.'

I smiled just as sweetly back. 'I'd carry a whistle, Robert; then you can summon help. She usually locks me in to prevent me escaping.'

Ignoring Eve's withering glance, I turned to Victoria. 'Are you going to continue the battle of the runes?'

I saw Robert wince, but it seemed Victoria was in an upbeat frame of mind. 'I am,' she replied, 'and hopefully the idea I had just before I went to sleep last night might help me achieve a breakthrough. I'm not going to say anything at this stage, though, I've been disappointed too often to make rash statements. I'm still relying on guesswork, but at least this time it will be educated guesswork.'

Seeing Robert and Alison getting up to leave, Eve asked, 'Where will we find you? In case the locksmith arrives, I mean.'

'We thought we'd make a start in the attics and work down from there. It'll be a novel experience for me, as I wasn't allowed up there as a kid. The rooms were always kept locked, but for what reason, I've no idea.'

'Perhaps we'll find your brother's deranged wife up there, along with her alcoholic nurse,' Alison suggested.

'I doubt that, anyone less like Edward Fairfax Rochester than my brother I can't imagine. Nor, by what I've heard about her, did Kathy King sound at all like Jane Eyre.'

Eve and I lingered over our breakfast, aware that we had nothing else to occupy us as we awaited the detectives' arrival. Tammy also took her time drinking coffee. She too seemed interested in DS Holmes' visit, but for a completely different reason, I guessed.

The police officers soon pulled up outside the house, their car followed by a white van bearing the logo of the local locksmith. Tammy went to summon Robert and Alison, while I checked the craftsman's credentials. Holmes and Pickersgill watched the precautionary measure with approval. Once I had introduced the locksmith to Robert, Eve and I adjourned to the drawing room for our meeting with the officers. Tammy had also joined the discussion group, principally to ask if the officers wanted tea. Not a bad excuse, I thought, given Johnny's immense capacity for the beverage.

'Robert told us there has been some development you're keen to share with us,' I prompted them.

'Actually, that's going a bit far. What we do have is some information that is puzzling us.'

'Oh goody,' Eve exclaimed. 'A puzzle, just as things were becoming so clear.'

I saw Johnny wince at Eve's sarcasm before she asked hastily, 'What's the information and why is it puzzling you?'

Keeping a wary eye on Eve, Holmes explained, 'Once we'd finished at Wharton's house we went to his office to search it and to talk to his secretary. It was obvious that the lady isn't a great fan of Wharton. She was happy to tell us what she could, which admittedly wasn't much. The firm is called Campbell and Price, but Mr Campbell died a few years ago, and soon after that, Price retired and sold the partnership to Wharton. He began practising there three years ago, and when we asked the secretary where he had been working before then she said she didn't know, which we found a bit odd. We checked with the Law Society, and they had no record of Arnold Wharton having practised law in this country prior to his acquisition of Campbell and Price.'

'Does that mean he wasn't qualified?' Eve asked.

'No, his law degree is genuine enough, that much the Law Society was able to confirm. When he graduated from Bristol University in 1964, he was based in Newark, but where he was living and working prior to his arrival in Barton-le-Dale is a complete mystery.'

Holmes paused and Pickersgill took over. 'Interestingly enough, at around the same time as Wharton took over at Campbell and Price, Graeme Fletcher opened his antiques shop, and within a couple of months, Kathy King signed the lease for her flat, so it seems that all three arrived here pretty much simultaneously. As you know, Fletcher is being exceedingly tight-lipped about anything and everything, and we haven't been able to find out anything about his background, or that of Kathy King.'

'It all seems very suspicious; three people arriving in a small town and deciding to set up a company together almost immediately afterwards,' Holmes added.

'I was going to suggest checking into their backgrounds,' I told them, 'but it seems that you had the same idea.'

'We did, but we got nowhere with our enquiries. Knowing where to look would be a massive help.'

'I don't suppose you've considered sending their fingerprints to other forces, have you?' Eve asked.

'It would be a slow, cumbersome process, if for example they've used other names. And where would we start? It isn't as if there was any evidence, either in Wharton's home or his office, or in Miss King's flat.'

His final words triggered a memory. 'It might be worth sending a telegram to the South African police with their names and descriptions,' I suggested.

My statement was greeted by astonished silence. It was Eve who recovered the power of speech first. 'Why South Africa of all places, Adam?'

'I remembered something I'd seen in Kathy King's flat, just after we discovered her body. I had a few seconds in

173

which to look around before Johnny threw me out. I noticed some items that interested me. It was a set of figurines that were standing on a display cabinet alongside the sofa. They were wooden sculptures of African natives. I spent some time in Africa as a correspondent, and saw a lot of similar work over there, created by craftsmen working in South African townships. I know this might seem rather a long shot, but I very much doubt whether she acquired them locally. That sort of artwork is about as rare in North Yorkshire as elephant droppings. I may be totally off the mark, but I still think it might be worth the cost of a telegram quoting those names to Pretoria or Cape Town.'

'I think Adam's right,' Pickersgill told Holmes. 'It might be worth trying.' He gave me a sly grin. 'It's telex, by the way, Adam. We're embracing new technology.'

'Gosh, you'll be replacing your bike with a Panda car next! Anyway, Eve has an idea you might find interesting.'

Eve described our search of the safe and what we'd found amongst the contents. Although she mentioned the family tree and the Latin manuscript in passing, she managed to convey the impression that we believed them to be incidental, concentrating instead on the letter from the young girl. 'Given what we've heard about Stephen Pengelly's reputation as a serial womaniser, we thought it seemed a little strange that he should have retained this above all the others he might have had.'

Eve was holding the letter as she spoke and lifted it to emphasise her next point. 'I'll show you it in a moment, and I think you'll agree that although the girl is quite explicit in her wording, the style implies she could be quite young. That being the case, we wondered why Stephen kept it, and also why he secreted it so carefully within the photo album. Then we remembered something Robert told us; an argument he overheard when he was a child.'

She repeated Robert's account of the row between

Stephen and his father. 'If you look at this letter, I think you'll agree that the girl might well have been underage. If that was the case and Stephen got her into trouble, that might provide a motive for revenge. I'm not sure how it would tie in with the other murders, but I thought it might be worth asking a few questions locally, to see if we can discover who the girl is, and what happened to her.'

'I agree that it might be worth tracing this girl, if only to rule her out,' Holmes told us, 'but if you're right and this is who the argument was about, it does seem unlikely that the revenge should take place now, after so much time has elapsed.'

'If the crime was an act of vengeance, I feel sure it would have been committed long ago,' Pickersgill added, backing his colleague up.

There were factors the officers had failed to take into account, but I decided against mentioning them at that point. 'Returning to our suspicions about the connection between the victims and Graeme Fletcher,' I said, 'we have a theory that the Pengelly family tree we discovered might have been fabricated to swindle Stephen Pengelly out of a large sum of money, using this company Overtring Ltd. If that wasn't the purpose of setting up that firm, the only alternative we can think of is blackmail.'

'Might that manuscript you mentioned be part of it, Adam? The one you said was in Latin,' Pickersgill suggested.

'It could be, but until I've had a go at translating it, I won't know, and even then there's no guarantee that I'll be any the wiser. As a way of shortening the procedure, we wondered if it might pay off for Eve and me to visit Fletcher and see if we can get him to talk. He might not have been prepared to admit anything to the police, but he could do so to us, as we don't pose a threat.'

'I suppose it might be worth trying. Let me mull it over during the weekend and I'll let you know after that,'

Holmes said.

We watched the officers leave, before I sought out Robert. I found him supervising the locksmith at work on the back door, and explained what their problem was. Eve and I returned to the drawing room. There, I told her what I believed was wrong with Holmes' dismissal of the revenge theory. 'If the girl had a lover, a brother, or a husband even – someone who had been abroad or in jail for many years – that would explain the delay in seeking retribution.'

Eve gave me one of her more brilliant smiles, the ones that always melt my heart, and said, 'I'm glad you agree, because I'm more convinced than ever that this letter is important in some way. Why else would Stephen lock it away? So if the police aren't in a hurry to discover who this girl is, I think we should make some enquiries locally.'

'A good idea, Evie, and I think I know the very place to start asking questions.'

'Don't tell me, let me guess. The village pub, by any chance?'

'Exactly, where better to get hold of local gossip than the lounge bar of the local? I think you and I should go for a pint sometime in the near future and see what we can discover.'

'I knew that beer would enter into your plans at some stage or other.' Eve smiled indulgently, 'OK, all we have to do is decide when to go. Of course, if you're driving, you won't be able to have a drink.'

That was a snag I hadn't foreseen.

Victoria's statement took everyone by surprise. 'I believe that I may be on the way to deciphering one of the runic inscriptions in the notebook. I know it seems to have taken forever. I was all but convinced that the whole thing was an elaborate hoax, a set of meaningless scribbles presented to give the appearance of runes.' She shrugged. 'That might well still be the case. There could be nothing more to the messages than someone writing "Kilroy was 'ere", or something equally banal, but until I've finished I won't know for certain.

'I thought it was beyond me, but today I realised why it has been so difficult. I firmly believe that someone was desperate to avoid both the messages being translated. It was only when I looked at the photographs carefully and compared them with the inscriptions in the notebook that I realised where the problem lay; or rather, problems, to be strictly accurate.'

'But why, and by whom?' Robert asked.

Victoria smiled. 'Even I am not old enough to determine who, but I strongly suspect it was the composer or composers of the texts. Alternatively, it could equally well have been the person or persons who commissioned them to be carved on the stone tablets. I have no way of knowing whether the source for both those messages was the same, or whether they are completely unrelated.'

'So you are saying there are two messages within those runic inscriptions, is that correct?' Alison asked.

'Actually, I believe there are three, possibly even four, but again, I can't be positive.'

'I'm getting confused,' Eve told her.

'If you're confused, how do you think I've been feeling for the past few days? Let me try and simplify matters. When they were inscribed, someone put all the symbols down, but jumbled them up – in essence creating a simple form of code. The message within the text would have been difficult enough to disentangle even at that, but as I discovered on examining them, someone else defaced the text. They did this by omitting some of the symbols and altering others by adding different characters. In essence, the effect would be similar to changing a letter I to a T in the Latin alphabet.'

'Why would anyone go to so much trouble?' Tammy wondered.

'It seems they were determined to ensure that the gist of the text did not fall into the wrong hands. That in itself is intriguing. I could understand the need to maintain the secrecy at the time these were created, but what I can't grasp is why someone went to all that trouble recently. Whatever the messages contain, they must have felt it was important enough still to be guarded after such a long time. Why that should be, I have absolutely no idea.'

'Perhaps it gives directions to the hiding place of some great treasure,' Tammy suggested.

'I rather doubt that,' Victoria told her. 'Such things don't exist outside the pages of fictional adventure stories.'

'What about the other inscription?' I asked.

'Ah, that would appear to present a different challenge entirely. The reason I can't be sure if it comprises one or more messages is that all I am able to say with some degree of confidence is that although the inscriptions are runic by nature, the language they are written in is not Celtic. Apart from that, I can also say that it definitely isn't Latin or Greek either. Where that leaves me, I have no idea at present.'

Victoria's news was good, and there was more to come when Frank appeared with a message for Robert. 'Mary asked me to remind you that Tony Bishop will be back from his holiday either later this evening or tomorrow. With everything that's happened, we'd quite forgotten that you haven't met him yet.'

Frank's statement gave Eve and me chance to discuss the idea of a jaunt to the pub in Barton-le-Moors. 'The manor is more secure now, and if there was someone else on hand in case of emergencies I think we could risk a visit to the Crown and Anchor,' I suggested.

Eve agreed, 'I'm beginning to think we'll never get anywhere with this investigation by staying cooped up

178

here.'

'That's true, and despite the charms of my lovely cellmate, I'm starting to go stir crazy,' I told her.

'I think we should tell the others what we plan to do, but let's leave it one more day. When we've met Bishop we can form a better judgement.'

Chapter Fourteen

I'm not sure what the estate manager expected on his return to work, but I'd guess the size of the reception committee wasn't what he anticipated. A few minutes after eight o'clock next morning the estate's Land Rover pulled up outside the front door and Tony Bishop got out. Frank had been deputised to lead the welcome party, which comprised six people. He opened the front door, allowed Bishop to enter, then closed and locked it, sliding the bolts home.

Bishop blinked with surprise at the sight of the gathering, but his attention quickly turned to Frank as he told him, 'We have some very bad news, and we're not taking any chances.'

'I did hear something last night, but I couldn't believe it. Emma's father phoned us when we got home. It was after midnight, and we thought there must have been a problem at their house, but then he told us a lurid tale about what had gone on here. Is it true? Has Stephen really been murdered?'

'It is, but before we go into that, let me introduce you.'

I watched as Robert greeted his new employee, and noticed that both men were assessing one another. In turn, Robert introduced Alison, then Tammy, and finally Eve and me, explaining that we were there to help with protection and to assist the police with their enquiries. 'I didn't mean that like it sounds,' he added with a smile. 'Apart from Adam and Eve trying to prevent us being murdered in our beds, the police have enlisted them on an unofficial basis to help solve the murders.'

'Murders?' Bishop looked aghast. 'Has there been more than one? I didn't know about anything other than Stephen's death.'

'The body count is three at present,' I told him, 'plus an attack on Tammy and two break-ins here.'

'Is that how you got that?' Bishop pointed to the plaster cast on Frank's arm.

'No, that was something totally different. A freak accident, you could say, but it happened at a most inconvenient time.'

Frank returned to the kitchen and we adjourned to the drawing room, spending the best part of half an hour explaining to Bishop everything that had gone on. I could tell he was struggling to take it all on board. Eve, Tammy, and I left Bishop alone with his new employers, and headed for breakfast.

'I think we can risk a trip to Barton-le-Dale this morning,' I told Eve. 'We won't be missed here, and I rather fancy buying you a Ming vase, or a nice mahogany whatnot.'

She looked puzzled for a second, then caught on. 'You're proposing that we visit Fletcher's antiques shop? Despite DS Holmes saying he wanted to think it over.'

'Yes, I reckon it's time we forced the pace a bit. Like you said earlier, the investigation isn't going anywhere. I think Holmes must be under enormous pressure not to make mistakes. There comes a point when that sort of stress makes you freeze, and you become unwilling to try anything in case you get it wrong.'

'What if *we* get it wrong?'

'Holmes can't be blamed for our actions. He has no control over us.'

Eve agreed a trifle reluctantly, and after we'd eaten, we asked Mary if she needed anything and informed Frank that we were going shopping. 'Keep the baddies away while we're out,' I told him, 'and if the worst comes to the worst you can always hit them with your pot.'

He glanced down at the plaster cast on his arm. 'I'd never have thought of using it as a weapon until you mentioned it, but I could do worse. I reckon it would give them a nasty headache.'

On our way to Barton-le-Dale, I asked Eve what she thought of Tony Bishop. Her opinion matched mine almost exactly. At one time this would have surprised me, but the longer we spent together, the more often our thinking seemed to tally on most subjects. I guess this happens with lots of couples. They either grow together or apart.

'I like him,' Eve said. 'He's considerably younger than I expected. He can't be much older than Robert, but that's no bad thing. I also think he cares more about the estate itself than he does about Stephen Pengelly. He didn't pretend to be devastated by the news of Pengelly's death, which shows he's not a hypocrite. I was a bit surprised that his girlfriend's father had already told them about the murder. I thought that DS Holmes was trying to keep a lid on publicity. But I guess that's village life for you. No point trying to keep secrets, because it just won't work. I can't imagine there will be many other topics of conversation in the Crown and Anchor of an evening at present, can you?'

'Not only at present. Gossip about what happened to Pengelly will keep tongues wagging for months. And when you add the other murders into the equation, talk will go on for years. Mind you, by if we go back in a couple of years and listen to it, we probably won't recognise the events, the way it will have been distorted.'

I'd anticipated needing to use the car park at the back of the main street, but despite the influx of Saturday morning shoppers I was lucky enough to see a vehicle pull out of a space almost directly opposite the antiques shop and manoeuvred the car carefully into the vacant bay. I sighed as I locked the car door. 'Getting back into my own car will be a wrench after driving the Mercedes.'

'Don't get ideas above your station, Adam. If you're not careful you'll start believing you're one of the landed gentry.'

'That isn't going to happen, Evie.' I took her hand and squeezed it gently. 'I'm too content with what I have to worry about things like cars, but I admit the Merc is a real temptation.'

The first sign that all was not as it should be was when we reached the shop door. Despite it being mid-morning on the busiest shopping day of the week, a market day at that, the sign was still in the closed position. That could have been an omission, I thought, but when I tried the handle, the door refused to yield. I looked at Eve and saw that her concern mirrored mine. She peered through the window, cupping her fingers to enable her to get a clearer view of the interior of the shop. 'There's no sign of anyone about,' she reported, 'the shop is neat and tidy, and the lights aren't on.'

I wondered if perhaps Fletcher had nipped out to get a sandwich, or had needed to use the toilet and locked up while he was absent from the shop floor, but if either of those had been the case, he would surely have left the lights on. 'Perhaps he's been taken poorly,' I suggested, 'he has nobody to cover for him now, following Kathy King's death.'

With hindsight, I think I was trying to come up with acceptable alternatives to what I feared might have happened. 'I suppose that's possible,' Eve conceded, but I could tell she didn't really buy into my theory. 'I think we should go round to the back and check, just to be on the safe side.'

I followed Eve towards the end of the terrace. There were five shops in the row, with Fletcher's occupying the central position. At the end, a road bisected the main street. We made our way along it, moving against the tide of pedestrians heading from the car park towards the open-air market that was a weekly feature in the town.

The rear of the properties comprised open yards, which served the dual purpose of providing easy access for deliveries, plus parking space for staff and customers of the shops. Eve pointed to a nearly new BMW that was parked at one side of the yard belonging to the antiques' shop. 'Holmes told us that Fletcher had recently bought a BMW, could that be it?'

'It could indeed.' My fear for the antiques dealer's wellbeing increased dramatically as I pointed to the back door, which was slightly open. 'Looks as if someone's inside. Perhaps he had a late night and has only just arrived.'

I'm not sure whether Eve believed me. My statement might have sounded more convincing if I believed it myself. I walked across and pushed the door further open, before calling for the owner. 'Mr Fletcher? Are you there?'

My words echoed back along the corridor, but provoked no response. I tried a second time, and then a third, but with no more success. 'I don't like this. I don't like it at all,' Eve muttered.

Neither did I. I was reminded of the previous occasion, only a few days earlier, when we had entered a property via an open door. That was when we had found Kathy King's body. I hoped this wasn't going to be a repeat of that grim discovery.

We inched our way cautiously inside, aware that if Fletcher was somewhere on the premises, he might not take kindly to strangers invading his shop uninvited, and that if it had not been Fletcher who'd left the back door open ... well, an intruder would have been even less kindly disposed to those who had disturbed him.

The corridor led to the back of the shop, and was flanked on one side by a storeroom, and on the other, by an office and toilet. If the shop had been in pristine condition, the same could not be said for the office. I pushed the door open, and was greeted with a sight reminiscent of the study at Barton Manor. Papers were strewn throughout the room; the desk had been smashed to little more than firewood, and the safe was wide open, its interior empty.

My suspicion that something untoward had happened to the antiques dealer hardened to near certainty. His car was outside, therefore he should be about, but our initial inspection of the shop, the office, the storeroom, and even the toilet had failed to discover Fletcher, either alive, or as I was becoming increasingly sure, dead.

It was only when we were standing in the storeroom on our second tour of inspection that Eve noticed a small, dark stain on the wooden floor. She grasped my arm and pointed to it. 'Adam, is that blood?'

It certainly looked like blood. An irregularly shaped patch, about the size of a dinner plate, had pooled alongside one corner of a very large blanket box, an ottoman. It might well have been Fletcher's blood, but if so, where was he? I moved closer and lifted the lid of the ottoman; then closed it hurriedly.

'Eve,' I gulped for breath. 'Eve, go back to the main street. There's a phone box near where we parked the car. Ring DS Holmes and tell him Graeme Fletcher won't talk –ever. Not without the aid of a Ouija Board.'

'Fletcher's dead? In there?' Eve pointed to the ottoman.

I nodded, and took another breath. 'The same as the others, I reckon. I couldn't see much. I didn't want to. There was blood all over the place.'

If DS Holmes was upset that we'd jumped the gun and attempted to interview Fletcher before he gave us the go-ahead, it certainly wasn't apparent from his opening remarks. Having viewed the grisly crime scene, he told us,

'It's as well you found him when you did. If his body had remained in that confined space for a few more days, it would have become really unpleasant in here.' He paused and added, 'It's bad enough having to look at what's in there, without the smell we'd have got if he'd not been found until after the weekend.'

Holmes appeared tired and stressed, I thought, and no wonder, given the circumstances. I felt immensely sorry for the young detective. The tally of victims was increasing with little to show by way of a motive, let alone a killer. I thought of my former colleagues in the media, knowing the sensational way they would treat the news of four people being slain by someone wielding a mysterious weapon. If they got wind of what was happening, Holmes' stress levels would go into hyper-drive. If ever a police officer needed help, Holmes certainly did.

As we watched the pathologist and the forensics officers preparing to enter the building, I remembered my thought about the company Fletcher had been partly instrumental in setting up. As much to distract Holmes from his current woes as to provide a way forward, I mentioned my idea to him. 'Have you any news about the victims? Anything back from South Africa, for instance?'

'Not yet, but given the fact that it's the weekend that doesn't surprise me. Added to which, I doubt whether an enquiry about someone who was murdered thousands of miles away will be high on their list of priorities.'

'That's true, but if and when you discover anything about Fletcher, or King, or Wharton, I would be very interested to know if any of them had an interest in, or had expertise in, genealogy.'

Holmes frowned. 'Why do you want to know that? Is it relevant to the case?'

'It might be, if their objective in setting up that company Overtring was to defraud Stephen Pengelly. Let's assume that was their intention, and to do so they compiled a fictitious family tree. From what we know of Pengelly, he was nobody's fool, so the document would have to be really convincing, and have a lot of equally genuine-looking back-up paperwork to prove what they were selling was the genuine article.'

'OK, I'm with you there, but can't see where you're going with it.'

'Whether the Pengelly family tree we found in is real or bogus, it would need someone with a deep knowledge of how genealogy works and the right places to research it, how to prepare it, and what to provide as back-up. And if none of them had the relevant expertise to do that –'

'They'd need someone else to do it for them,' Holmes finished my sentence for me. 'Now why didn't I think of that? If there was someone with that knowledge, they might either be the killer, or be able to lead us to him.'

'Or her,' Eve interjected. We stared at her in surprise. 'I know you've been busy with other aspects of the case,' she told Holmes, 'which is why you missed the connection Adam has just made. However, while you were talking, I started to wonder if we've had tunnel vision about the murderer all along. Thinking about Stephen Pengelly's unsavoury reputation as a womaniser, isn't it just as likely, perhaps more so, that the killer might be a woman? Certainly if revenge over his sex life is the motive.'

Holmes looked stunned by Eve's suggestion. Hardly surprising, because the more I thought about it, the more sense I could see in her argument. 'That's something else I didn't stop to consider,' he admitted. I could see by his crestfallen expression that self-doubt was creeping in.

'Nobody has a monopoly on ideas,' I told him. 'Eve could well be right, but I certainly didn't think about the killer being a woman. That's one of the reasons major investigations involve a team of detectives. You don't have a team; all you have is Johnny Pickersgill and a couple of interfering busybody amateurs.'

'Gifted amateurs, I'd say. And please believe me; I'm glad of your help. I need all the help I can get, and I'm not too proud to accept it from wherever it comes. I'm dreading my next step, which is to report this,' –he indicated the antiques shop –'to my superiors.'

It was almost dusk by the time we returned to the manor. The news that the killer had struck again left everyone horrified, and re-awakened the fear that had lessened with the tightening of security around the old house. I don't think my graphic description of how I'd discovered Fletcher's body did anything to allay those fears, which made broaching the subject of a jaunt to the Crown and Anchor even trickier than previously.

'Eve and I were thinking of going to the pub tonight,' I told them, 'but it seems a bit unfair to leave the manor without adequate protection. This killer seems prepared to strike wherever and whenever he wants, and appears unconcerned about being challenged.' That's right, Adam, I thought as I was speaking, you go ahead and cheer everyone up.

Tony Bishop, who had spent the whole day closeted with Robert and Alison, provided a solution that quelled everyone's concerns –and offered the opportunity for me to have a couple of pints too. Not that the thought of beer was a prime consideration, of course. 'If you want, I could stay at the manor for the time being. Would that help? If there's a spare room, and you'd like me to, I could ask Emma to join us, that way there will be two more people here most of the time. I think that should deter even this murderer.'

Robert glanced at Alison, who nodded. 'Brilliant idea.'

'OK, I'll phone Emma and let her know. She works on the bar at the Crown and Anchor, so if I drop Adam and Eve off, then Emma can phone me when they're ready to return, and I'll collect all three. That means nobody has to go without a drink, and the manor will only be at risk for a few minutes. Overall, the more people there are seen to be here or hereabouts, the less likely anyone is to try and force entry.'

'I think that makes perfect sense,' I agreed.

With our trip to the pub in mind, Alison had asked Mary to serve dinner earlier that night. As we assembled, Victoria emerged from the study, waving a piece of paper triumphantly, rather in the style of Neville Chamberlain's return from Munich. 'I've done it,' she announced. 'I've translated the first of the runes. However, I have absolutely no idea what the message means. Do you want to hear it?'

That had to be one of the most rhetorical questions of the century, I thought.

'OK,' she said. 'Here goes: *My time is almost at an end. I have passed to my sons the secret that has been handed down through the generations. It will be for them to carry it and in the end, they must decide whether it is prudent to reveal it or let it rest. I have counselled them to think long and choose wisely.* That's all it says.' Victoria lowered the paper and looked around.

We had listened to the translation, and at Robert's request, we listened to it a second and third time, and to ensure we had absorbed every nuance, each of us in turn examined the paper containing the translation, but, like Victoria, the meaning of the message was totally lost on us.

Fortunately, Bishop was insured to drive the Mercedes, so we were able to complete the short journey to the village in luxury. 'Emma will be behind the bar,' he told us as he negotiated the last band before reaching the houses at the end of the single street that comprised Barton-le-Dale. 'The landlord and his wife are taking care of a shooting party, so Emma has been deputised to look after the regulars.'

The Crown and Anchor was typical of so many country inns in the county, a long, low, stone building set back from the road. Behind the pub, the ground rose steeply towards the moor that gave the village its name. Inside proved to be as traditional as the exterior; with low, oak-beamed ceilings that had been darkened by centuries of cigarette and pipe smokers. A dark-haired young woman I guessed to be Bishop's girlfriend was pulling a pint for a middle-aged man as we entered the bar. I waited then placed my order, adding, 'You must be Emma? Tony Bishop asked me to make myself known to you. I'm Adam Bailey.'

'I sort of guessed that.' She shook hands and smiled. 'And you must be Eve.' Once the formalities were over we looked around as Emma got our drinks. Apart from two young couples seated at tables in front of the bow windows, the room had only one occupant, the man Emma had just served. 'There don't seem to be many people in for a Saturday night,' I remarked as I pocketed my change.

Emma glanced at the clock. 'It's early yet; wait until ten o'clock, the place will be heaving then. If you're really desperate for someone to talk to; there's always my dad.' She indicated the gentleman she had just served, who was inspecting a notice advertising a darts tournament.

'Why not,' Eve said, 'it'll make a nice change to have someone different to chat to, and we can catch up on all the village scandal.'

'You've certainly picked the right man for that job,' Emma said.

I knew Eve's comment was an excuse to get talking to someone who might be able to tell us more about the mystery girl in the photo. Who better than someone whose daughter categorised them as a gossip. As Emma had been sorting our drinks out, Eve had been staring at a series of framed photos that were hanging on the wall alongside the bar counter. Barton-le-Dale, it seemed, was proud of its cricket team.

Emma introduced her father, whose name was Chris Ellis, and explained that we were guests at Barton Manor. 'I recognised your face from one of the cricket team photos,' Eve told him. 'It was taken twenty years ago, but you hardly look any older.'

I admired Eve's strategy. Not only had she flattered Ellis, but she had immediately established his long-term residence in the village. That, together with his natural tendency to discuss local characters and events, made him the ideal person to extract information from. And so it proved; Ellis was more than happy to discuss the village and its past, but first we had to prime him with information regarding the current spate of murders. He'd heard of two, it seemed, that of Stephen Pengelly and his mistress.

'I'm not surprised that Pengelly came to a bad end. No more than he deserved, I reckon. He was just like his father; a nasty piece of work who thought he was God's gift and above everyone else.' He paused and looked at us. 'What's the brother like? Not another from the same mould, I hope? That would be a shame, because as I remember him, he was a nice, polite little lad; but scared of his own shadow. Can't say that surprised me, knowing what he had to put up with up there at the manor.'

He saw my look of surprise and smiled. 'It was no secret the way he was treated. The gardener and the cook used to come in here regular away and tell such horror stories. Folk felt really sorry for him, losing his mother the way he did. But when they heard how Stephen and his father treated him, I tell you there were some who wanted to get a lynch party together and string Stephen and his father from one of those oak trees in Home Wood.'

Eve told Ellis that we liked Robert. 'Whatever they did to him hasn't embittered him. He's a really nice bloke, engaged to a lovely girl.'

'That's good to hear. They say that breeding will

always tell in the end, and I reckon it must have done in this case. By that I mean Robert must take after his mother. She was a lovely woman, beautiful in looks and with a caring nature. A real lady.'

Having told him all we dared about current events, I let Eve broach the subject of the letter, which she did by mentioning the rumours surrounding Stephen Pengelly. 'We heard he was a real ladies' man,' Eve suggested, 'especially in his younger days.'

'I don't think his age altered his behaviour one bit,' Ellis told her. 'Stephen was exactly the same as his father. He'd chase women until his dying day.' He suddenly realised how inappropriate that remark sounded and added hastily, 'I mean, if he'd lived to be eighty he'd still have tried it on if the chance arose.'

'Were there any girls in particular that he was involved with when he was younger?' Eve asked. 'Someone from the village, perhaps?'

'Knowing Stephen, picking one girl from his conquests might be harder than looking for a needle in a haystack.' But Chris Ellis was astute enough to spot Eve's fishing expedition. 'You have someone particular in mind, don't you?'

'The trouble is, we don't know anything about her. All we have is a letter that was at the manor. We were hoping we might find someone who had lived here long enough to know of her, a girl called Annie.'

'Well, well, well,' he said. 'It just shows you never know with people. I'd have thought he would have burned that letter at the first opportunity. I know his father would have done if he'd caught Stephen with it.'

'Why? Who is it, and what's so special about that girl?'

'Her name is Annie Flood. Her father used to be gamekeeper on the Barton estate. He and his wife were from the Midlands somewhere. Nottingham, as I remember. They moved up here when Joe Flood got the keeper's job. The girl would have been about three or four then.'

'Was Annie their only child?'

'Yes and the locals reckoned she was spoilt rotten because of it. She thought herself a cut above the rest of the village kids. She was a pretty girl and knew it. Used to flaunt herself and everyone said she'd get into trouble, if she didn't mend her ways. Not that she'd let any of the village lads near her. They weren't good enough for her.'

'I take it she and Stephen were in a relationship?' I asked.

My question seemed to tickle him. 'I reckon that's the understatement of the year. At it like rabbits they were, by what I was told. Of course, they couldn't do it in his house or hers, so they had to find other places to get together. Unfortunately, a couple of the places they chose weren't quite as private as they thought, and word got round like wildfire.'

'We did hear that old man Pengelly had to fork out a lot of money because of a young girl Stephen was involved with,' Eve told him. 'Do you think that might have been Annie Flood?'

'That sounds right to me. People reckoned she had an eye to the main chance, which was why she was only too happy to let Stephen have his way with her. The gossip is she thought he'd be bound to do the right thing by her; maybe even engineered things in the hope that if she fell pregnant he'd be compelled to marry her.'

'Is that what happened? Did she become pregnant? Is that why Stephen's father had to pay her off?'

His answer surprised me. 'Not that I'm aware. I mean, it's possible, I suppose, but I've never heard anyone suggest she was in the family way. What caused the bother was that someone let on to Annie's father what she and Stephen were up to and he hit the roof. What father wouldn't in the circumstances?'

194

'I can understand anyone getting upset if he heard that someone had seen his daughter misbehaving like that, I suppose.'

Ellis shook his head. 'That wasn't the only thing that got Joe riled. It was the fact that Annie was only fourteen at the time. To hear that she had lost her virginity while underage was bad enough, but when he knew that the man who had deflowered her was someone with a reputation as bad as Stephen's, he was livid. Rumour has it that it was only his wife who stopped him going looking for Stephen with his shotgun.'

Ellis saw the look of distaste on Eve's face and nodded, as if in agreement with something she'd said. 'Aye, when his wife got him calmed down a bit, Joe was all for involving the police, but she told him that would mean a lot of scandal, and their name being dragged through the mud, so in the end they packed Annie off out of harm's way while Joe dealt with old man Pengelly. I can't swear to what happened between them, but local rumour at the time was that Pengelly paid Joe a lot of money on condition that they move out of the area and stop Annie having any further contact with Stephen. The story was that they moved back to Nottinghamshire. Much good it did them, from what I was told.'

'Why do you say that?'

'Again it's only gossip, but round here gossip usually turns out to be true. Someone said that Joe and his wife were killed in a road accident soon afterwards.'

'So Annie would have been on her own?' Ellis seemed to be knocking all the potential suspects for a revenge attack out of the running with every sentence.

'Not exactly. I think her grandparents were still alive. I seem to remember them visiting here now and again. And then there was her uncle, of course. He doted on Annie. I used to see him regular away cycling down from the moors to Joe's house. The keeper's place was too small for him to stay, so he went to the trouble of buying a cottage in Langstrop village. It's let out as a holiday place nowadays. Anyway, I heard it said that the reason he was so fond of Annie was because he couldn't have kids of his own, but that's speculation, I reckon.'

Did you know anything more about the uncle? Was his name Flood too?'

'No; I can't remember his name, but it wasn't Flood. He was Annie's uncle on her mother's side.'

'It would be useful to trace the family if we could,' Eve told him, without revealing the reason for our interest. 'Can you think of anyone in the village who might know whereabouts Annie Flood and her family moved to? Nottinghamshire is a big county and the surname Flood isn't that rare. It's quite important that we trace them.'

Ellis thought for a moment. 'I suppose I could ask Carrie. She and her husband used to keep the village shop and post office. Carrie kept the business on after her husband died. She might have been given a forwarding address at the time. If so, with a bit of luck she might remember it.'

'Do you think she'd be prepared to release that sort of information?'

Ellis cast a wary glance towards the bar, where his daughter was busy serving a group of customers who had just entered. Reassured, he gave us a sly grin. 'Carrie would tell me. Don't let on to Emma, but Carrie and I have been seeing one another since my divorce. I'll talk to her tomorrow. If I find out anything, shall I ring you at the manor?'

Chapter Fifteen

Conversation on the return journey was restricted with Tony and Emma being in the car, and only when we reached the privacy of the Rose Room were Eve and I able to discuss what Emma's father had revealed.

'The more I hear about Stephen Pengelly's character; the more I believe his murderer had ample justification.' The anger in her eyes and in her voice was unmistakeable.

'I agree that he comes across as unspeakably vile, but I don't think that's enough of an excuse for killing him.'

'You're not defending Pengelly, surely? There can be absolutely no excuse for taking advantage of a child that way.'

'I'm neither defending him nor making excuses for what he did. It was just that something Chris Ellis told us that made me wonder if the blame was all one-sided.'

Eve, to give her due, paused and considered what I'd said. 'What was it: what did I miss?'

'Ellis said people thought Annie threw herself at Stephen in the hope that he would marry her. Maybe in her naivety she saw it as a great romantic love affair with her ending up as mistress of Barton Manor. That certainly doesn't excuse Stephen Pengelly's behaviour, but we already know from what we've been told about him that where women were concerned he was unable to resist temptation.'

'Six of one and half a dozen of the other, you think?'

'Maybe nine of him and three of her would be more accurate. I'm also willing to bet Annie Flood *was* pregnant when her family shipped her off to Nottinghamshire, despite Ellis saying there was no evidence to that effect. Certainly if his statement about their behaviour is anywhere near accurate.'

'Why are you so convinced that she was pregnant, though?'

'Because I don't think anyone as hard and unfeeling as Pengelly senior would have paid out unless he absolutely had to. Joe Flood might well have threatened him with police action, but that would have involved a lot of unsavoury publicity, and even if the girl wasn't mentioned by name in court, word would have spread like wildfire, especially if Pengelly senior had disputed the case and insisted on paternity tests, or proof that his son had been screwing her. Stephen wouldn't have cared if she got pregnant, and if she did have eyes on the manor, Annie might have thought that represented her best chance.'

'I see your point, Adam, but where does it leave us regarding Stephen's murder?'

'With two, maybe three potential suspects, I reckon.'

Eve looked startled. 'How do you work that out?'

'There's Annie Flood herself, plus the doting uncle. Additionally, if she was pregnant, there could be a third, in the shape of Stephen's illegitimate son or daughter.'

'That's a whole lot of assumptions with very little to back them up,' Eve remarked, 'but some of our wildest theories have been proved right too often for them to be dismissed.' She smiled. 'Just one of the many things we have in common. Sometimes, when we're talking like this, it's a bit like hearing an echo of my own thoughts. Do you feel that way?'

'Of course I do, and perhaps it has to be mutual for it to work.'

The terrible discovery at the antiques shop weighed heavily on my mind, added to which I felt curiously disturbed by our conversation. I was left with the feeling that we were nearing the crux of the whole problem, and that it represented something truly evil; truly frightening. The consequence of my disquiet was that I was unable to sleep. Alongside me, Eve's rest was again troubled by dreams.

Eventually, rather than lie awake listening to the rain, which had returned in full-force and was lashing against the manor windows, I slipped out of bed, and reached the fireplace, where I switched on the table lamp alongside the armchair. I donned dressing gown and slippers and looked around for something to read. I didn't feel in the mood for *Le Morte d'Arthur*. There had been little honour or chivalry in anything we had seen or heard that day. On the contrary, it seemed that evil had triumphed over good rather than the other way round.

Instead, I picked up the ledger we had retrieved from the safe and began, rather laboriously, to attempt a translation. The journal would either grab my attention or send me off to sleep, I thought. In the end, it achieved both. It aroused my curiosity within the first few sentences, but the long periods of intense concentration eventually wearied me, causing my eyelids to droop as I fell asleep in the chair.

I was awakened by a sound. It was a dull thud, as if someone or something had either fallen or been knocked over. For a few seconds, as I struggled to recover my wits, I was convinced something untoward had occurred. Then I realised that the tome had slipped from my grasp as I slept and had landed on the parquet floor alongside the fireplace. The noise had also woken Eve.

She sat up, blinking in the light. 'What happened? What was that noise?' her voice was heavy with sleep.

'Sorry, that was my fault. I dropped a book.'

'Come back to bed, Adam. It's still pitch black outside.'

I obeyed, and my presence provoked an immediate

protest. 'How long have you been sitting there? You're absolutely frozen.'

'I've no idea. I couldn't sleep, so I started translating that journal. I must have nodded off.'

'Come here and let me warm you up.'

Now that is true love.

Next morning, Eve sat on the edge of the bed as I read the translation I'd made of the first journal entry. I took it slowly, because my Latin was rusty, and without a dictionary I could only guess at the meaning of some of the words by their context.

'I can scarce believe; as I recall the events that have befallen me over the past four years, and the adventures I and my companions have endured; that our adventure began in such mystery; and with our hopes and expectations set so high.

'As is only to be expected during the travel through life, one encounters death in her many forms. The silence of the tomb has overcome every member of our small band in diverse ways, coming from the sword to the plague.

'It is sometimes difficult to comprehend that of the eight of us who set out on this quest; I am the only one remaining to recount our adventures and misadventures; the only survivor with hope, if not a burning flame, at least a flickering ember, hope that I can still claim the prize we were charged to discover and to bring it to its rightful home.

'I will not bore any reader who might chance upon this volume in later times with a wearisome account of the journey that brought us here; for the moment I will only recount the most germane facts. The chief of these being that of the eight of us, who set out with the greatest blessing available to man speeding us, only five of our company reached our destination and the sanctuary offered by our Holy Brothers in Christ with safety.'

'What does all that mean? What was this prize they

were seeking? Do you think it was something valuable?' Eve asked.

'I've no idea, beyond guessing that it might have had some religious connotation, because I feel sure they were either monks or priests.'

On Monday morning we got a phone call from Johnny Pickersgill. DS Holmes, it transpired, had been summoned to a meeting with the chief constable, and would be absent until lunchtime.

'Did you advise him to wear two pairs of underpants?' I asked.

'Oh, very droll, Adam. Anyway, he asked if you would come into the station this afternoon. Both you and Eve, I mean.'

'Any particular reason?'

'A small matter of some written statements. As amateur detectives such trivial items won't concern you, I know, but they are an essential part of police procedures. We need statements from you both regarding your discovery of Fletcher's body, and also that of Kathy King.'

'I shall have to consult my diary first. I have a really hectic schedule, so fitting something like this into it could be quite tricky.'

'See you this afternoon then.'

I replaced the receiver and went to relay the news to Eve. She looked concerned for a moment. 'On the last two occasions we travelled to Barton-le-Dale we ended up staring at corpses, but I don't suppose that will happen this time.'

On hearing of our intended visit to town, Mary asked if we would mind visiting various shops to collect food she would order. 'I need supplies from the butcher, the baker, and the greengrocer. I need to restock far more frequently with their being so many more people to cater for.'

Robert, who was listening to our conversation, said,

'This must be causing you a lot of extra work. I hope it isn't proving too much for you.'

'Not a bit of it, Mr Robert. It's great fun, and I love seeing the old house full of life. Apart from that, I get a kick from seeing how much everyone enjoys what I've made for them. Added to which I do get a lot of assistance in the kitchen, even if one of my helpers only has one usable arm.'

Robert eyed Mary's husband. 'I understand now why Frank has to work so hard on the grounds. He needs to burn off all the calories you feed him. Have you ever considered catering as a career? Not that I want to lose you,' he added hastily.

'We did talk about it once over,' Mary admitted, 'but we don't have the money for one thing, even with the bequest in Mr Stephen's will. And, to be honest, we're really content here.'

'I'm relieved to hear it.'

Tammy volunteered to go along with us. 'I could collect the food that Mary orders while you're giving your statements, then meet you at the police station. That would save you time, and you wouldn't have the bother of finding parking places.'

'Are you sure?' I asked. 'I wouldn't want you to go to all that trouble just for our convenience. Especially if there are things to do here.'

'No, no, it would be no trouble, and I've nothing here that won't keep.'

Afterwards, when we were alone, Eve accused me of sadism. 'You knew very well that Tammy was only using it as an excuse to see DS Holmes again. Teasing the poor girl like that was cruel.'

We reached the police station and had finished giving our statements when Holmes walked in.

'How did your meeting go?' I asked. Tact has always been my strong point.

'It was nowhere near as bad as I feared. I expected to be hauled over the coals for failing to find the killer, especially in view of the latest murder, but the chief constable was extremely understanding.'

I glanced at Johnny Pickersgill, who was the chief constable's cousin. He was staring out of the window, a look of innocence on his face. My bet was that Johnny had interceded on Holmes' behalf. However, I certainly wasn't going to humiliate Holmes by mentioning it.

'We're almost done here,' Johnny told him. 'We're only waiting for the statements to be typed and then they can be signed. I doubt whether they will reveal anything we didn't already know.'

'I didn't think for a minute that they would. It's purely for the record. But, as you're here, I have some news that will interest you.' Holmes paused and smiled. 'And that's putting it extremely mildly. I'd like your opinion, because quite frankly, I don't know what to make of it.'

He glanced down at the papers he was holding, which I could see had been torn from the telex. 'I heard back from South Africa a short time ago. You were quite correct with your theory. The police there did recognise the names of all three. Apparently they have quite bulky dossiers on Graeme Fletcher and Kathy King, and a similar one on Arnold Wharton.'

'I take it they weren't exactly pillars of society?' Eve asked.

'Far from it; Kathy King and Graeme Fletcher disappeared just as warrants for their arrest were being issued. Police reckon they were tipped off. Having read the file extract, that doesn't surprise me. The charges being brought against them were blackmail and, in Kathy's case, prostitution. There is one fact that knocks the sexual jealousy motive on the head. Unless Fletcher added incest to his other crimes, that is. Kathy was his half-sister.'

Holmes paused to allow us to think about that. 'There

was nothing original in their scheme. Kathy was a high-class call girl, with a clientele of rich and powerful men; most of them in positions of authority. According to the report, there were businessmen, politicians, high-ranking police officers, lawyers, doctors, and even judges in her little black book. Many of them were married. Almost all of them would be highly embarrassed should their liaisons with Kathy be made public. Graeme's part in the conspiracy was to shoot compromising videos of their activities in Kathy's bed and threaten the victims with the resulting porn movies.'

'As you say, hardly original, but by the sound of it very effective. What went wrong?' I asked.

'They worked the racket for quite a while without problem. Their success was down to them not asking more than the victim could pay without having to give awkward explanations. They never attempted to bleed them dry. They tried it once too often, though, because one of their clients called their bluff and got the police involved. When they went to interview the couple, they'd vanished, leaving all the evidence behind. It was only by examining this that police were able to assess the extent of their crimes.'

'Was Arnold Wharton part of their scheme?' Eve asked.

'Not directly. He was a client of Kathy's, but not one that got blackmailed. He was also their lawyer.'

'Why do the police have a dossier on him?'

'Wharton had taken a law degree in South Africa to allow him to practice there. He built up a good clientele, but couldn't keep his hand out of the till. By that I mean he embezzled a large amount from the client accounts. In doing so, he upset some very unpleasant people, and as a result he'd received a number of death threats.'

Holmes paused, he seemed to be enjoying his role as narrator and was making the most of the drama in it. 'Five years ago, it seemed that someone had carried out one of those threats. Arnold Wharton was crossing a street in Johannesburg when he was knocked down in what at first appeared to be a hit-and-run accident. That was until police heard from an eyewitness. They reported that having hit him, the vehicle stopped, reversed over his body, drove over it again and then zoomed off into the distance. Wharton was so badly disfigured that it was only possible to identify him by the driving licence and other personal items in his pockets.'

'What about dental records?' I asked.

'The police checked, but either Wharton had perfect teeth or he hadn't visited a dentist in the time he lived in South Africa.'

'Hang on, though,' Eve interjected, 'if Wharton was killed five years ago, who was the man using his name here?'

'That is a very good question,' Holmes acknowledged, 'and one I don't have an answer to, unfortunately.'

'Did those eyewitnesses mention noticing anything unusual in Wharton's behaviour prior to him being struck by the vehicle?' I asked.

Holmes stared at me, his surprise obvious. 'How on earth did you work that out?'

Eve and Johnny looked equally perplexed, although to me, the answer was clear. 'I take it from that the answer is yes?'

'It is indeed. Had the car not gone back and forward over the body, police would have marked it down as an accident. Eyewitnesses reported that Wharton appeared to be drunk. He was reeling around, totally unsteady on his feet, and actually fell over a couple of times. However,' Holmes turned the page, 'when the pathologist sent a blood sample for testing, it came back negative for alcohol.'

'Did they conduct any other toxicology tests?'

'No, it wasn't deemed necessary, given that the cause

of death was so obvious. Where that leaves us, I have absolutely no idea.'

'I don't suppose it's relevant after all this time,' I remarked, 'but it would have been interesting to know who the dead man was.'

Eve was first to catch my drift. 'You don't think it was Wharton, do you?'

'I'm damned certain it wasn't. It's all far too convenient. Wharton was being hounded on all sides. It was only a question of who got to him first, the police with an arrest warrant, or an aggrieved client with an elephant gun. Either way he was a marked man. Time for him to disappear, and the best way to ensure nobody came looking for him would be to play dead. You can be fairly sure that you're safe if everyone believes you're occupying one of the drawers in the mortuary cabinet. It's a shame those other tests weren't carried out, though. I'll bet the victim's blood would have tested positive for hallucinogenic drugs.'

'Let me get this straight.' Holmes held up the telex as he spoke. 'You believe that Wharton set out to fake his own death, making it appear like murder. He did that so suspicion would fall on one of the clients he'd swindled.'

'That's broadly it, yes.'

'Who would he get to use as his substitute?'

'He'd need someone with no close friends or family. Moreover it would have to be someone who was either out of work or in a lowly paid, menial job. In other words, someone who wouldn't be missed.'

'It's all hypothetical, though. There's no way we could prove that was what happened.'

'There is a way,' I told him. 'It wouldn't prove beyond doubt that Wharton faked his death, but it would make it a near certainly.'

'How can we do that?'

'If it isn't mentioned in the telex, you might be able to

find out via the South African police. Either way, you need to establish whether Wharton emptied his bank account in the days or weeks before his so-called death.'

Holmes scanned the three-page telex for several moments. 'Yes, here it is. Wharton withdrew large sums of money, almost the full balance in each case, from four different accounts he had throughout the country. The money was never traced.'

'How much was it?' Eve asked.

'I've no idea. The amount they quote is in rand, but I assume it must be a lot because of the number of noughts after it.'

'He would need a lot of money. First he'd have to buy a car to use for the hit-and-run, and then to obtain paperwork for his new identity with which to make his escape. He couldn't simply book a plane ticket in the name of Arnold Wharton, deceased.'

'Wouldn't it be risky for him to set up as a solicitor here?' Johnny asked.

'Why would it be? He couldn't have foreseen what was going to happen to him, and if he hadn't been murdered, none of these questions would have been asked. And if we hadn't been lucky enough to make the African connection to Kathy King, nobody would have linked a North Yorkshire solicitor to a man who was killed in Johannesburg five years ago.'

'Unless someone did find out and delivered their own form of belated justice,' Eve suggested.

'Phew! You two are good,' Holmes said. 'I'm glad you're on our side.'

At that point the station's clerical officer returned with the statements for signature. 'There's a young woman in reception asking for you,' he told Holmes.

The young woman in question was Tammy, and once we had signed the witness forms we went to collect her. She was standing talking to Holmes, amid a large collection of carrier bags. Although I couldn't be sure, it sounded as if Holmes had asked her for a date. I began picking up carriers.

'I'd no idea Mary had ordered as much as this, otherwise I'd have thought twice about volunteering,' Tammy told us.

'Never mind, I feel sure your efforts will have their reward in due time,' Eve told her, glancing towards Holmes.

I made a mental note to take Eve to task about her display of double standards. Calling me a sadist and then making a cruel remark like that was definitely hypocritical. Before we left the station, we received a panicky phone call from Barton Manor. I had just loaded the last of the carriers into the boot when Holmes came out with a message. Mary, it seemed, had seriously underestimated our appetites. We were to return to the butcher where another order was awaiting collection.

When we got back to the manor, unloading and stowing the voluminous amount of shopping took a fair while. Mary acted as commander-in-chief, directing her troops' activities between freezers, fridges, larder, and store cupboards. Once the hectic spell of activity was over, we gathered in the kitchen for a well-earned cup of tea.

Victoria shattered this oasis of calm by flinging the door back and announcing with glee, 'I've done it. I have deciphered the second of the inscriptions.' Her enthusiasm ebbed faster than any tide as she added, 'Unfortunately, the message makes as little sense as the previous one, and I still have absolutely no idea about number three.'

'Let's hear the second message anyway,' Robert told her.

Victoria began to read, and as I heard the second sentence, I felt a chill such as I had never experienced before. I'd always considered that the expression, 'my blood ran cold' was an exaggeration, until that moment. I looked across the table at Eve, and saw that she was similarly affected. Our eyes met, and I saw the fear in hers. I wondered if it was matched by my own. 'Would you read that again please, Victoria?' she asked. Her voice sounded hoarse, which I guessed was due to the emotional impact of one word in that message.

Victoria read the message a second time. *'My choice is made, for good or ill. I will follow the way of The Bear. This thing is all too powerful a matter to leave to chance. Let fate rather than the hand of man decide.'*

'Are you sure you got that wording correct? Are you absolutely certain it mentions a bear?'

Victoria was too engrossed in the message to take offence at my question. 'I am sure. It definitely refers to the bear. Not a bear, but The Bear, which I would guess means that it refers to someone or something in particular. Why do you ask? Is there some significance?'

Even as she was speaking it seemed as if Victoria had realised what that significance might be. I noticed her expression change, and the look on her face mirrored Eve's of a few seconds previously. I had been wrong, though. It wasn't fear that either of them were experiencing. It was awe.

Taking it in turns, Eve and I explained, beginning with what DI Hardy had thought he'd seen shortly before crashing his car. Then I told them what Frank and I had seen in the woods around the time of his accident. Finally, Eve related her recurring dreams. 'It would be wrong to call them nightmares,' she ended. 'I thought so at first, but then I realised that the bear wasn't malevolent. Quite the opposite, as with what Frank or Hardy experienced. Had they not seen the bear, neither of them would be alive now.'

Eve's remark caused my memory to return to a time years before, when I'd been working as a foreign correspondent. 'When I was in America,' I told them, 'I visited some of the Native American tribes. Their belief is that when you see a standing bear, the animal isn't preparing to attack or to run away from you, but simply protecting those he cares for. Perhaps the bear is protecting us.'

There was a long silence after I finished speaking. Finally, Tammy broke this. 'What can it all mean? Why should a bear suddenly appear to people like that? What is special about the bear and how is it connected to Barton Manor?'

I was already aware that Victoria was holding something back. Now was the time to encourage her to open up. 'Out with it, Victoria. You haven't told us everything, have you?'

She cleared her throat, and began to speak, her voice low and hesitant. 'If you hadn't told me those stories I'd have probably have dismissed it as coincidence; or me being fanciful. However, having seen the supposed Pengelly family tree, I can no longer ignore the possible connection.' She paused, running her tongue around her lips nervously, before adding, 'The word I translated from Celtic; the word that means bear in the Celtic tongue – is Arthur!'

Chapter Sixteen

Conversation over dinner that evening was sparse. Everyone seemed immersed in their own thoughts, which I guessed, not unnaturally, would be centred on Victoria's dramatic revelations. How strange it was that one simple four-letter word should have such a powerful effect. It being Monday night, there was a darts match at the Crown and Anchor, which Tony Bishop, as team captain, was obliged to attend. With Emma also absent, there would have been ample opportunity to discuss what we'd learned, but it seemed that no one was in the mood.

'One thing is plain,' I said to Eve when we were alone, 'we're going to have to revise our thinking about the Pengelly family tree.'

Eve frowned. 'The one we thought had to be a fake, you mean?'

'I do, and incredible though it must seem, what little evidence we have, if you can call it evidence, tends to suggest that the family tree might not be fake.'

Eve followed my line of reasoning. 'Unless the runes are also fakes, and the plot is far more elaborate than we suspected. Planting the word bear in them, with its translation to Arthur, would lend it the right air of authenticity. Let's be fair, whatever else people say about Stephen Pengelly, nobody has suggested he was a mug, or the slightest bit gullible, so it would take something really convincing to persuade him to part with enormous sums of money.'

'That might be true, but it wouldn't account for those random sightings. Nor would it explain your dreams,' I pointed out.

'I know, and that's what bothers me. There is absolutely no rational explanation for them. It just seems so far-fetched.'

'What was it Conan Doyle wrote? One of Sherlock Holmes' pearls of wisdom was something on the lines of, *"when you have eliminated the impossible, whatever remains, however improbable, must be the truth"*. Admittedly this is at the furthest reach of unlikely happenings, but there is just the slim possibility that it might be the truth.'

Neither of us was at all sleepy, our brains still buzzing with all we'd learned that day. Instead of going straight to bed, we curled up together in the large armchair alongside the fire. Eve held the ledger as I translated more of the journal.

'It seems that our friend Domenico was an Italian priest. No surprise there, the name sort of gives his origin away, plus the fact that few people apart from the clergy were able to read or write in those days.' I was paraphrasing what the journal contained, both because of my rustiness with Latin, and as I explained to Eve, because of the archaic phraseology. 'Some of the things Domenico has taken from the English and translated into Latin are as foreign as if they were in another language, such is the difference between what we speak nowadays, and what they spoke then.'

'That sounds very much like an excuse to me,' Eve said provocatively.

'Don't push your luck. Remember, you're in a very vulnerable position.' As she was seated on my lap at the time, that threat cut both ways, as I soon found out. After a short but enjoyable scuffle, a truce was called, and I returned to the journal. 'Domenico was assistant to a bishop. I know little or nothing about the offices in the Catholic Church back then, but the word he uses is "cappellanus" which I'm not familiar with, but I guess it sounds very much like chaplain in today's clergy. Domenico and a small group of other priests were chosen to conduct a special mission. He doesn't specify what the objective was, not in this part of the journal at least, but it must have been something way out of the ordinary, because those who were picked for the task had to be vetted by a panel consisting of five cardinals and the Pope's chancellor.'

'Wow!' Eve exclaimed. 'That's some selection committee.'

Reading on, I told her, 'It sounds as if the whole mission was fraught with danger. Some of the group never even reached England, let alone their destination here. Domenico was told that he would be the only one who knew the purpose of their journey; the others would only be given directions to the place they had to head for. Each of them had copies of the instructions given to Domenico secreted somewhere in the clothing that had been specially made for them. That way, if anything untoward were to happen to Domenico, the mission could still succeed because the head of the order of monks they were to meet in England had been told of this and would be able to retrieve the information. However, from what I can gather, even he was unaware of what the mission was meant to achieve.'

'It's beginning to sound a bit like a spy film script,' Eve said.

'It does a bit,' I agreed, 'but there's nothing new in that. Even in those days there were conspiracies and plots.'

Eve's presence so close to me was beginning to affect my concentration. Very un-priestly thoughts were crossing my mind, a fact that Eve was aware of. She put her hand on the back of my neck and began to caress me. 'Why not leave the journal for tonight and let's go to bed?'

That was probably the easiest decision I've ever had to

make.

Next morning, Emma had news for us. 'Last night I was talking to my father and he asked me to tell you something, but I forgot when we got back here. It was to do with a family you were talking to him about. He said that when they left Barton-le-Moors they gave a forwarding address in Newark-on-Trent.' She smiled. 'He'll have found that out from Carrie at the post office. He's under the impression that I don't know what's going on, and the silly man dare not tell me in case I disapprove. Why he thinks that, I've no idea. If it makes them content, then good luck to them, I say. It's far better for them to be happy together than miserable and lonely apart. Anyway, he says he can't be more specific because it all happened so long ago, but he hopes that it helps.'

'Thanks, Emma, I'm sure it will be useful.' As I spoke, I glanced at Eve and saw a frown of concentration on her face. I knew that expression. Something Emma had told us had provoked an idea, or a memory. At that moment, however, Robert and Alison entered the room, and my mind switched to more immediate matters. 'If I could borrow the safe key, Robert, I'd like to take a look at the other parts of that journal and attempt a translation.'

'Of course. Here it is.'

Eve came along with me as I went to the cellar. As we were descending the steps, I said, 'Something in what Emma told us caught your interest, didn't it?'

'It certainly did that. Don't you remember what Holmes told us about Arnold Wharton?'

'The South Africa bit, you mean?'

'No, it was earlier than that. He said that before Wharton went to Bristol University he lived in Newark-on-Trent. The fact that Annie Flood and her family also moved there is a bit too much of a coincidence, don't you think?'

I agreed. 'Do you think Arnold Wharton might be Annie Flood's mysterious uncle?'

'I don't know, but I suppose he could have been. The age would be about right, if he was her mother's younger brother.'

'Also, if there was a family tragedy, such as his sister and brother-in-law being killed in a road accident, that might have decided him to leave Britain and start a new life in South Africa.'

'Possibly so, but it all depends on what happened to Annie following her parents' death. If he doted on her as Mr Ellis said, he'd be unlikely to simply leave her to fend for herself, would he? He'd want to know she was being taken care of. That would tend to imply that another relative, perhaps a set of grandparents, might have taken charge of the girl; in which case he might have felt redundant.'

'Of course, we're assuming an awful lot on very little evidence. Wharton might not have been any relation of Annie's.' I paused, before adding, 'Having said that, I think it's highly probable that he was her uncle. It's simply too coincidental otherwise.'

When we returned from the cellar, we tried to contact DS Holmes, but neither he nor Johnny Pickersgill were available. I learned later that they were attending the latest post-mortem, following which they were going to conduct a detailed search of the antiques shop.

Having left a message for one or other of the officers to call us, Eve and I set to work attempting to translate more of the journal. 'I feel sure somewhere in this manuscript, Domenico will provide us with some clue as to why Stephen had the journal, and why he considered it important enough to lock away,' I told Eve.

She was of the same mind. 'It can't be from historical value, because it isn't the original document. Nor, from what we know of Stephen Pengelly, was it likely to be from sentimental reasons.'

To be fair, opting to spend the day on the journal wasn't exactly a difficult decision to make. The weather had worsened again overnight, with strong south-westerly winds driving heavy bursts of rain before them. In short, it was what the locals would refer to as a 'right fireside day'.

Even by the use of skim-reading, which is a technique most journalists learn early in their career, translation was difficult, and it was mid-afternoon before I closed the first of the ledgers and gave Eve a précis of what it contained.

'A lot of it seems to contain Domenico's self-recrimination for the failure of their mission, and repining the fact that their task hasn't borne fruit. What it doesn't give, unless I've lost it in the translation, is any indication of what their objective was. It must have been something extremely important for a party of that size to travel all the way from Rome. They couldn't exactly hop on an airliner to Heathrow.'

Eve smiled at my flippancy, but asked, 'Is there anything else, anything more pertinent?'

'There's quite a lot about Domenico's conversations with the head of the monastery where they were staying, a man he refers to as Abbot Henry. That name's ringing vague bells, sort of, and making me wish I'd paid more attention during my history lessons. Domenico discusses local politics with Henry; all to do with the struggle for the English throne and the disputing factions.'

'Why did the mission fail? Does Domenico give any hint as to the reason?'

'Not really, at least not in the first part of the book, although by the sound of it, disease or plague of some description took its toll on a number of them before they could complete their assignment.'

We started on the second volume once we had been fortified with mugs of tea brought by Frank, who was now able to use his injured arm without the need for a sling. We had chosen the manor's small library for the task. It was a comfortable room, protected from the elements by virtue of its position to the rear of the drawing room. Knowing we were to occupy it, Robert and Frank had been thoughtful enough to light the fire, so that by pulling two armchairs close to the blaze we were warm and cosy.

Once we had finished our drinks and the homemade scones Mary had provided, Eve switched the lights on. The winter afternoon was already drawing to a close as I commenced reading the second volume. After much of the same stuff, I decided to try a different approach. I jumped to the tenth journal entry, and then moved swiftly to the eleventh section. 'Domenico and one of his colleagues from the Rome delegation have been consulting a monk named Brother Boniface,' I told Eve. 'Now, Domenico has gone to Abbot Henry to discuss what Brother Boniface told them.'

Eve must have seen the change in my expression as I was in the throes of translating, 'What is it? What have you found?'

I continued, my finger moving from word to word as I struggled with the difficult handwriting. My finger stopped as I noticed two words that were in English, not Latin. I read them once; then again, and as I grasped their significance, I gasped aloud. 'Evie, this is incredible. It's as if myths and legends are coming to life before our eyes. I know where Domenico and his colleagues came to in England. Not only that, but I have just read something that was apparently as much of a rumour in the twelfth century as it is today. Listen to this.

'I had cause to visit Abbot Henry, whose advice I needed to solicit. I told him one of my companions had been talking to Brother Boniface and I believed the story he told merited consideration. Some centuries past, I am not certain quite when, for I am lamentably ignorant of English history, there was a great chieftain here whose

deeds are still recounted by local people. It is said he was Celtic by birth and commanded a great host of valiant soldiers whose achievements in battle repelled the Saxon invaders for the best part of one hundred years. Much of what Brother Boniface had to tell me was based on little more than gossip and rumour but it appears that many myths and legends have grown up about this man. Accounts seem to vary wildly, but on one thing most are agreed; that the chieftain was named Arthur and that he was married to a queen called Guinevere.

'Many of the legends are contradictory and none more so than regarding his fate. Some say that Arthur did not die, but that he rests asleep until such time as England's need of him is great again; then he will rise and lead another rebellion against the invaders and thrust them back into the sea. Another legend relates that Arthur was mortally wounded in his last great battle and that he and Queen Guinevere lie buried together close by or inside the grounds of the Abbey, for this is said to be both his spiritual and ancestral home.

'The worthy Abbot told me he knew of the stories surrounding King Arthur, and also knew the legend of his ancestry. He saw me looking blank and continued, 'It directly concerns the reason for your mission here, and lends great credence to the possibility of discovering that which you seek.'

'He looked at me, his gaze keen, piercing almost. 'Do you recall, before the snow came, at the turn of the year, I took you to that place, the one they call Wearyall Hill and showed you a thorn that was in blossom? We were fortunate, for although all else was heavily rimed with frost nothing could disguise the purity of the flowers on that thorn. That is no native tree, for there is none other that flowers at this time of year; all others blossom in the month of May. There is a legend surrounding that thorn, for the locals insist it grew from the staff of St Joseph

218

which he planted in the ground when he and his small band of companions arrived here. It is from his line that King Arthur is reputed to have been descended.'

Eve started at me in disbelief. 'I don't know what to make of that, do you? And what's all that about hawthorn and blackthorn, they don't flower until around May, do they?'

'There is one that does. Only one tree, and only in one place. It is called the Glastonbury Thorn, and it is on Wearyall Hill, close to Glastonbury Abbey. Legend has it that when Joseph of Arimathea came to Glastonbury, he planted his staff there and the thorn grew from it. That is the legend that Abbot Henry has been recounting to Domenico. And what I find extremely interesting, according to Abbot Henry, is the popular superstition that King Arthur was descended from Joseph or one of his followers.'

'This is fascinating, but what does it mean, even if it is true?'

'I'm not really sure, but it has given me an idea. This journal entry could mean that Victoria is having no success with that third inscription from the stone tablets because she's using the wrong language to decipher it.'

Robert was delivering fresh coffee to the study and we followed him in. The only language we heard on entering was Anglo-Saxon. Victoria looked up from the paper she had been scribbling on and apologised. 'Sorry for the unladylike phraseology but this final message has got me so flummoxed, and is having an extremely bad effect on my temper. I hate to admit defeat, but if I don't get a breakthrough soon, I'm going to have to give in.'

'Before you do that, may I make a suggestion?'

'Does it involve throwing this onto a blazing fire? Because if so, I've already thought of it –several times.' Victoria paused, then relented, 'Go on, give me your

219

suggestion, and please make it an inspirational one.'

'What languages have you used?' I grinned at Robert and added, 'Apart from Anglo-Saxon.'

'All the Celtic ones, including any dialect variations I could think of. I even dipped into some of the old Germanic tongues.'

'Is it possible that the runes aren't Celtic at all? Could the message have been presented in runic form simply to throw people off the scent by disguising the true origin?'

'It's entirely possible, I suppose, and if that was the intention, I have to say it has worked remarkably well, at least as far as this translator is concerned.'

Robert looked puzzled, so I explained. 'Suppose I was to write down, "My name is Adam Bailey and I live in North Yorkshire," but instead of using the Latin alphabet I wrote it in Cyrillic; then showed it to a man in Leningrad or Vladivostok, how likely is it that they would understand it?'

'Oh, I get you.'

'I take it there is a specific point to your extremely open question?' Victoria asked, a trifle sarcastically.

'There is indeed. My suggestion is that you try using Aramaic.'

'Aramaic? Why on earth would it be written in an ancient Semitic language that hasn't been in use for around fourteen hundred years, and then only in a few regions thousands of miles away? This is Britain, not Babylon, Adam.'

'I know that, and I agree that it's a long shot, but I still think it's worth a go. I have evidence, if that's not too strong a word, that visitors to Britain who would be familiar with the Aramaic language might have commissioned the carving of that message.'

'Very well, as I've reached desperation point and tried everything else I can think of, I'll give it a try. I'll be sure to let you know if I'm successful – or otherwise.'

The fiendish grin that accompanied her final remark told me that if she were to fail, her rich vocabulary of invective would be directed at me. With that in mind, as we returned to the library, I told Eve that I was almost dreading encountering Victoria later. 'Don't worry, Adam, I'll protect you,' she consoled me.

Much of the second volume of Domenico's gave details of the dangerous situation the visitors faced; not by virtue of their mission, but simply because of the warring factions in Britain at that time. England during that period was a land of division. The power that was William I had long gone, and in his place the dying King Henry II had just been replaced by Richard I. Although Richard was portrayed by history as a courageous warrior leading his troops on crusades against those who had captured the Holy Land, at home, all was far from well. In fact, Richard detested England, spending as little time in the country as possible. Into that vacuum stepped his younger brother, the ambitious Prince John.

I explained this to Eve, and was surprised by her response. 'It sounds like one of those war reports you did from Africa.'

I stared at her in surprise. 'When did you see those? I didn't know you when I worked there.'

She blushed slightly, but admitted she had found the video tapes the TV company had given me of several of my dispatches. 'If you watched those you must be a masochist,' I joked, but I saw her point. There was a similarity between the civil wars I had covered in Africa and the lawless state of Britain towards the end of the twelfth century.

'However interesting these facts might be, they do nothing to advance our knowledge of the purpose of Domenico's mission,' I added.

'What do you suggest?'

'I think we should leave them until a later date and seek enlightenment towards the end of the journal, in the latter part of volume three. By then he might have decided to come clean about their objective.'

I was dead right, and almost immediately we opened volume three I found what we had been looking for. As with the previous occasion, it was a two-word phrase that almost leapt from the page, only this one was in Latin, not English. 'Oh my goodness,' I exclaimed, not having Victoria's gift of invective.

'What have you found?'

I pointed to the phrase. Eve peered at the crabbed, tricky handwriting for a second, her lips moving as she read each letter. She looked at me, and I knew from her startled expression that she had performed her own translation.

The phrase did far more than explain the reason for the priests having travelled to England. It explained Stephen Pengelly's desperate search. It explained his willingness to spend a huge amount of money in attempting to find it. Above all, it provided a motive for the murders that none of us could have foreseen. What it did not do was point to the identity of the killer.

It was early evening when Victoria came into the library, where Eve and I were still sitting in quiet contemplation of what we had learned. 'You were right, Adam,' she told me. 'It is Aramaic, and I have completed the translation. What I am now hoping is that you can shed more light onto how you came to guess so accurately, and what the message refers to –although I have my suspicions.'

'I think everyone should hear it, but before they do, I think you should take a look at this.' I pointed to the journal.

Victoria was as startled as we had been, and agreed with my interpretation. 'Let's call the others and get this over with.'

I smiled at the retired professor, who was as excited as a six-year-old on Christmas morning. Small wonder, having read what we had found. I went to summon everyone, and when they arrived, Victoria explained her success with the final rune, and how it had come about.

She picked up the piece of paper and prepared to read out the translation. 'I was baffled to begin with as to the meaning, but what Adam and Eve found in that journal' – she pointed to the ledger –'explains it all. Here goes.

'*Our small group came to this strange, cold, inhospitable land in fear of our lives for we refused to recant our belief in face of the barbarians. It was as well our leader knew these shores else the seas hereabouts would have accounted for us. Fortune favoured us on reaching this place, for our leader knew the local warlord before whom we were brought, having traded in metals with him. These people are wondrously clever in metal-craft and this stood us in good stead.*

'*So we have made our home with them and have achieved a form of status. With the passage of time the power of that which we brought became known and the force it gave to sustain the body against all manner of maladies and ailments spread far and wide. Although it did much good for us, for we were made safe by its power, it became a target for those who would steal it, careless of its true significance.*

'*To protect the wonderful object our leader entrusted it to me before his time was over and charged me to do all within my power to protect it. Now my time too runs short, so I have devised a place where the object is secreted, away from the acquisitive gaze of men. The whereabouts of its resting place I will pass to the son of our leader, for none has a greater right, with these words of warning for the generations that follow.*

'*Heed this, you who come after. The power of this thing*

is great, so great you cannot comprehend it. But as it is a power for good, in equal measure it may be a power for evil. Think well and well again before you risk unleashing such power, for as it saves, so may it also destroy.'

She put the paper down and looked at the others, before turning to Eve and me. 'I now understand what this is all about, but I'll let Adam and Eve explain. This is more their success than mine.'

All eyes turned to me and I began by directing my explanation to Robert. 'I can now see why your brother invested so much money in the company Overtring. He obviously believed he was on the verge of discovering something of incalculable value. By way of confirmation, towards the end of Domenico's journal the priest reveals why he was sent here.'

I told them our more recent discovery. 'The place he describes is Glastonbury, and towards the end he explains why they had been sent here by the Pope and his emissaries. Their mission failed, but the objective was to recover the most sacred relic of all time and take it to Rome. Domenico refers to it as the "Sacro Catino", which roughly translated means sacred dish. In other words, the Holy Chalice from the Last Supper, or as it has also been called, the Holy Grail.'

There was a long, stunned silence. It seemed an age before Alison spoke. 'That is incredible. Think of it, Robbie; think of the effect this discovery would have. How much would an object like this be worth? I'm not sure you could put a price on it. It must be without doubt the most precious religious and historical artefact the world has ever seen, the vessel containing the sweat, the tears, and the blood of Jesus Christ; The Holy Grail. Not only that, Robbie, that's only a part of it.'

'She's right, Robert,' Victoria added. 'Remember when I told you what Professor Gladstone said? "The true story would be revealed at last of the most mysterious and charismatic leader and his entourage, King Arthur. Not only that but the story of Merlin the wizard, father of both Cerdic of Wessex and Arthur, a story that will make every history book of the time just worthless scrap paper." If this is true and not a confidence trick, the possibilities are endless.'

Robert looked troubled. 'I'm not sure where all this is leading to? I really can't comprehend it.'

'Hang on though, Robert, I'm afraid there's even more to this than you've taken on board yet,' I told him. 'Have you worked out who the leader referred to in that message is?'

Robert shook his head. I looked at Eve and Victoria, who both obviously had.

'Tell him, Adam, it's not fair to keep him in the dark,' Eve encouraged me.

'Very well, I think the leader refer to in the runes is Joseph of Arimathea, St Joseph. He was a trader in metals and visited Cornwall regularly to buy tin. Rumour has it that on one of those journeys he brought Jesus along with him. 'That's what William Blake's poem refers to.' I hummed a snatch of the hymn *Jerusalem* to emphasise my point.

'Jesus was Joseph's nephew, or so it's believed. There is evidence that after the Crucifixion, Joseph travelled from the Holy Land through Europe with a group of Christ's followers, escaping persecution and carrying the sacred vessels with them. The group split up, but Joseph and a small party came to England, where they settled at Glastonbury. It is believed that Joseph and other members of the party intermarried with people from the local tribes, partly as a means to avoid persecution. When you read that message, and take it in context with the other runes, and if we believe Gladstone's tale, I think it's safe to assume that the man who passed the secret to his sons was Merlin, and the two sons were Arthur and Cerdic. That would also bear out the rumour that was prevalent as early as the twelfth century, that Arthur was descended from St Joseph. It is mentioned in another part of the journal.'

I paused for a long time to allow the full implication of my theory to sink in. It clearly hadn't dawned on Robert, so Alison prompted him. 'Robbie,' she whispered, her voice a mixture of awe and terror, 'if Arthur's ancestor was St Joseph, and St Joseph was Christ's uncle,' she paused again, unable to comprehend the implication of her own deduction.

'Go on, Alison, say it,' Eve told her, her voice almost inaudible.

'If all the details Stephen researched are correct, if that family tree happens to be accurate, do you realise what it means? Robbie, if by some,' Alison gulped, 'I was going to use the word miracle but that doesn't seem appropriate really, if by some remote chance the genealogy happened to be correct, do you realise what a special person you would become in the eyes of many? Merely at the thought that you might be the last person in a direct line from the Holy Family.'

Chapter Seventeen

Reaction to the revelations of the previous evening had been intriguing. Whereas many might have considered we should have been in high spirits; the converse was true, and for much of the time, everyone seemed more inclined to quiet introspection I think we were all somewhat overawed by the possible implications.

One of the few comments made was by Alison, who professed to be a little sad that one of her favourite childhood stories now seemed less credible. Faced with cold hard fact, the fiction withered, according to her. 'I used to love reading about those brave knights that King Arthur sent to do battle with dragons and rescue damsels in distress. In particular I loved the story of the quest for the Holy Grail, but if King Arthur knew where the Holy Grail was hidden, he wouldn't need to send his knights to search for it.'

'Actually, your theory might be wrong. The quest for the Holy Grail might just show Arthur's real wisdom. Think of it this way, if Arthur and Cerdic had been told the secret by Merlin of where the Grail was hidden, Arthur might have been concerned as to how secure that hiding place was. Those were uncertain times, the Saxon menace was growing, and he would be desperately keen that the Grail should stay safe until the time was right for it to be revealed. In order to test the security of the hiding place, Arthur might well have ordered the Knights of the Round Table to search for the Grail, reasoning that if they failed to discover it, the secret was safe.'

'That's an exceptionally good, well-reasoned argument,

Adam,' Victoria said. 'You would have made a good historian.'

'That's because he's lived through more of it than most people,' Eve said, sarcastically.

'What puzzles me,' Tammy interjected hastily, 'is why Arthur and Cerdic weren't persecuted for their beliefs. If they were Christians amongst tribes of pagans, how did they end up becoming such powerful leaders?'

It was Victoria who provided the answer. 'If they were as wise as we are led to believe, and by that I mean worldly-wise, I think they might well have chosen to hide their true beliefs, knowing that if they owned up to being Christians they would speedily end up as martyrs. They might even have gone so far as to renounce their Christianity. As a religion, Christianity was in its infancy, remember, and no one at that time could possibly have foreseen what a massive worldwide effect, be it for good or evil, it would have in the coming centuries. It would have been far more pragmatic of them to merge with the local tribes and by their superior skills and weaponry become leaders. Once they had attained that, then few would dare to challenge their authority, or question their beliefs, their roots, or anything about them. As proof that they could well have adopted such attitudes, you have to look no further than the way Cerdic founded a Saxon dynasty.'

The delay in DS Holmes returning my call of the previous day, gave us chance to discuss matters with Robert, Alison, and the others. Between us we decided it would be best to refrain from telling the police about our latest discoveries.

'You mentioned earlier that we'd probably get locked away if we repeated what Victoria told us about Professor Gladstone's story,' Robert said. 'If we were to go to them now with this tale, I doubt whether we'd ever be let out again.'

'Robbie's right, Adam,' Alison agreed. 'This would be far too much for them to take in.'

'I have to agree,' Victoria added. 'The police mind does not readily cope with anything as surreal as this. To be fair,' she conceded, 'I doubt whether many people would give such a fantastical yarn much credence. It is far too close to the supernatural for comfort.'

I bowed to the majority view, and when eventually I was summoned to the phone, confined my discussion with Holmes to what we'd learned about Annie Flood and her family. In a strange way, even this relatively straightforward story underlined Victoria's comments about the way the police mind works.

'It's all a bit circumstantial and with little but local gossip and hearsay,' Holmes commented. 'Newark is a fair way from here. I would rather concentrate our energy on trying to find a killer who doesn't have to travel over a hundred miles every time he wants to commit a murder.'

Had I been of a more sensitive nature I might have taken offence at Holmes' dismissive attitude, but my years in journalism had thickened my skin. I also made allowances for the pressure he must have been under to get results. Eve was rather less forgiving when I reported the conversation to her. 'The stupid, arrogant whippersnapper,' she snarled. Eve does a very good snarl when she's roused. 'Doesn't he realise this is the best lead he's got? In fact it's probably the only lead he's got.'

'I think his problem is that although the Flood connection might establish a good motive for Stephen's murder, there's no way he can see how it links to the other two deaths. To be fair, apart from the information we decided against telling him, we couldn't see a motive for all three crimes. We can now, because we know the immense value of what they were searching for. But as we opted not to reveal that, we can't really complain if Holmes is unconvinced.'

'I suppose not,' Eve agreed, somewhat reluctantly. I think her feisty nature was goading her to make an issue of it, but better judgement overcame that desire. 'What do you suggest we do now?'

'If Holmes isn't prepared to take the Newark connection seriously, then I guess our only option must be to travel there ourselves and try to find some trace of Annie Flood or her relatives. It might not be easy. We can't simply walk into the local nick and enlist police help.'

'No, I guess not. The first thing they'd do probably would be to phone the cops here and that would shoot us down in flames.'

'The other problem we have is that if Annie's maternal family are the ones who remained in Newark, we have no idea what their surname is. It could be Wharton, but we've no guarantee that's a fact.'

'The more I think of it, the more annoyed I am that DS Holmes wouldn't simply pick the phone up and ask the local force to cooperate. Instead of which we'll have to trail all the way down there and knock on doors.'

'On the other hand, it might be fun. It will give us chance to be alone together in a hotel where no one knows us. A couple of nights together, it will be a good chance to rehearse.'

'Rehearse? For what?'

'For our honeymoon.'

'Honestly, Adam, don't you think of anything else except sex?'

'Not when you're near me, Evie.'

At one time I'd have got my hand slapped for that remark, but it seemed she took it as a compliment. She had a point, though; it was irritating that Holmes wouldn't take up our suggestion regarding the Flood family. However, had we not travelled to Newark, and had we not followed up our only lead, the mystery surrounding those deaths might never have been solved. More to the point, had we not taken that course of action, the greater mystery would never have been revealed. Such, as the old saying goes, are the strange paths down which fate leads us.

Getting away to Newark wasn't as easy as simply loading the car and driving off. First, we had to ensure that everyone at the manor was fully aware of the need for continued vigilance. I placed the automatic pistol in the care of Frank Jolly. 'Tony Bishop won't always be available. He has his job to do, but you'll be in and around the house more or less full time.'

'Aye, don't fret, I'll make sure nobody gets past me.'

Our next task was to find suitable accommodation. After perusing the AA Book, and following several phone calls, we managed to get a room in a hotel close to the town centre that sounded ideal for our short stay.

'We have to go home and collect more suitable clothes,' Eve told me. 'It's one thing having something that will pass in a private house, but I for one am not going to be seen in public wearing a sweater and jeans. Besides which we need to check to ensure our own house is in order.'

I remembered that on the last occasion we'd been away from Eden House for a few days there had been a burglary and a nasty attack of vandalism. That had been only a few months previously, but the memory still rankled. 'I don't think we'll have been burgled again,' I reassured her. 'That alarm we had fitted will deter anyone who isn't stone-deaf.'

'I wasn't just thinking of that. We need to ensure the heating oil was delivered and that the central heating is running OK. If we keep getting cold nights it would be just our luck to get a burst pipe. Added to which there will be mail to see to.'

In the end we agreed to spend one night at Eden House

before travelling to Newark-on-Trent. 'I'll have to get used to driving the Range Rover again,' I told Robert, who had come outside to see us off.

'Is there a lot of difference between your car and Stephen's?' he asked, 'I wouldn't know, not being a driver.'

'There certainly is. The Mercedes is much more luxurious, but the Range Rover is ideal for the sort of road conditions we get around here in winter.'

Eve listened to the conversation, but when I stopped by the main gates to allow a tractor to pass, she pointed out that I'd failed to mention the most important thing about the Range Rover. 'What's that?' I asked.

'Have you forgotten that the Range Rover was how we met?'

'How could I? At the time, you were furious, and mistook me for your sister's chauffeur. I think it was when you were tearing a strip off me that I began to fall in love with you, despite your ferocious glare.' I risked a quick sideways glance. Eve didn't look angry now. On the contrary, she looked content, serene almost.

When we reached home, everything was in order. The oil had been delivered; the house was warm and comfortable. 'I have to admit, I wouldn't swap for a manor house or a castle,' Eve told me.

'Nor would I. To be honest, I don't care where I live as long as you're with me.'

Eve eyed me suspiciously. 'That's twice today you've made sentimental remarks. Are you feeling poorly, or are you after something?'

I hastened to assure her that neither of those was the case, which was almost the truth. I mean, I certainly felt well.

There had been quite an accumulation of mail during our short absence, but most of it was destined straight for the waste bin. About the only item addressed to me that was worth commenting on was a note from my publisher which made me laugh. 'What's funny?' Eve asked.

'I have been asked to speak at a prestigious event, but my publisher, in her wisdom, has turned it down on my behalf.'

'That doesn't sound very funny. Why did she do that?'

'When I first read it, I thought the event was in South Wales. Then, when I read it a second time, I realised it was in New South Wales. I'm prepared to bet they wouldn't pay the travelling expenses.'

Eve chuckled, but resumed her study of the letter she had just opened. I'd noticed the foreign stamp when I passed her it. 'That looks interesting,' I commented.

'It's from Harry; she and Tony are away on a skiing holiday, taking advantage of the kids being at school. She's worried about them.'

Eve's sister, Lady Harriet Rowe, was a born worrier. 'Which of them is she fretting about?'

'All three, by the sound of it. She's worried about the twins going to university next year. Reading between the lines, she thinks that Sammy has developed a craving for anything that wears trousers and shaves daily, while Becky seems totally unprepared for life away from home, but her main concern is with Charlie.'

'Why? What's wrong with Charlie? He isn't poorly again, I hope.'

'No, it isn't his health she's worried about. Harry's getting her knickers in a twist because Charlie and Trudi are still writing to each other regularly. Added to which, when he's home from school and Trudi isn't on tour they talk on the phone for hours at a time.'

'What on earth is there to worry about in that? Trudi's a very nice, well-brought-up young girl. It's hardly her fault that she's a pop megastar. At least Harry doesn't have to worry that she might be a gold-digger, after Charlie because he's heir to a fortune.'

'I know that and so do you, but try telling Harry. It sounds as if she thinks Charlie will be getting involved in sex, drugs, and rock'n'roll.'

'Has she met Trudi or her parents yet?' The family were friends of ours, and it was through us that Charlie had met Trudi.

'No, they were supposed to visit the castle a month ago, but Trudi had to jet off to the States for a TV appearance, and they went with her. Now they're due to meet sometime over Christmas and Harry is worried that they'll turn out to be hippies or beatniks, smoking illegal substances and indulging in free love all over the place.'

'Does this rant of Harry's warrant a reply?'

'I ought to, if only to refute her senseless slurs.' Eve glanced at the date on the letter. 'Actually, I could ring her tonight. This letter was posted ten days ago. She'll be back home by now.'

'Do that, and tell her to wake up to reality for goodness sake. Charlie is a very intelligent young man. He must get that from his father, because his mother is an idiot. Put her mind at ease. Tell her Sammy isn't going to become a nymphomaniac, Becky isn't training to be a nun, and Charlie isn't saving up to buy heroin.'

'That's a good idea. Shall I tell her you think she's an idiot?'

'Why not, I've already told her once.'

'Really? When was that?'

'When she accused you of climbing into bed with me a few hours after we met.'

'Oh yes, I remember now.'

'Whereas I had to wait much longer before I got the chance. Still, I'm not complaining; the best things in life don't come easily.'

'Sometimes you say the nicest things, Adam Bailey. It doesn't happen very often, admittedly, which makes it all the more worthwhile when it does happen. Unless of course you're doing it simply to get your evil way with me.'

'I wasn't even thinking of it,' I protested, hotly.

Eve turned away as she muttered a reply. If I'd been able to hear it better, I might even have thought she'd said, 'That's a shame.' I dismissed that idea as wishful thinking.

Being conscious of the social mores surrounding our stay at the manor, we had discontinued our regular practice of having a lie-in when the mood took us. Free from the constraint of politeness, we took advantage of our freedom to be lazy. After a leisurely breakfast, we were on the road by mid-morning. Once we were clear of the narrow, twisting country lanes, Eve asked if I had made any plans for when we got to Newark.

'I went to the trouble of stipulating a double bed, if that's what you mean.'

'Your trouble is that you have a one-track mind. That wouldn't be so bad if it weren't a dirt track.' Despite her censure, I could see that Eve was smiling. 'I *meant* have you any plans regarding the reason for our visit to Newark.'

'Yes, I thought it might be worthwhile visiting the local newspaper office. There might be someone there who remembers the road accident and they might even recall the family's details. They're bound to have covered it, because that's the sort of human interest story a regional newspaper thrives on. Even if there is no one who remembers the event, they might extend a former journalist the courtesy of allowing me to trawl the graveyard.'

'The what?'

'Sorry, that's journalists' slang for the archives.'

'Oh, that's OK, I had a momentary vision of us tramping around from church to church examining tombstones.'

Eve glanced out of the car window. A few flakes of snow were beginning to fall. 'It's not exactly the weather for that sort of thing. One question, though. Is there a newspaper in Newark, or would we have to go to somewhere like Nottingham.'

'There is indeed, an old-established and excellent paper it is too. It's called *The Newark Advertiser.*'

'I think that's a great plan. You do have some good ideas when you can get your mind out of the bedroom.'

Eve has this knack of making praise sound like a thinly disguised insult. I have enough masochism in me to find it endearing. The snow had all but petered out, and was in places replaced by wet, sleety rain. To distract herself from the drab scene outside the car, Eve turned her attention to the guidebook we had brought from Eden House. She found the relevant section and began to recount the attractions of Newark-on-Trent.

'It sounds like a really nice town,' Eve reported. 'There's a twelfth-century castle, which from the photo looks really imposing.'

'It's sobering to think that the castle had been built before Domenico and his companions travelled to England.'

'I wonder if he learned much about England during his stay.'

'At a guess, I'd say he learned quite a lot. Obviously the language would have been a barrier to begin with, but I seem to recall that monks and other members of the clergy, would travel from place to place far more than we might assume. They even took religious relics from place to place in order to encourage local people to worship.'

'I always thought attendance in church was compulsory.'

'No, I don't think it was. Regular absence would have been frowned on, certainly, and there is no doubt the Church wielded enormous power and influence in those days, but I think commanding attendance at church was beyond even them.'

'So the things Domenico was told would be from other members of the clergy.'

'Not necessarily, there would have been lots of other visitors to the abbey. Travelling merchants would be an almost daily occurrence. In those days shops were virtually non-existent, and even the clergy and those associated with the Church would need provisions of one sort or another.'

'Speaking of churches, Newark has one of the largest churches in England,' Eve reported. 'It is the church of St Mary Magdalene, and has an impressive spire that can be seen for many miles. It's quite close to where we're staying, near the market place, so I wouldn't mind looking inside, if it's open.' She read a little more of the guide book and told me, 'There is also a Georgian Town Hall, and Belvoir Castle is only twelve miles away. That's the ancestral home of the Manners family, the Dukes of Rutland.'

She paused and then chuckled. 'Apparently the Normans named it Belvoir, but the locals couldn't pronounce that so they called it Beaver Castle, and it's still called that to this day. Newark is also on the Fosse Way, the Roman road that linked Exeter with Lincoln.' She paused and thought for a moment. 'I suppose that bears out what you said about people travelling large distances.'

I smiled. 'Yes, but in the Romans' case it was most likely to have been used for troop movements.'

Eve resumed her reading. 'The town owed much of its prosperity to the wool and cloth trade, and during the reign of Edward the Confessor, Newark belonged to Leofric, the Earl of Mercia and his wife. I bet you can't tell me what her name was.'

'Yes, I can. It was Lady Godiva.'

'Trust you to know all about a woman who rode naked on horseback. I bet you'd have been staring out of your window as she went past.'

'No I wouldn't, I value my eyesight too much. Besides which, that story probably never happened.'

'You're going to have to explain that.'

'The legend is that she rode naked to protest against the oppressive taxes imposed by her husband on the people of Coventry, but that seems a bit improbable. I feel sure she could have found better ways of persuading him. As for watching her, the other part of the legend is that one voyeur was struck blind as a result of his misbehaviour. His name was Tom, which is where the expression Peeping Tom originates.'

'You are an absolute mine of information. I'm going to give up reading this, because I can learn far more listening to you.'

'Good, because you're starting to sound like a package tour rep,' I told her. 'Incidentally, a lot of towns owed their prosperity to the wool trade. Back in those days it was a very valuable commodity.'

'If I'm starting to sound like a tour guide, listening to you is like sitting in on one of Victoria Riley's history lectures.'

Eve has a superb talent for retaliation.

Chapter Eighteen

We arrived early in the afternoon, and before checking into our hotel strolled through the streets hand in hand like a couple of regular tourists. I was admiring the many fine buildings when Eve said, 'The guide book didn't exaggerate. This is a really nice town.'

I squeezed her hand gently. 'You're right; I have an affinity for market towns, with their being so many in Yorkshire, but this has to be one of the finest I've visited.'

We dined in the hotel restaurant that night. The food was good, and we shared a bottle of red wine. Having lingered over coffee, we retired early. If I'd thought that our absence from Barton Manor would bring an end to Eve's disturbing dreams, I was very much mistaken. The phrase 'rude awakening' was literally true that night, as, at some point in the early hours, Eve pinched me – hard.

'Adam,' she whispered, 'it's dark in here. You must let me out. The bear has warned me. If you don't we'll all die. Do you understand?'

'OK, Evie,' I told her.

'Watch out, Adam. Watch out for the dagger.'

Up to that point I'd thought Eve's dreamed was sparked off by a random memory of the time we'd been imprisoned in a dark place that had almost become our tomb. I reached out and located the bedside lamp. I switched it on; her mention of the bear and the dagger convinced me this wasn't a bad dream from the past. This dream was very much of the present – and equally chilling.

She spoke again, her voice still only a whisper. 'We have to protect Robert. The bear says so.'

Then, without warning, she rolled onto her side and faced me, blinking sleeping in the glare from the lamp. 'What's wrong, Adam? Couldn't you sleep? Or were you having a bad dream?'

I was astonished. Eve clearly had absolutely no recollection of her dream; or of the cryptic warning she had uttered. I pondered whether to tell her, but decided against it. It was bad enough for me to know what she'd said, without burdening her with it.

Eve had returned to our room to freshen up after breakfast, and I seized the opportunity to place a call to Barton Manor from the public phone in the hotel foyer. Eve's dream troubled me more than I wanted to admit. I was immensely relieved when Robert answered the phone, and the reassurance was amplified by his cheery assurance that all was well. I explained briefly how we proposed to go about researching Annie Flood's family.

Although at first it seemed as if we were going to be stonewalled in our attempt to access the newspaper archives, our efforts to cajole the receptionist were curtailed when the outer door opened and a middle-aged man entered. She greeted the newcomer with a warm smile and explained why we were there.

He introduced himself and asked if he could help, then did a double-take. 'Aren't you Adam Bailey?' he asked.

Eve chuckled. 'Fame at last, Adam.'

I explained that we were there looking for information about a local family. We were fortunate that we had mentioned the story to the man who had covered it. Even luckier that his photographic memory rendered a prolonged search of the dusty archives unnecessary.

The information came at a price, but it was one I was more than happy to pay. 'Would you mind if I ran a feature on you?' he asked. 'Your previous career and the various dodgy goings-on the pair of you have been involved with more recently will make fascinating reading.'

I glanced at Eve and saw that she was all for it. As she explained later, 'Who knows, it might even enhance your book sales, which can't be a bad thing.'

He led us to an empty office. 'This will do. Make yourselves comfortable and I'll try and rustle up some tea.'

We talked for almost an hour, mostly about ourselves, but in the process we also elicited the facts we had come to Newark to discover. It was at the end of the conversation that I brought up the subject of Annie Flood's parents. The reporter gave us chapter and verse; far more than we could have hoped to glean from the back numbers of the paper.

Emerging from the building, I took a deep breath of the cold, crisp air. It was a clear, bright November day that to me had suddenly turned dark and unwholesome. The sun was bright, but my mind was filled with dark clouds. Eve, I could tell, was also struggling to come to terms with what we had learned. 'Do you think we should go to where they lived and talk to the neighbours?' Eve asked. 'We might find out more of what happened afterwards?'

I agreed, reluctantly. So grim were the facts that we had already learned that I wasn't sure I was prepared for any further revelations. However, as usual, Evie was right, but our initial attempt to discover anything met with no response, principally because we had chosen that time of day when almost everyone was out at work. 'Let's go back to the hotel and try again after teatime,' Eve suggested.

Our second foray met with more success, and we returned to the hotel with little appetite for dinner as a result of what we had learned. 'I reckon we should set off back first thing tomorrow morning,' I said. 'There's nothing to keep us here now, and I think we ought to return to Barton Manor as soon as possible.'

Eve, it seemed was of the same mind, but we didn't dwell on it. It was only once we were en route back to

Yorkshire that either of us felt able to discuss what we had been told. 'So now we know it all,' Eve said. 'We know who and we know why. What a terribly wicked, sad story. What is it they say about evil begetting evil?'

I agreed, but as I pointed out, now that we did know who was responsible, the information we had been given, together with what we already knew made the motive two-fold. I explained my reasoning, and Eve admitted she hadn't thought along those lines.

'If anything, that makes it even sadder,' she commented.

The thought acted as an effective conversation stopper, and the rest of the journey back to Barton-le-Moors was completed more or less in silence.

We reached Barton Manor shortly after lunchtime, where Robert and Frank greeted us. I noticed with approval that Frank kept one hand in his pocket until he was certain there was no threat, following which he removed the Glock and gave it to me.

'I take it you've been trouble-free in our absence.'

Robert nodded. 'Yes indeed, in fact so much so that Alison and Tammy, who were going stir crazy from being cooped up within these four walls for so long, have made a break for freedom. They heard Tony telling me he had errands to run in Barton-le-Dale and they insisted he should take them with him so they could have a day's shopping.'

He saw the look of concern that passed between Eve and me and hastened to reassure us. 'Don't worry, I warned them that they must stick together at all times and to avoid alleyways and anywhere they could be at risk. I begged them to stay in or around the market place, the shops and cafes. If they followed that advice they surely couldn't be in any danger, could they?'

'I certainly hope not.' In hindsight, I suppose he was

right to think that way. It didn't seem likely that Alison and Tammy would come to any harm in such public places. However, when that decision was made, neither Robert nor the girls were aware of what we had learned in Newark. To be fair, even had they known some, or all of it, I doubt whether they or anyone else could have foreseen what would happen.

'What time are they due back?' Eve asked.

'Tony arranged to meet them at around four thirty, depending on when he got finished with his calls, so I reckon they should be back here by five o'clock.'

'In that case I think it would be best to phone DS Holmes and ask him to come here this afternoon. That way we can explain what we've found out to everyone.' Holmes raised no objection to my demand that he and Johnny Pickersgill come over. My comment that we now knew the identity of the killer certainly galvanised Holmes into action. He and Pickersgill arrived less than half an hour later. Eve told Robert it would be best if everyone in the household heard what we had to say.

He looked surprised, and asked, 'By everyone do you mean Frank and Mary, or Professor Riley?'

'Everyone,' Eve insisted, 'especially Professor Riley.'

'But what about the girls?'

'You can tell them later.'

Eve began her story. 'To understand what's behind all this we have to go back a long number of years, to when Stephen Pengelly began an affair with a young girl by the name of Annie Flood. Her father was outraged, by all accounts, not only because of Stephen's murky reputation with women, but because his daughter was under the age of consent. He confronted Stephen's father, who agreed to pay the family a large sum of money, because the girl was pregnant.

'Soon after that, the family moved back to Newark-on-Trent, which was where they hailed from originally.

Whether that was from choice or whether Pengelly senior insisted on it isn't clear, nor is it relevant.' Eve stopped and looked at me, a clear invitation for me to take over the narrative.

'When we went to Newark we spoke to someone who lives a couple of doors away from where the Flood family moved to. The woman was most informative, and told us that after the birth, Annie suffered severe post-natal depression, which lasted for a long time. The last straw for Annie came when her mother and father were killed in a road accident. Their car was in a head-on collision with an oil tanker. Soon afterwards, a week or so following their funeral, Annie left her home. Nobody knows the exact sequence of events, but a week later a rambler discovered her body in Sherwood Forest. She had hanged herself.'

'What happened to her child?' Holmes asked.

I left it to Eve to answer him. Knowing her love of the dramatic, I sensed that she would want to save the best until last. She seemed to ignore his question as she began to speak. 'Annie had an uncle; her mother's younger brother. He doted on Annie, and after her death he transferred that love to her offspring, becoming guardian, mentor, and surrogate parent to all he had left of his beloved niece.'

She barely paused, but Holmes was determined to seek a reply to his question. 'What became of the child?'

'Not child,' Eve corrected him, 'children. Annie Flood gave birth to twins.'

I heard a gasp from my right and saw Robert's astonished expression. 'That's right,' I told him, as if confirming something he had said, 'just as Alison discovered from the Pengelly family tree.' I explained the significance of this remark to the others. 'Alison noticed an unusually high incidence of twins stretching back many generations. It must be a genetic thing, and I guess it is probably the clearest indication that Stephen was the

244

father.'

I allowed Eve to continue the story while the detective pondered the relevance of this. 'We had already been told a little about the uncle, although our informant here didn't know his name. Our guess is that the man hated the Pengelly family; believing Stephen in particular to have been responsible for all the bad things that had happened; the death of his sister and brother-in-law, the suicide of his niece, and for the children to be left as orphans. We think he must have instilled in the twins a deep loathing for everything the name Pengelly stands for.

'Although our local informant here in Barton-le-Dale didn't know the uncle's name, he did say he thought the man was a professional person, and it was only when we spoke to a newspaperman in Newark that we discovered his identity.' She looked at Holmes and asked, 'Do you remember Adam's theory that the family research might have been an attempt to defraud Stephen?'

Holmes nodded, but I could tell he was puzzled as to where this was going. Eve continued, 'Whether that was the case or not, Adam's other point *was* accurate. He believed the people involved, and by that I mean Graeme Fletcher, Kathy King, and Arnold Wharton would need the assistance of someone with expertise in the subject. We are uncertain whether Wharton dreamed up the plan, or whether it originated from a man he went to university with, his former neighbour. I'm speaking of Annie Flood's maternal uncle, a man by the name of Rufus Locke.'

Eve's revelation was without doubt a bombshell, but it only reached one target. Victoria gasped aloud and stared at Eve with astonishment. Robert frowned, no doubt trying to remember where he had heard the name before. Frank and Mary looked bemused, while Holmes and Pickersgill, although obviously interested, were evidently awaiting further elucidation.

'You're talking about Professor Locke?' Victoria asked, her tone incredulous. 'My successor as history tutor?'

'Absolutely correct,' Eve told her. 'Rufus Locke is Annie Flood's uncle. It's easy to understand how he developed such a deep loathing for Stephen Pengelly. It's our belief that it was Locke who hatched up a scheme to exact revenge on Stephen, by first defrauding him of a small fortune, and then by murdering him. However, in order to cover up that crime and ensure there was no one who could reveal what he'd done, the others involved in the plot had also to die.'

'This is all theory, though,' Holmes said after a while. 'You have no proof that this man Locke committed the murders, have you?'

'We thought we might leave such tiny details to the police,' I told him.

'We can't charge him without proof. We need a whole lot more than just a theory, no matter how likely it seems. But it certainly gives us sufficient grounds to pull him in for questioning, and to apply for a search warrant for his premises. Does your information stretch to where he lives?'

Eve shook her head. 'Unfortunately not, although I suggest somewhere in Leeds might be a good place to start.'

'Perhaps I can help,' Victoria offered. 'I can ring the university and find out the address from them.'

During the latter part of Eve's monologue and the exchange between Holmes and Victoria I had been watching Robert closely. On a couple of occasions he looked as if he was about to say something, but I was able to attract his attention and warn him off with a slight shake of my head.

When Victoria had made the call and given Holmes the address, he declared their intention of returning to Barton-le-Dale immediately. 'I'm going to have to liaise with our colleagues in Leeds on this. On reflection, I'm not sure whether we have sufficient evidence for a search warrant, but I do think we ought to get him into a police station and ask him some pertinent questions regarding a potential charge of conspiracy to murder.'

Eve and I escorted the detectives to the front door. As they were leaving, Johnny Pickersgill hung back long enough to say, 'Perhaps one day you'll tell me the whole story. I'd be interested to hear the bits you left out.' With that parting shot he closed the door behind him.

On our return to the drawing room, we were immediately questioned by Robert and Victoria about the omissions Pickersgill had hinted at. 'Why didn't you want us to go into detail about the family tree?' Robert asked.

'Yes, and why did you avoid the subject of the runic inscriptions completely?' Victoria backed him up.

'It's back to the question of credibility,' Eve told them. 'Adam and I discussed it as we were driving back from Newark, and we thought it would be sensible to concentrate on provable facts such as the hatred motive, rather than making any mention of King Arthur, or the Holy Grail.'

Victoria picked up on Eve's comment about motive. 'When you said it would be sensible to concentrate on hatred, what other motive could there have been? If Locke and his cronies had already milked Stephen Pengelly for a huge sum of money it could hardly have been for profit. That would be like killing the goose that lays the golden eggs.'

'It was an even bigger motive than profit, or hatred,' I told her. 'The motive was survival. We believe Locke was desperate to get his hands on the Holy Grail for precisely the same reason as Stephen Pengelly. Both men were ill; both had been diagnosed with conditions for which there is no known remedy. In effect, Stephen Pengelly and Rufus

Locke were dying, and they looked to the Grail as the sole means of providing a miracle cure. Even if the Grail exists; and even if it can be found, whether it has that capability, or whether both men were merely being delusional is a question we'll probably never know the answer to. I think it's very much open to question. All it seems to have done thus far is provoke people to committing acts of extreme violence and murder.'

'What happens now?' Robert asked.

'Nothing much; I guess, all we can do is sit and wait to see what the police find out when they interview Locke. I'd be interested to know what happened to the twins, though.'

'Were they boys or girls, or didn't you find out?'

'They were both boys,' Eve told him. 'One was named Joseph, after his grandfather on the paternal side, and the other was called Lionel. What became of them, we couldn't discover in Newark, so all we can do is await news from the police. Luckily, now they have all that information, we can relax in the knowledge that we've done all we can, and that the danger is past.'

Should Eve accuse me at any future point of tempting providence, I will remind her of that statement.

Chapter Nineteen

As we adjourned to the kitchen, lured by Mary's offer of freshly baked scones I reflected on the power of people's habits. Most families foregather in their kitchen, except when the television draws them together, and it seemed that even in a house like Barton Manor with elegant, comfortable reception rooms, that tradition still held.

The scones were delicious, and it was only when I had finished the second and was pondering the wisdom of going for a third, and risking Eve's condemnation, that I glanced out of the window and noticed that it was already dark outside.

I looked at the kitchen clock. It was just after five o'clock. 'Shouldn't Tony and the girls be back by now?' I asked.

Robert glanced at his watch. 'Yes, they should, but I don't think they'll be far away. Tony would have called if there had been a problem.'

He was right of course, and I relaxed. If Robert wasn't concerned there was no point in me becoming anxious. I made the difficult decision to forego a third scone, opting instead for another mug of tea. With the others also partaking, we discussed the outcome of the case, as we saw it. Victoria was the one who was most upset by our revelations, expressing her sorrow that her successor was suspected of being a cold-blooded serial killer.

'I never had much to do with Rufus Locke. I met him on one or two archaeological digs when he was a student, and recall that he was fascinated by the Arthurian legend. Later, when I read various papers he'd written, I found it hard to come to terms with the way he allowed supposition and theory to enter his work and presented them as facts. Having said that, I would never have thought him capable of the sort of wickedness you have ascribed to him.'

She looked at me, and it seemed almost as if she was pleading for the right answer as she asked, 'Do you think those runic messages were part of the plot to defraud Robert's brother, or do you believe those carvings actually exist? I mean as ancient inscriptions, not as modern ones fabricated as the basis for deceit?'

'I can't say that they are definitely genuine,' I told her, choosing my words carefully. 'I think it's highly probable that even if it did start out as a plot to defraud Stephen, somewhere along the way it got overtaken when someone discovered that at least part of what they were putting together was actually true.'

'How do you work that out?' Robert asked.

'The key lies not only with the runes, but also with Domenico's journal. The fact that someone; and we must assume it to have been Stephen, went to so much trouble to encrypt the messages and hide the journal so carefully suggests that they believed them to be valuable and worth protecting. Any doubts I had were more or less removed when I learned what Domenico and his companions were sent to England to retrieve. Of course, it may have been pure wishful thinking on Stephen's part, knowing the reputation of what they were seeking and how it might offer a miracle cure for what ailed him. That would make him susceptible to fraud; but only if the confidence tricksters were aware of his illness.'

'I'd be very interested to take a look at that journal,' Victoria remarked. 'Having wrestled with those runes a straightforward translation from Latin should be far easier. The journal might offer a fresh insight into certain areas of life in Britain in the twelfth century, as seen from an outsider's point of view. There is never a point when a historian can have too much evidence to work with.'

'I would also like to know where on earth Stephen obtained the manuscript,' Robert said. 'I somehow can't imagine him spending countless hours delving through dusty archives.' He shrugged. 'But then I barely knew him, so who am I to say.'

'There could be any number of places where he might have found it,' Victoria told him. 'I can think of dozens off the cuff. Some are places where a vast majority of the works they store haven't seen the light of day for centuries. Much of the stuff is mundane, I grant you, but the sheer volume of the material means that it would take a team of historians decades to wade through every manuscript.'

As she was speaking, the telephone, which had an extension in the kitchen, rang. Robert answered it, and as he listened to the caller I saw tension in his expression that hadn't been there earlier. 'Better stay where you are and ring me back one way or the other.'

He looked up, his expression bleak. 'That was Tony. The girls haven't turned up at the place he arranged to meet them. He's been waiting there almost an hour.'

'Could they have gone to the wrong place?' Eve asked.

'Hardly, they were to wait by the town clock in the market place.'

We attempted to reassure him, suggesting that Alison and Tammy had probably been so engrossed in their shopping expedition that they had failed to notice the time, but I don't think Robert was convinced. Nor do I think we really believed that was what had happened. A measure of Robert's concern was that when Bishop rang back soon afterwards, reporting that the girls still hadn't turned up, his immediate reaction was to involve the police.

However, his call to Barton-le-Dale didn't produce the result he wanted. He was informed that Holmes and Pickersgill were out, and would not return until next

251

morning. Having declined to leave a message, Robert put the phone down and told us the bad news. Frustrating though it was, the inability to contact the police actually worked in our favour, although it didn't appear that way at the time.

Within minutes of Robert's abortive call, the phone rang again. He grabbed the receiver, obviously hoping that it would be Bishop with good news, or failing that Alison and Tammy to say why they weren't at the rendezvous.

Although we were unable to hear the caller's words, Robert's expression spoke volumes. It was obviously not Bishop or the girls, and what he was hearing was certainly not to his liking. He signalled to Eve and me to join him and tilted the receiver so that we could catch what was being said. If he had looked bleak earlier, his face was now grim; etched with fear.

The voice of the caller was harsh, grating; the message uncompromising, the threat potent. 'You have something of mine, Pengelly. Now, I have something of yours. I'm talking about your two pet whores. Which of them is your favourite, or do you take them in turn? They are safe –at least for the time being. However, some of my associates have ideas about them, and restraining their animal instincts might take some doing. So, their continued health and well-being is up to you. Here's how it works. If you involve the police – your pet whores will die. If you fail to follow my instructions to the letter – they will die. You must be aware by now what that dreadful weapon is capable of. Your brother discovered that to his cost. It was a just reward for the evil life he had led. Even to the bitter end he attempted to cheat his way out of trouble, but he paid the price for one deceit too many. Believe me, I shall not hesitate to do the same to these whores once my associates have slaked their desire on them. I can make theirs a quick ending, or I can ensure they suffer long hours of torment, with such agony that they will plead for the release that death will bring. Their lives are in your hands.'

'Tell me what you want.' Robert's voice was flat, seemingly emotionless.

'What I want is simple. I want the runic inscriptions your brother stole from me when I was unable to get to them. Not the fake ones he tried to palm me off with; I want the originals. Do you understand what I am talking about?'

'Yes, you're talking about the ones in the photos. The ones carved on stone tablets.'

'Correct, and I want you to deliver them to me personally. I will call you tomorrow to give you instructions regarding the time and place.'

The caller hung up.

Although we tried to console Robert, it was of no avail. He wouldn't listen to our platitudes, nor could I blame him. It was only after Tony Bishop had phoned again, been advised of the situation, and told to return to the manor that Eve took control of the situation, displaying that combination of care and determination I have heard referred to as tough love.

'Self-recrimination and mooning about feeling sorry for yourself and going frantic with worry isn't going to help Alison or Tammy. You must demonstrate your resolve and show you can cope with a crisis. Believe that they will be freed and returned to us unscathed, anything less than that is untenable. Whatever you fear might be the outcome and no matter how had it might seem at the moment, the surest way of bringing about a bad ending is by caving in and bowing to the kidnappers' demands.'

'It's all very well you saying that,' Robert protested, 'and I do know that I must try and be strong, but what can I do? I feel so helpless, sitting here waiting for that sick bastard to phone. He holds all the cards. No way can I do

253

anything that might endanger Alison.'

'I agree; there is nothing you can do at the moment. It must be terribly frustrating and heart-rending, having to wait. The worst part is that as things stand we're unable to make any sort of plans. We have to see what he comes up with in his instructions.'

'Eve's right,' I told him. 'If you panic, you play right into their hands. I read an article about abductions in America, and kidnappers rely on their victims' nearest and dearest caving-in as the surest way of forcing home their demands. The advice the writer gave is that the best way to combat the threat is to stay calm and make what plans you can while appearing to be doing exactly what they tell you to.'

It was all sound advice, even though the part about the article came purely from my imagination, but as things stood, I dare not reveal my most chilling thought. It was only later, once I had managed to get Eve alone that I was able to voice my deepest fear. 'We have to ignore the kidnappers' demands, whatever the instructions are. We have to rescue the girls at all cost.'

'Why do you say that? If he really is prepared to trade Alison and Tammy for those runic inscriptions, wouldn't it be far easier and much less dangerous to allow the exchange to go ahead without interference?'

'He isn't going to let that happen. Locke has no intention whatsoever of exchanging the girls. He will murder them as soon as he gets his hands on those photos.' I paused before adding the thought that even I had refused to entertain up to that point. 'That is, if he hasn't already killed them.'

'How do you know that? You can't possibly be certain that's what he'll do. Or is this some more words of wisdom from that imaginary American writer you dreamed up?'

I smiled. 'I didn't imagine for one minute that would

fool you. As to me being certain of what he intends, the answer is simple, and has nothing to do with a normal kidnap scenario. The plain fact is that Alison and Tammy will have to die because they will certainly have recognised Rufus Locke as the man who abducted them. I bet that's how he staged the kidnap. They might have been slightly surprised to see their history tutor in Barton-le-Dale today, but they wouldn't have been suspicious because there was nothing to connect him to the murders. Not without the information we discovered in Newark. All he would need to do is spin them some tale about his presence; something along the lines of going to view a valuable artefact dating back to the reign of King Rudolph the Red-Nosed or whatever, and inviting them to come along. Once he got them away from the main streets the rest would be easy. Barton-le-Dale is hardly a bustling metropolis.'

'And having given himself away he can't afford to let them live, because he believes they are the only ones who could point the finger of suspicion at him. Is that correct?'

I nodded. 'OK,' Eve continued, 'I accept that. So how do we stop him?'

'There's only one way, and that involves danger for Robert. When that phone call comes tomorrow morning, he must make sure that Locke understands that Robert knows who he is; knows all about him and Annie. That way, if Locke is capable of rational thought, he will see that there is no mileage in killing the girls, at least not until such time as he has disposed of Robert. If we can get Robert to achieve that, we might be buying ourselves a bit more time to try and figure out where he's holding them prisoner and how to rescue them.'

'I suppose you're right, but it sounds very risky.'

'Maybe, but it's very much the lesser of two evils.'

Neither of us got much sleep that night. Next morning we

were up and about far earlier than normal, aware of the crucial phone call that could come at any time. Nevertheless, Robert was up before us, and from the haggard expression on his face I wondered if he had been able to sleep, or even if he had gone to bed.

Whether it was Locke's intention to exert the maximum possible pressure on Robert I will never know, but as time passed without the call coming in, we were able to tell him of what we had determined the previous night.

The instructions we gave him with regard to the phone call were explicit. 'Whatever he says, no matter where the conversation is heading, at some point you must address him as Professor Locke and if you can achieve it, make it perfectly clear that you know everything there is to know about him. By that I mean that you know he's related to Annie Flood, and that you know about Stephen's affair with her, and the resulting twins. Also mention Locke's illness if you get the chance.'

'Won't all that stuff enrage him and make him more desperate?'

'On the contrary – it should make him realise there's no point in trying to hide his identity any longer. It's absolutely essential for Alison and Tammy's sake that you do this, Robert. He knows that they will have identified him, and therefore he might stand a chance of getting away with it if he eliminates them. However, once he realises that you also know who he is and everything about him, with luck he should know that violence against the girls would be futile.'

I tried to put the last part as diplomatically as possible, but on seeing Robert grimace I guessed that I'd been less than successful. Nevertheless, with Eve's endorsement of my policy, Robert accepted the need to put the message across. It was the first fragment of our burgeoning plan to rescue Alison and Tammy. The second, far larger piece came courtesy of DS Holmes.

It wasn't until shortly after ten o'clock that the phone rang. Robert answered it, and I saw the tension ease from his face. This wasn't Locke calling. 'Yes, he's here. Just a second, I'll get him.'

He held out the receiver, and I noticed he had the mouthpiece covered by his free hand. 'It's DS Holmes. You won't tell him what's happened, will you?'

'I'll be as discreet as I can.'

I listened as Holmes brought me up to date with events in Leeds. 'We went to that address along with a couple of officers from Leeds CID. There was no sign of either Locke or the twins. We did establish that they lived there, but a neighbour we spoke to said she hadn't seen them for weeks. However, nobody seemed to know where they've gone or when they're expected to return.'

I thanked Holmes and before ending the call, asked him, 'Will you be in your office all day? I'm only asking in case I get any more ideas that I might want to share with you.'

Holmes confirmed that he and Pickersgill would be available should I require them. As I repeated what Holmes had said, once I reached the part about Locke's whereabouts I noticed a frown on Eve's face. Past experience taught me to wait, knowing that she was developing a line of thought. After a few minutes she looked at me.

'Adam, do you remember what Emma's father told us that night at the Crown and Anchor? Didn't he say that Annie's uncle bought a cottage in Langstrop and used to cycle down to Barton-le-Moors?'

'That's correct, and if I remember rightly he also said that the cottage was now being used as a holiday let, didn't he?'

Eve nodded, adding, 'What Emma's father didn't say was if the property had been sold. I'll bet that's where he and the twins have been holed up all this time; and I also reckon it's where they're keeping Alison and Tammy.'

She had barely finished speaking when the phone rang again, and this time it was the call we'd been expecting; the one we feared. As Robert went to answer it, Eve had a last piece of advice for him. 'Remember, don't let Locke intimidate you. Be a bit arrogant –like Adam. Most important of all, make sure you get your message across. He must understand that you know virtually everything there is to know about him.'

At any other time I might have objected to that slur on my character, but the situation was far too tense to be picky. The insult served its purpose though. Robert smiled faintly, squared his shoulders, and picked up the receiver. He listened for a moment, then cut in, interrupting the caller in mid-flow. 'Good morning to you, Professor Locke. How are you today? Ill, I hope. You've left it a bit late to call, haven't you? Not an early riser, perhaps, or is the illness getting the better of you?'

Although we couldn't make out what Locke was saying, the agitated tone of his voice told us that Robert's strategy was working –so far. Robert listened for a few seconds before replying. 'Yes, of course I know who you are. I know all about you – and about your harlot niece Annie's little bastards, my darling nephews? Although come to think of it, I don't suppose the bastards are so little anymore, are they?'

I hoped that Robert's initial success hadn't gone to his head. It was one thing to get Locke rattled, but driving him too far might push him over the edge. I tapped Robert on the shoulder, then made a downward motion with my hands. He nodded, accepting my signal to ease off. He listened again, before telling Locke, 'No, I'm sorry, I can't do that. It simply isn't possible.'

More agitated squawking followed, to which Robert said, 'If you'll let me get a word in edgeways, I'll explain. This isn't one of your lectures, you know. The reason I can't do as you ask is because I can't drive. I don't have a driving licence; I've never owned a car, never even sat behind a steering wheel. I wouldn't know the difference between a gear lever and a handbrake.'

Locke's voice seemed marginally calmer as he responded to Robert's statement. After listening to what he had to say, Robert told him, 'Yes, I know where that is, but I'll need a bit longer. Stephen's chauffeur has broken his arm so I'll need to find someone else to drive me.' He listened for a moment. 'Yes, that should be OK. I'll make sure my driver knows how to get there. Of course I'll bring the runes, but before I agree to anything, I want to speak to Alison. I need to be sure that you haven't hurt her.'

There was a few seconds' silence, then we heard a different voice; obviously Alison's. Although neither Eve nor I could make out what she said from the few words she could utter before the receiver was taken from her, at least we knew she was alive, and we could plan our strategy properly. Hopefully, Robert had ensured her safety for the time being by telling Locke his identity was no longer secret. That, together with the knowledge of where they were being held captive should give us an advantage. I had a sudden sense of déjà vu; of having been through a situation such as this before. On that occasion, Eve and a friend of hers had been the hostages. It was plain that she remembered it too, for as Robert was telling us what Locke had said and repeating Alison's plea for help, Eve nudged me and whispered, 'I think the divide and conquer strategy we've used before might work if we can take them by surprise, don't you?'

If I had reservations, they were about the calibre of our allies, and the state of mind of the enemy. Dealing with a criminal who is only seeking a fortune is a world away from tackling a potential psychopath. My blood ran cold as I corrected the equation: a trio of potential psychopaths.

Chapter Twenty

'Locke has instructed me to meet him at Bleke Mire in two hours' time. He wanted me to go alone, but as you heard, I told him I don't drive.'

'Where is this place, Bleke Mire?' Eve asked.

'On the high moor beyond Langstrop village, so it sounds as if your theory about where Locke is hiding out might be correct.'

'Did he say that he would bring Alison and Tammy along when you meet him?'

Robert looked surprised by the question. I knew I would have to explain my reason for asking it, unpalatable though it was. 'Yes, he said that as soon as he was satisfied that I'd given him the runic inscriptions he wanted, he would release the girls.'

'What's this place like? It sounds like a marsh.'

The answer to Eve's question came from Tony Bishop. 'That's exactly what it is, a highly dangerous marsh at that. It stretches for almost half a mile with a small tarn in the centre, and the marsh is capable of taking a man under within minutes, or so I believe.'

'Do I take it there is no cover around there?'

'Actually, you're wrong. There's a small brake of trees about half a mile, maybe less, from the top of the moor, and alongside the copse is a row of shooting butts used by the guns on the Barton grouse shoot.'

'Those shooting butts, are they nearer the marsh or further away?'

Bishop hadn't missed the implication. 'A little bit nearer. There's a dirt road leading to them, it's a spur from the road that takes you past the marsh. I'd say they were close enough for a decent shot, certainly for someone with a stalking rifle equipped with a telescopic sight.'

Robert was horrified that we were even considering such a course of action. 'Surely you're not seriously considering mounting an ambush? That would be far too dangerous. No way could I sanction putting Alison or Tammy at risk through ill-advised or reckless action. I'm not prepared to go along with such a mad scheme.'

There was no alternative but to spell it out for him. 'I'm sorry, Robert, but you have no choice. Why do you think I asked you if Locke intended to bring the girls along? He intends to kill you, to kill Alison and Tammy, and to kill your driver.'

'I don't believe Locke would do that. The hue and cry when the bodies are found would make it impossible for him to continue searching for the Grail.'

'You're missing the point, Robert. Why do you think Locke chose Bleke Mire for the handover? You heard what Tony just said about how dangerous the marsh is. Once Locke has those photos, either Locke or the twins will murder everyone. They will then load the bodies into your car, drive it into the marsh, and let it sink. No bodies will ever be found, and when questions are asked, the rumour will probably start that you were abducted by aliens.'

I've remarked several times about my talent for reducing an audience to silence. It seems that my ability hasn't waned with time.

Victoria had been listening to the conversation. She stepped forward and put a reassuring hand on Robert's arm, looked straight into his eyes and, with a steady voice, said, 'Listen to Adam, Robert. Let him help you.'

Eventually, and with considerable reluctance, Robert accepted my hypothesis and agreed to listen to the scheme we were planning.

'The idea is for me to drive you there in my Range Rover. At the same time, Tony, if you agree, I'd like you to take up position in the closest of the shooting butts. The only problem, and I admit it is a huge one, is that at some stage, one of us must be prepared to take another human being's life.'

'Why take your car? Why not use the Mercedes?'

It seemed that Robert was prepared to accept the need for direct action. There were several reasons for the choice, and I explained a couple. 'For one thing, going on what Tony has told us about Bleke Mire, the Range Rover's four-wheel drive will make it far more suitable in such terrain. In addition, my guess is that Locke will be on the lookout for the Mercedes. I know it isn't much, but when a car turns up that isn't the one he was expecting to see, it might give us an advantage, even if it's only momentary.'

I didn't disclose the main reason, which was that the Range Rover would contain my secret weapon.

We were ready well ahead of the time scheduled for the rendezvous. My last act before getting into the car was to brief Tony Bishop. 'Wait ten minutes after we've gone, then set off, but don't rush. If my guess is correct, Locke will have left the cottage before you get to Langstrop. The last thing I want is for him to see a stream of vehicles passing through the village. That would certainly arouse his suspicions. Apart from that, he might recognise your car, which would be disastrous.'

No matter how carefully you plan, and even if you believe you have catered for every eventuality, there is always the risk that some unforeseen factor will upset your meticulously thought-out scheme. In this case, it was the local climate that threatened to put a huge spanner in the works.

It wasn't until we had passed through Barton-le-Moors and were heading for the higher ground that I noticed the change in the weather. Whereas in the lower reaches of the dale the day had been a bright, cold, sunny morning, as we climbed the hills the sun vanished behind a wall of low cloud and mist. 'This isn't good,' I commented. 'If it's foggy on the tops, Bishop won't be able to take a clear shot, and if he tries to get closer, that could give the game away. The problem with fog is that it swirls about and, although you might think you're safely hidden one minute, if it lifts without warning you'll be totally exposed.'

'Do you think Tony might try that?'

'I hope he's experienced enough to work out the danger and stay at the butts. If that's the case, it looks as if it will be down to us.'

I drove slowly through Langstrop, which hardly counted as a hamlet, let alone a village. Less than a dozen small dwellings clustered around a small patch of wispy grass, huddled together as if trying to protect themselves from the weather, which I guessed could be extreme during the winter months. I wondered how many, if any, were occupied the whole year round. That thought spurred me to look for signs of life.

I saw none until the far end of the cottages. The last one had an old, grey van parked in front of it, facing our destination. 'I wouldn't be surprised if that van belongs to Locke. It's facing the mire, and it's the only vehicle in sight.'

As we left the village, I saw that the fog was becoming denser. There would definitely be no chance of Bishop being able to see clearly enough to take a shot if this weather didn't clear. Within a few minutes we had reached the pre-arranged meeting place. It was distinguishable by a sign that conveyed a grim message. '"Bleke Mire,"' I read aloud, '"Hazardous marshland. Danger of death. Keep off." I think that gets the message across.' The image of a skull and crossbones drawn on a piece of wood nailed to a stake added a suitably macabre finishing touch.

There was a small patch of bare ground almost opposite the sign where it looked as if vehicles had stopped frequently. Birdwatchers, perhaps, or walkers; I doubted that even the most ardent of lovers would have chosen so desolate a location for their trysts. I manoeuvred the Range Rover to face the village.

'Why are you doing that?' Robert asked.

'It'll be better should we need to make a hurried getaway – plus the fact that if they park in front of us, they won't be able to see the back of our vehicle.'

I saw Robert fidget uneasily in the passenger seat. Time for a pep talk, I thought. 'Remember what we discussed earlier. This is no time for half-measures. You must carry the fight to the enemy. We have nothing to lose, so don't hold back. No way are they going to allow any of us to leave here alive. We cannot fail.'

We waited for over a quarter of an hour with the windows open, listening for the slightest sound, our eyes straining to make out any movement in the swirling fog, but there was nothing until we heard an engine in the far distance, the sound almost indistinguishable but growing slowly more noticeable.

'That must be Locke. Are you ready to do this?'

'I am, as ready as I'll ever be.'

'OK, let's get out of the car but make sure you leave your door open.'

He did as instructed, waiting by the front passenger wing. I also climbed out and stood alongside the vehicle, my back resting against the edge of the open driver's door. 'I can't see anything yet,' I said loudly.

'Neither can I,' Robert replied.

A couple of minutes later the van came into sight, being driven very slowly. 'Well, this is it,' I remarked, 'at least they've been kind enough to let us prepare ourselves.'

The grey van we'd noticed in the village pulled to a halt

a few feet from the front of the Range Rover. The driver was a young man, barely out of his teens, if that. The passenger seat was occupied by a much older man whose face was grey with the pallor of ill health. I had no doubt in my mind that this was Rufus Locke, and that the driver was one of the twins.

The passenger opened his door and got out, moving slowly and with obvious pain. The driver made no attempt to leave the vehicle, but stayed, his arms crossed over the steering wheel, staring fixedly at us. Once outside, the passenger leaned heavily on a walking stick. In his free hand he was holding an old but serviceable-looking revolver. I'd planned for Locke to bring Excoria with him; I hadn't bargained for the firearm as well. That altered the odds against our survival dramatically. My hopes were now pinned on the preparations we had made. 'I see Locke has a gun,' I announced loudly, 'that's not good.'

Locke ignored me as completely as if I wasn't there. He made no attempt to approach us, merely saying, 'Where are the photos? Have you brought them?'

Robert reached into his pocket and instantly Locke raised the revolver, pointing it directly at him. 'Move slowly and carefully,' Locke stated. 'I won't hesitate to use this.' His voice was harsh, but far from strong. The cancer must be close to its terminal stage, I thought.

Robert pulled out the packet of photos and held them up for Locke to see. 'Where are the girls?' he demanded. He sounded angry. That was exactly what I wanted.

Locke tapped the side panel of the van with his stick. Through the window, I saw the driver say something, but he still made no effort to leave the vehicle. A couple of seconds later the back door of the van opened wide and three people emerged, walking slowly along the side of the van to stand alongside Locke.

Alison and Tammy's hands were tied in front of them. Their eyes were wide with fear. The reason for that became obvious when we saw what their companion was carrying. Had the circumstances been different I might have admired the skill of the craftsman who had forged that weapon, but I had seen the terrible wounds it could inflict. Apart from that, my attention was not so much on the blade Excoria, but on the man holding it.

He and the van driver were twins, that much was obvious from their features, but although the faces might have been alike, that was where the similarity ended. Their eyes told a vastly different story. Whereas the van driver looked more scared than angry, the twin carrying the weapon looked to have long since abandoned any form of sanity. Whatever experts argue about the possibility of seeing madness in a person's face, I had no doubt that I recognised it instantly in his.

I think it was only at that moment, when Robert saw for himself the deep hatred in Locke's face and the insanity in that of the girls' captor, that he finally accepted the truth of what we had told him. His response to the challenge that realisation presented was all that I could have hoped for.

'I see you've brought the bastards along for company, Locke. Which of Annie's brats is which?'

He looked at the twin holding Excoria. 'Which are you, Joe or Lionel? You don't look much like your father, if my brother actually was your sire. Come to think of it, you don't look much like your slut of a mother either.'

I heard a hiss of pure venom from the twin holding the girls prisoner, and feared that Robert might have gone too far.

'Steady, Lionel,' Locke ordered. He looked at Robert. 'Enough of that nonsense. Stand perfectly still.' He turned slightly and peered at me, and I realised that along with the other symptoms of his ailment, his sight was failing. That didn't help much given the close proximity of that revolver. 'You! Go stand alongside your employer. That's it, shoulder to shoulder.'

He obviously believed me to be one of the estate workers. Whether that was to our advantage or not, I wasn't sure. Perhaps it might lull him into a false sense of security. 'Lionel,' he almost gasped as he gave the instruction, 'go collect the photos, but watch out for tricks.'

As Lionel stepped forward, Locke placed the revolver against Alison's temple. With that deterrent, no one was going to try anything rash. Locke was obviously not prepared to take even the slightest chance. Robert handed the photos over. As he did so, I glanced down and saw Excoria clearly for the first time. Despite our desperate situation, I had to bite my lip to avoid laughing out loud; such was the comic irony in what I'd just seen.

Lionel retreated, walking backwards, one step at a time, never taking his eyes off us. On reaching the van he passed the photos to Locke, who turned away from the girls and began to examine the images one by one. At length, a smile of satisfaction crossed his face, before he looked up. 'These are what I wanted, but your evil brother cheated me of them, just as he cheated Joseph and Lionel out of their inheritance, and cheated them of their mother's love. It's important that you know that, Pengelly, and your minion too.'

He shifted his gaze to me. 'I actually feel sorry for you. It's a shame you have to die, simply for being in the wrong place at the wrong time, and working for the wrong person.'

I smiled sweetly at him. 'You're wrong, Locke, so wrong that it's laughable. You've been wrong about everything.' I spoke confidently, because when Lionel had approached us, the last piece of the puzzle had dropped into place. 'You're wrong about me being an employee of Barton Manor estate. You're wrong if you believe those runes are going to lead you to what you seek, and most important of all, you're wrong if you think that you're going to find the Holy Grail and be miraculously cured of cancer. None of that is going to happen. Oh, and one other thing; you're wrong if you think that Sonny Boy there is going to kill us.'

'We'll see about that. So you're not an employee, you're an interfering busybody. Soon you'll be just as dead, whichever you are. Lionel, it's time to liberate Excoria once again. Take Pengelly first. I will enjoy watching that.'

We stood in silence as Lionel approached; a grin of pure sadistic evil on his face. Beyond him, in the van, I could see that his twin brother had turned away, obviously dreading what was about to happen. His face was averted, but even then that wasn't sufficient. He covered his eyes with his hands. 'Time for Mr Glock,' I said, as loudly as I dared.

Lionel stopped for a second with Excoria raised as he tried to work out the meaning of my strange remark. He must have decided it posed no threat, for he moved forward once more to stand in front of Robert. I saw his arm go back, ready to strike, and I pushed Robert as hard as I could, just as Lionel thrust the blade at him.

My action took Robert clear of that deadly weapon's path. Unfortunately, it put my left arm directly in it. I felt a sharp, burning sensation run up my forearm as the sword ripped through my coat and shirt sleeves, removing a long strip of skin as it caught me a glancing blow.

Lionel turned towards me and once again I heard that venomous hiss of rage, saw the fury in his eyes as he raised Excoria again. Is this it, I wondered? Then, as he brought his arm forward to deliver the killing lunge, sight and sound seemed to merge. I saw blood spurt in a small gushing fountain as the sound of the Glock reverberated, thrown back by the fog in a thousand decreasing echoes. I thought I'd been stabbed, then realised the blood was from Lionel's chest, not mine. I glanced back towards the rear of the car. Slightly to one side, my beautiful Eve crouched in classic gunfighter pose, one arm bracing the other, the Glock pistol unwavering in her hand as she turned towards her next target. Our plan to conceal her in the back of the Range Rover had worked. She had undoubtedly saved my life, but it wasn't over yet.

As Eve raised the Glock once more, Alison threw herself sideways, her full weight catching Locke, knocking the stick from his hand. The old man collapsed sideways, the revolver hanging from his limp hand.

Eve's shot had struck Lionel high in the chest, just below his right shoulder. He screamed with pain and the weapon dropped from his hand. He clutched at the wound. Blinded by pain, he staggered towards the mire, heedless of our warning shouts. On and on he went, until the fog engulfed him. Then we heard a fresh scream, this time of pain and panic combined.

Eve walked forward and kicked Locke's gun out of his reach. 'Adam, get the other twin,' she commanded.

Before I could do so, the driver's door opened and Joseph hurtled out. He ran towards where Lionel had vanished, but Robert, with a rugby tackle that would have been applauded at Twickenham or Cardiff Arms Park, pulled him down and held him there by sitting on his back. I walked across and relieved Robert of his prisoner.

'Behave yourself and you won't get hurt,' I told him. I wasn't sure how much of the message got home. Joseph whimpered and looked to where Lionel had gone, his distress increasing as he heard the desperate cry for help that emerged from the gloom. He struggled against my grip, and tried to free himself as if to go to Lionel's aid, but I pulled him back. I thrust him aside and scooped Locke's revolver from where Eve had kicked it. 'Sit down there,' I told him, pointing to a spot alongside Locke's prostrate form.

Robert began untying Alison and Tammy. I told Eve to

keep watch over Joseph, although it seemed obvious to me that he no longer posed a threat. How strange, I thought, that one twin should be so docile while the other had been capable of such unspeakable violence.

I think Eve had worked out what I intended to do. She nodded to me. 'Get it over with, Adam, make it quick.'

I walked slowly towards the mire, intent on ending Lionel's suffering. When I reached the nearest point to where he was floundering, I saw that any attempt to pull him out would be fruitless. He had already sunk up to his armpits in the oozing mud that was sucking him inexorably to his doom. I raised the gun but before I could fire, he gave one last struggle. His scream was replaced by an obscene gurgling sound as the marsh claimed its victim. There was a long, terrible silence.

Chapter Twenty-one

I walked slowly back through the gloom, picking my way carefully. Even at the edges, the mire looked dangerous, and after what I had just witnessed I wasn't about to take the slightest chance.

When I reached the vehicles, Tony Bishop had joined us and was examining Locke.

'He's alive but unconscious,' Bishop reported. I handed him the revolver and told him to watch the prisoners. Only then was I able to thank Eve for her intervention. I took her in my arms. 'That was good shooting, my darling. You saved my life.'

'How bad is your arm?' Her face was etched with concern.

I showed her the injury, which must have looked worse than it felt.

'What shall we do now?' Robert asked.

'I think if Tony brings his car up here and then takes you and the girls back to the village, you can phone the police from there. If we tie these two up and lock them in the van, Eve and I will stay here and stand guard over them.'

'What do you plan to do with that?' Robert pointed to Excoria.

'I think you know what I have in mind.'

He nodded. 'Do it, then. The sooner the better.'

As he and Bishop were tying up Joseph and putting him with the still-unconscious Locke into the van, I picked up the blade, Excoria. It was lighter than I expected, exhibiting the expert craftsmanship of the master metal worker, and as I held it I felt a curious sensation of peace, that there was nothing I might not achieve while I held this. I looked at Eve, who was eyeing the weapon apprehensively. 'Do you remember those inscriptions that Victoria translated?' I asked.

'Yes, what about them?'

In order to show her what I meant, I balanced Excoria on my injured arm and gestured towards the blade. Eve looked at me, then at the weapon, then back at me and as I told her what I thought, we both began to laugh. 'Now, I'm going to do as Robert wants and chuck this thing into Bleke Mire.'

'But won't the police want it for evidence?'

'I'll tell them that Lionel staggered into the marsh carrying it with him and they both sunk without trace.'

'Shall I come with you?'

'No way, it's treacherous.'

I walked forwards, picking my way with extreme care, my eyes searching the ground for firm footholds. I knew that one false step could end in disaster. The grim reminder of what had happened to Lionel was still fresh enough to act as a potent warning. It was only when I reached a point where I judged it was unsafe to go any further that I looked up. The fog had lifted sufficiently for me to be able to see the small tarn ahead. Obviously I was close to the centre of the mire.

I knew it would take a supreme effort to reach the water from where I was standing. The last thing I wanted was for the weapon to fall short and be picked up by some adventurous wildfowler. As I stood there, shuffling my feet to ensure I was properly balanced, I looked towards the reeds at the water's edge, and was suddenly aware of the eerie silence of this place. I remembered John Keats' poem 'La Belle Dame Sans Merci': *'Oh what can ail thee knight-at-arms, alone and palely loitering? The sedge has withered from the lake, and no birds sing.'*

I shivered, but not from cold, rather from an unnamed dread of things beyond my comprehension. Suddenly, I wanted to be away from this awful place. I swung my arm back and hurled the blade with all the strength I could muster. The effort almost caused me to lose my footing, and I struggled to regain my balance. As I did so, I looked up, in time to see the bright steel glitter in the weak light as it traversed an arc to the pond. There was a sudden movement in the rushes, then the blade splashed into the water. I stayed there, motionless, my eyes blinking with surprise. I stared at the spot where Excoria had vanished for several moments, then turned and made my way with great care back to Eve. As I made my way from clump to clump of the sturdy grass I dismissed the movement I'd seen as no more than the stirring of the reeds from a sudden gust of wind.

There was only one flaw in that argument, and I had almost reached the vehicles before I acknowledged it. There was no wind; not even the merest zephyr of a breeze. Nothing to create that movement, unless it had been a fish, or an otter, perhaps. Even now, as I record this for the first time, I can feel once more that cold shiver from the thought that it might have been something else; something far beyond my understanding. We waited for the police to arrive, and I told Eve what had happened. I was a little hesitant, wondering if she might have thought that all we'd been through had finally affected my sanity, but she accepted my version of events without question.

'There's definitely something strange about this place,' she said, looking around. 'I've felt it ever since we arrived. I don't know what it is, but I'm glad we're together. I wouldn't want to be alone here, or with someone I didn't love or trust. Perhaps that has something to do with why all Locke's plans came to nothing and ended in disaster.'

'Love rather than hate, you mean?'

'Or good triumphing over evil, more like.'

It was less than half an hour before Holmes and Pickersgill, together with a posse of uniformed officers, arrived to take the prisoners from us. Locke had regained consciousness by then, but looked dreadfully ill, and I guessed there would be little or no chance of him ever standing trial. Not before an earthly judge, that is. After we had given a brief, strictly edited version of what had occurred, Holmes allowed us to return to Barton Manor to rejoin our companions. 'We'll be along later after we've interviewed these two.' He indicated the police van, into which the uniformed men were loading the prisoners. 'They'll be held in custody pending a remand hearing, so once we've got the formalities out of the way we'll be up to see you all, complete with pads of statement forms.'

It was one of the few signs of humour I'd seen from the young detective, and I guessed it was relief from the stress of the case that had caused him to relax somewhat.

Despite Holmes' promise, the day passed without any sign of the detectives' arrival. As we waited, we were able to discuss the case in depth and agree on the content of the statements we would have to give. Eve expressed the need succinctly. 'We have to ensure our stories tally,' she told them. 'It would be easier if we were able to reveal everything, but as there are elements we don't want the police to know, that makes the need for uniformity even greater.' She looked at me, knowing I had several points to put over.

'We will have to explain about Excoria,' I began, 'but what we can't say is how it disappeared, otherwise one or more of us would face a charge of tampering with evidence, or obstruction, or whatever the term is. As far as the police are concerned, all they need to know is that

Excoria finished up in Bleke Mire along with Lionel. That isn't exactly a lie, just not the whole truth.'

'It seems strange that after all that we've been through, the mystery is still as baffling as it was when we started,' Alison stated. 'I mean the location of the Holy Grail. I think it would have been wonderful to have been able to present it to the world.'

I looked at Eve, and then at Robert, and saw that both of them were awaiting my response. Eve nodded slightly, and I decided to tell the truth. 'Do you remember the wording of the runic messages that Victoria translated. In particular, the first one, which read like this, *"My time is almost at an end. I have passed to my sons the secret that has been handed down through the generations. It will be for them to carry it and in the end, they must decide whether it is prudent to reveal it or let it rest. I have counselled them to think long and choose wisely."* That wording baffled us. It's hardly surprising that we've been foiled in our attempt to interpret that message, because all along we've been deceived by a very astute old man with a long white beard.'

'Who on earth are you talking about?' Robert asked.

'That's how Merlin is usually portrayed in popular fiction. The secret lies in the words, *"it will be for them to carry it"* which should have been read literally. When I examined Excoria, I found there were markings all around the blade and hilt. Unless I'm very much mistaken, I think that Merlin inscribed the location of the Grail on the metal of Cerdic's Excoria and Arthur's Excalibur.'

Victoria interrupted me. 'I thought you said the killer took Excoria into the marsh with him? When did you examine it?'

'No; I said that all the police need to know is that it finished up in the mire. With Robert's approval I threw it into the tarn in the centre of the marsh.'

Victoria looked apoplectic, so I hastened to add,

'Before you condemn what I did as sacrilege, consider what Cerdic and Arthur's wishes might have been. When Merlin told them the location of the Grail, the world was an unstable place. Old empires were dying, new ones being formed. Isn't that very much how things are today? Only the weapons have become far more lethal. Now consider the effect that discovery of such a valuable artefact might produce. An excuse for new crusades, new holy wars perhaps. That was why Cerdic acknowledged the danger such a relic might represent, and followed Arthur's example, leaving it for fate to decide whether to reveal it.'

I paused to let everyone dwell on this, before adding what I hoped would be a clinching argument. 'If you are still in any doubt, all you have to do is think about all that has happened since this began. Even without the Grail appearing, there have been two near-fatal accidents, one to DI Hardy and the other to Frank Jolly. Then there was the break in here, the kidnap of Alison and Tammy. Add to that total, four murders, and the planned murders of four more of us, and finally the violent death of one of the killers.'

The others seemed prepared to accept my logic readily enough. My only misgiving was that as a professional historian, Victoria might not be swayed by the emotional argument. I was concerned that she would regard the destruction of so valuable a piece as a criminal act. I was therefore more than a little surprised by her response.

'There is a legend that the soul of a warrior lives on after his death; being captured in the blade of the weapon he carried into battle. Perhaps that was so with Cerdic and Excoria. It might even be that your action today was not quite so much of your own free will as you imagine. Isn't it quite possible that you were directed to that mire today, not by Locke, but by other influences, so that the original intention of making sure that secret would be hidden for all time could be fulfilled? Or, if not for all time, at least until powers we cannot begin to understand deem it more appropriate?'

She had only one question; and it was not difficult to answer. 'What I fail to understand is, if Locke had the weapon in his possession, why did he fail to translate the inscription. I may have been highly critical of his abilities as a historian, but I do know he had a working knowledge of the Ogham, the Celtic alphabet.'

'For the same reason that you struggled with the final runic inscription,' I told her. 'I'm no expert, but I believe the markings on Excoria would have turned out to be something other than Celtic.'

Victoria groaned. 'Not bloody Aramaic?'

'Yes, I told you he was a very cunning old man, was old Merlin.'

'That's damned clever of him, but it also shows how determined they were to guard that secret, which in turn underlines how right your decision was.'

It was the following morning before Holmes and Pickersgill arrived, and after we told them about the Pengelly history, their opening remarks explained why they had been delayed, as well as filling in some of the gaps in our knowledge. 'That tallies with what Locke told us,' Holmes said. 'Unfortunately, he wasn't able to give us the whole story. We began to interview him, but had to suspend it because he was taken ill. From what we were able to gather beforehand, it seemed that he devised the scheme to defraud Stephen Pengelly in revenge for the treatment his niece had received. To do this he co-opted his old friend Wharton and his associates. However, once he started to research the Pengelly family history to lend credibility to the confidence trick, he discovered something amazing, and the whole scheme took on a different slant. All the money Stephen paid to that company Overtring was to provide funds for more research, and visits to some previously undiscovered sites. It seems Locke uncovered the dagger and then they found something at another of these, but Locke never got to see it; he was too ill to travel, and only learned of the fact much later.'

Johnny Pickersgill added, 'For some reason, Locke believed Pengelly had found something that would cure his illness, and was determined to get hold of it, but Stephen wouldn't let him in on the secret. He mentioned something about stone tablets with writing on them, by which we thought he meant tombstones.' Johnny looked around, but as no one spoke, he continued. 'Locke felt that Pengelly had cheated him, because when the stone tablets were found, Locke was having treatment for his cancer. He said he chose that point to have the treatment because he thought that the site Pengelly wanted to look was unlikely to yield any result. I think that peeved him a bit. When he'd recovered, Pengelly had ordered the stones to be re-buried and wouldn't tell him what was written on them.'

'To be honest,' Holmes added, 'we thought this was a bit far-fetched, thinking that something written on a tombstone could provide a miracle cancer cure, but Locke obviously believed that to be the case. He was about to tell us what it was, but before he could do so, he collapsed and had to be rushed to hospital. He got really angry as he was talking about it, and I honestly believe that caused his collapse, or at least hastened it. That was part of the reason we didn't get here until now. I spoke to one of the doctor this morning,' Holmes added, 'and the news isn't good. Locke is in intensive care, and by the sound of it he only has a very short time left. We're talking days, not weeks.'

'Does that mean that Joseph will have to stand trial alone?'

'Nobody will stand trial. Joseph has been committed to a secure mental institution. He will never be considered competent to understand what is going on in a courtroom. The psychiatrist believes the trauma of his brother's death was the tipping point.'

We had been back at Eden House a few days, the only unsolved mysteries centred around where Stephen Pengelly had found those runic tablets and where he had discovered Domenico's journal, but as Eve commented, 'No doubt if we tried hard enough we could locate both places, but why bother? Life without mysteries would be far too boring.'

I agreed, adding, 'And maybe the timing of Locke's collapse during his interview was a little more than pure coincidence, because it happened before he could reveal the rest of what he knew.'

She shrugged. 'You may be right, but we'll never know. Let me take look at your arm. I need to change the dressing.' When Eve removed the bandage, she stared at the wound site and gasped. 'Adam, look at your arm.'

I did so, and was astonished to see there was no mark, no scar where Excoria had taken the skin off. The injury had healed remarkably quickly, and with no trace left. 'That is really weird,' I said.

I looked at Eve and smiled as I drew her into my arms. 'I've been meaning to say this for a few days now, but it is really nice to be home. Barton Manor is a very fine house, with very pleasant company, but I prefer Eden House.'

It was a week or so later after our morning walk when I asked her as to when she thought we should arrange the wedding. Eve was a good organiser and had promised to start planning, but something always seemed to get in the way.

'I've been thinking about that and decided we should get married now,' she told me.

'That suits me. Any particular reason?' I asked.

'Because if we delay any longer, someone will come

along with another problem for us to solve.'

A month later, on Christmas Eve, three years to the day since we met, we were back at Mulgrave Castle, back in the private chapel, but this time there were no unknown murderers, just close family and a priest.

Eve looked radiant as she came up the aisle on the arm of her brother-in-law Sir Anthony while Harriet stood with Becky and Sammy. The girls hid their disappointment at not being bridesmaids at what I'm sure would have been billed as the wedding of the year, if they had anything to do with it. Later, Charlie, acting as best man, dug me in the ribs and with a cheeky grin announced, 'Nice one, Adam!'

When we boarded a train at King's Cross to return home from our honeymoon, for the latter part of the journey, there was only one other occupant in our First Class compartment, an elderly woman who looked very upset. 'I'm going to see if that lady's all right,' Eve told me.

She spent a long time talking to the other passenger before returning to her seat. 'She's heading for Elmfield, and was going to take a taxi from York, so I offered her a lift. Did I do right?'

'Of course you did.'

'Anyway, you'll never guess what she told me ...'

The Eden House Mysteries
Bill Kitson

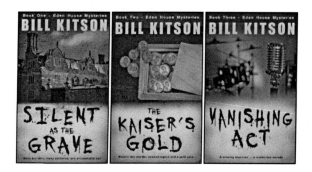

For more information about **Bill Kitson**

and other **Accent Press** titles

please visit

www.accentpress.co.uk

Lightning Source UK Ltd.
Milton Keynes UK
UKOW04f0803200316

270472UK00006B/8/P